SING LIKE A CANARY

CANARY ISLANDS MYSTERIES BOOK 5

ISOBEL BLACKTHORN

Copyright (C) 2021 Isobel Blackthorn

Layout design and Copyright (C) 2021 by Next Chapter

Published 2021 by Next Chapter

Edited by Graham (Fading Street Services)

Cover art by CoverMint

This book is a work of fiction. Names, characters, places, and incidents are the product of the author's imagination or are used fictitiously. Any resemblance to actual events, locales, or persons, living or dead, is purely coincidental.

All rights reserved. No part of this book may be reproduced or transmitted in any form or by any means, electronic or mechanical, including photocopying, recording, or by any information storage and retrieval system, without the author's permission.

Dedicated to my mother and all retired police officers who worked hard to keep us safe.

ACKNOWLEDGMENTS

My eternal gratitude to my mother Margaret Rodgers. This book could not have been written without her. My heartfelt thanks to Miika Hannila and the team at Next Chapter Publishing.

Parts of this story are loosely based on real events. All of the characters are completely made up.

1

PLAYA BLANCA, LANZAROTE, THURSDAY 14 MARCH 2019

I HAD NO IDEA WHY I LIED ABOUT MY NAME. I HAD NEVER, EVER, not once in all of my sixty-seven years given a false name. Why start? A reflex? I realised with sudden force that now could well be the time to lie about who I was. There was a pretence to maintain. Even on this far-flung rock of an island. I had to remind myself of that. I could be too honest.

My eyes had already taken in his signature on the letter. It was unmistakable even after forty years.

Edwin Banks.

Billy Mackenzie had practised that signature over and over in the days leading up to his departure. I'd watched him do it. He wrote in large childlike alphabet letters, the sort you would expect from a kid in Grade One – I hadn't liked to ask if he was at best semi-literate, I'd just assumed it watching his cack-handed efforts – and for the fun of it he'd come up with a way of making the E much larger than the rather large B and underscoring his new name with a pronounced zigzag trailing under the S.

And there it was, the signature of Edwin Banks plain as day beside the stranger's fingertips, the letter itself splayed out on the café table, its corners lifting thanks to the sea breeze.

I'd always enjoyed keen eyesight. Ever since I was a child my eyes would home in on little bits of evidence – the shoelace of Carl Fisher's school shoes in the bushes where Fiona Macintyre was molested, the missing tooth of Wendy Fraser in the gravel edging the school driveway after her skirmish with notorious school bully Sharon Weare – and it was this natural talent that had led me to join the constabulary. You'd make a great detective, my mother had said, which was a progressive thing to tell a daughter in the 1960s. I had a habit of finding myself in the right place at the right time, too, and I had a good nose for sniffing out clues. You're a natural, Marjorie Pierce. Isn't that what they'd said, back in the days of my police training. It was 1977 by the time I joined the force at the tender age of twenty-four, and indeed they had. That was what they'd said when they weren't being lewd.

On that warm afternoon in March, I had gone for a drive down to the island's southern coast to meet up with an old colleague. He was on holiday here and had managed to get a message through to me when I was back in England that he had some information about Billy. Once I'd arrived on the island, we arranged to meet. But he didn't show. On my way back to my car, I was passing a café near the ferry port when hunger grabbed a hold. It was lunchtime and the café's outdoor area was crowded with holidaymakers, and I was forced to head for the only table with a vacant chair. I didn't want to have to share a table with anyone, but the woman seated with her back to a potted succulent looked harmless enough.

And there the woman sat, her mature and stately visage replete with wavy grey hair framed by the plant's fleshy leaves as she pored over a letter from Billy Mackenzie née Edwin Banks. He was writing to his son Alvaro. Dear Alvaro. That was all I was able to read. That and the date. 1989. To have continued would have appeared rude and inappropriate. Besides, a waiter came with the woman's coffee, and I'd had no choice but to accept the proffered menu as I sat down. The woman then tucked away her letter and held out her hand and introduced herself. And I, Marjorie Pierce, had said Edna Banks. Edna, Edwin, it was as though I had temporarily fallen under some sort of hypnotic spell. Either that or I'd had a brain freeze. Why not say my real name? And if I felt I had to lie, why then choose a name almost identical to the fake name of the individual I had come to find? Clumsy. Not one of my sharp-witted moments. Truth is, the woman's unexpected hospitality had left me momentarily flustered. The curse of ageing.

At least Clarissa had no idea I had seen, let alone recognised that signature. She thought it was pure coincidence that my name was so similar, and her face filled with astonishment.

What were the chances?

'Banks is a common enough name,' I said.

Even so, I suspected the similarity was the sole reason Clarissa had shown a good deal of enthusiasm for exchanging contact details. Perhaps she thought I was this Edwin's sister and was trying to hide it. Still, when Clarissa said she was on her way back to Fuerteventura and she would look me up next time she was on the island, I, Marjorie now née Edna, decided it unlikely I would ever encounter the woman again.

I thought I had hidden my own astonishment well. A different sort of astonishment, founded on the presence of that letter. What were the chances? I kept coming back to that. What was Clarissa doing with that letter anyway? Then I realised Alvaro's death had been all over the newspapers. And the articles had mentioned an Englishwoman who had managed to escape a heinous ordeal at Villa Winter, thought to be a secret Nazi base on Fuerteventura.

My memory was hazy when it came to that Englishwoman's name. An inner voice prevented me from simply asking Clarissa if she was that very woman. In her shoes, if it *was* her, I would not want to be probed. Do as you would be done by. Isn't that what they say. At any rate, I gave her the privacy she no doubt craved. Which meant I was forced to make chitchat for the duration of my ham sandwich and orange juice, chitchat in which I managed to divulge far too much to cover my inner embarrassment at calling myself Edna Banks. Then there was my eagerness to find out what I could about the Villa Winter case. The combination had thrown me off-kilter. Fortress Marjorie had let down the drawbridge.

Making a bad situation even worse, Clarissa seemed to have a knack for loosening tongues. It had a lot to do with her own divulgences and how she had come to Lanzarote on a day trip to visit a prisoner. How he'd been wrongly convicted of murder. Poor sod, but it happens. In the telling, she'd created common ground. It felt natural letting her know I was a retired copper who back in the day had been instrumental in nailing a notorious London gang. A gang rightly convicted, no mistake there. I'd even told my new acquaintance I had come to the island to settle a score with an expatriate criminal. Sounded like bragging when I thought back on it later. Would Clarissa put the two together, the gang and the man? Even if she did, it wouldn't matter. There was nothing to link any of what I'd said to Billy Mackenzie.

After some brief observations about the weather – there'd been one mother of a dust storm a couple of days before I arrived – I promised to keep in touch, paid, and left.

There was a newsagent on the next corner. I wended my way past the usual tat and cheap novels on display at the entrance and browsed the newspaper rack inside. I didn't need to search hard to find what I was looking for. Clarissa Wilkinson's name and photo were on the front page of a local newssheet. I bought the newssheet and headed back to my car.

The drive to the holiday let was, for the island, a long one. I had the aircon on full blast, and I had to concentrate the whole way, not accustomed to driving on the other side of the road.

The eastern portion of the island was mostly given over to tourist resort towns and the traffic was steady. A stretch of dual carriageway circumnavigated the capital Arrecife and then there was a string of roundabouts heading out through the wealthier suburban enclave of Tahiche. After that, the traffic thinned a little, the main road continuing on to Teguise and the central towns, the turnoff, which I took, coursing along a coastal plain beside steep-sided hills. The lure of the north, with dramatic landscapes further on and several renowned tourist sites, meant there wasn't that much of a let up in the traffic. Here, the drive was complicated by the cyclists, loads of them, and there wasn't enough road width for them and us, causing no end of tailbacks and risk-taking by irate drivers. Once I'd turned off onto the old road to my village, the traffic thinned to near zero and I relaxed.

Not being one for the tourist enclaves, I had rented a detached house on the eastern edge of the pretty village of Guatiza, on land backing on to Las Calderetas, a low sprawling volcano sheltering Guatiza from the east coast. There were volcanoes everywhere you looked on this island but the ones in the north were a lot older. The locale was known for its prickly pear farms – cultivated for cochineal traditionally, and also for cactus jam – and there were fields of cactus to either side of the house. I loved the area. The village was neat and tidy, the houses cuboid and white. The cacti – lending a permanent green to a bone-dry landscape – contained by low dry-stone walls. The house I had rented was a new build constructed in the traditional fashion and very well maintained by its German owner who had been more than happy to let me lease the place for three weeks at a reduced rate because there was one of me.

There was another reason I'd picked Guatiza. Billy would have holed up somewhere remote but accessible. Not for him the wilderness, the cliffs, the churning ocean. He had a horror of heights, having once been suspended upside down from the roof of a high-rise housing block. The price you pay for the people you choose to mix with. Which had ruled out all of the Canary Islands bar Fuerteventura and Lanzarote when he was choosing where to run to, where to hide. I had joked with him at the time that La Gomera would be his best pick. Near vertical cliffs and ravines, no beaches to speak of – at least not the sort sporting swathes of white sand – the island rising up out of the ocean like a raised scab. They'd managed to flatten a portion of land near the coast for a runway. The island was favoured by the Germans, there were almost no English there, and the guidebook talked of some interesting cave dwellings. An ideal location to disappear to as no one who knew Billy would ever think he would pick such a place. He was having none of it. I had him rubbing his palms on his trouser legs in the imagining. Hilarious.

Neither of us had heard of any of the islands other than Tenerife before studying the map. He'd vetoed Fuerteventura – even though it looked much flatter than most of the other islands – saying it sounded like a total backwater, which it was in 1980, according to *Let's Go*. As for Lanzarote, which became his choice after he'd eliminated all the others, there were not that many places on the island off the beaten track that were not half-buried in a lava flow. The island was barren and exposed – you could be seen for miles practically anywhere – and a foreigner had little choice but to mingle a little. In 1980, lone foreigners outside the tourist areas and the capital would have been known individually by the locals. I did alert him to that, but he didn't listen.

After studying maps and descriptions of the island when I was planning my trip last week, I had taken a punt that Billy would have headed north, away from the tourism in the south, but still within easy range of shops and banks in the capital Arrecife. Even back when Billy had come here, the pocket of land at the beginning of the island's northern tip – where the island narrowed to just a few kilometres wide, ending abruptly on the west coast in a dramatic cliff – boasted a small German enclave in the village of Mala and a nudist colony at nearby Charco del Palo. The Germans had established themselves as had the nudists, and both groups would have suited Billy as neither would have taken the slightest bit of interest in a scrawny, bearded weasel of a Brit.

2

OLD SALT WORKS, LOS COCOTEROS, LANZAROTE, THURSDAY 14 MARCH 2019

Billy yawned over his toast. He took another slurp of coffee, hoping to shake off the tiredness. He'd had a rough night, a rarity for him. He hadn't had a disturbed night's sleep in decades.

He'd got off to sleep fine, but he awoke in the small hours from a nightmare. He never had nightmares. And this one had him sweating. As the various disconnected elements of the dream had presented themselves in his half-awake awareness, he'd hunkered down beneath the covers, spooked. His hearing had grown sharp. A distant knock and he was convinced he had an intruder. He got out of bed and crept through the house in the dark, checking every door and window. He even checked in the cupboards. On his return, his dog Patch looked up at him from her bed in the corner of his bedroom, cocking her head to one side. It was only her nonplussed expression that caused him to get back into bed, reassured there was no intruder. It had all been a dream, first one faceless guy after him with a gun, then another with a knife. He'd escaped being shot, and narrowly avoided having his throat slit, and he'd woken up as he was hiding, terrified, in some property's cistern, convinced he was about to drown. He had a horror of drowning. Only equalled by his fear of heights.

The nightmare was cinematic, vivid, blood-curdling and all too real. If he hadn't known better, he would have treated it as a premonition.

But a dream was just a dream, only a dream.

A dream that, even in the clear light of morning, had left him rattled.

Forty years had passed since he'd had to think about the likelihood of his own violent death. Forty years of relative tranquillity. What had triggered that nightmare? Nothing, as far as he could tell. It was that nothing that instilled him with unease.

Patch sat dutifully by his side as he ate. The toast had gone limp and the coffee tepid. He took another bite and washed it down. Then he took his plate and cup to the sink before putting a handful of dog biscuits in Patch's bowl. She always ate second. Patch knew her place.

He'd found her in a pound five years back and trained her well. She was a pint-sized Labrador-dominant mongrel, black and tan with one floppy and one pointy ear, and a large white patch over her left eye. She looked odd and none of the rescue-dog browsers had wanted her at the pound, mostly on account of her eye patch. Their loss. His gain. She had turned out to be his ideal companion. And after he lost Natasha last year, that dog had been a huge comfort to him.

He went and slipped on the flip flops he wore outside, and she came trotting over.

It was still early, but the wind was up. In the cool of the shade cast by the house, he took in the expanse of white-painted concrete that had taken on a yellowish-brown patina. Dust. He'd been putting off the task for days. As he surveyed the obvious, he had to lecture himself into action. No one else was going to come along with a yard broom. Natasha would have had a fit seeing it in such a state. All that dust, tracking into the house, making more work, for her. The grit underfoot wasn't that pleasant either, especially for Patch.

In the end, he did it for Patch.

It took him the next half hour, sweeping and hosing. Patch sat in the shade and watched.

He should have gotten houseproud in his old age. Not that he was old. Seventy-five wasn't old, was it? Or maybe it was. His back thought it was. As did his knees and his hips. He wasn't the agile man he once was. But he ignored the twinges. Doctors were expensive, he had no private health cover, and he was hardly going to announce his whereabouts to the British government and claim free health care under the reciprocal agreement with Spain. He couldn't claim the aged pension for the same reason. He would rather rot on Lanzarote than be one of those poor bleeders who disappeared shortly after their arrival back in the motherland, or one of those crims arrested on their hospital bed back in London twenty or thirty years after the fact. Eyes never stopped watching. The mind once crossed never forgot. A bunch of elephants with very long memories. You couldn't escape it. If Billy had known in the 1970s what he'd come to know as he aged and aged some more, he would have chosen a different path. A straight and narrow path. Stuck with his legitimate job as a milkman and nothing more. Would that even have been possible? Probably not. Not for the likes of Billy Mackenzie.

Still, he thought, leaning his arms on his broom and looking around at his handiwork, he'd done all right for himself on this desert island.

The patio was large and skirted by a concrete-block wall about two metres high, rendered and painted white, marking the perimeter of his property. Entry was via a pair of rusted metal gates positioned in the southern wall. The solid panels matched the height of the walls, with a decorative metal grille in the form of a cactus inserted in the centre of the left gate at about eye level. In the north-western corner of the patio was a garage, also built of concrete blocks, rendered, and painted the same. Everything was rendered. Everything was white. So much white. Reflected the heat but hard on the eyes. That starkness was broken up by three raised beds fringed with basalt boulders, containing a cactus, a palm tree, and a drago tree. He could see the mountains and the volcanoes above the patio wall to the west. In all, the property was private, sheltered, and very pleasant.

An unexpected noise, a rustle maybe, and he was instantly alert. He cautioned Patch to stay and went over to the gates and peered warily through the decorative grille. Maybe it was nothing, but he opened the gates and stepped outside. He scanned up and down the length of wall that stretched all the way down to the cliff. There really was nothing. Even so, he remained wary.

As he lifted his gaze, he spotted his neighbour or rather his neighbour's hat – a white bucket hat hiding his near-bald head – poking up above his own patio wall. A loud woof followed by a faint, 'What is it, Penny?' and the neighbour Tom looked over, and, seeing Billy outside his gates, he waved. Billy was forced to wave back, which he did as he closed his gates, hoping to make it clear the brief encounter was not a signal to visit. Billy didn't much like Tom, and Patch didn't much like Penny, a barely trained pure-bred Weimaraner.

Billy knew Tom could no longer see him, but he felt the man's eyes on his back anyway. He deposited his broom and dustpan in the garage and went inside with Patch, embracing the ambient feel, the cool, the absence of wind.

The house was more than adequate for the needs of a

family – it had five large bedrooms – which was why Billy was able to devote one of the bedrooms to his jigsaws.

Forty years incognito on a desert island? A man needed a hobby. Jigsaws were time-consuming, soothing, and suited the solitary life.

Some he'd had framed – a still life, a castle, a map of the world. He only did two-thousand-piece puzzles and in that dedicated puzzle room, he had four on the go at once. He found it relaxing. He'd become something of a collector, too, favouring the most difficult puzzles, the rarities, the relics. As long as they had all their pieces.

He eyed the castle puzzle nearest the window and spotted a portion of the crenelations in among the masonry pieces lying outside the frame. The piece fit. He looked for more pieces and found three. After that run of luck, nothing.

He went over to the window and gazed out at the deep blue ocean. He was listless. The dream still lingered in the recesses of his mind. Then there was Natasha. The constant gnawing heartache of missing her. And, lodged smack in the middle of his mind, there was something else he did not want to think about. Another death. Alvaro. His son.

He left the puzzle room and wandered back through the house. The living room was spacious and peaceful. Something about the dim interior facing the brilliance outside. Glass sliding doors looked out over the ocean beneath a deep open porch. Close to the house was a swimming pool. Billy kept the cover on unless he wanted to use it. He had never felt entitled to such luxury. A large home with a pool and a stunning ocean view – who would have thought? Although life here wasn't all sunshine and daffodils. You can be lonely in paradise, that much he knew all too well as he went over and drank in the ocean blue, one loss compounding another until he didn't know how to position himself mentally. The avoidance was draining.

Patch came and pressed her nose against the glass then looked up at him expectantly. He slid open the door.

The land sloped down to the low basalt cliff. Billy had landscaped the slope into a series of low terraces that he'd planted up with groundcovers and succulents. The perimeter walls reduced in height by shallow increments, the rear wall only a metre high. Down there at the property's coastal edge, Billy saw no point in attempting any sort of beautification. The trade wind was too strong, the salty air too harsh and corrosive, and the only plants that would survive the exposure were euphorbias which tended to look scrappy unless watered and cared for, and he couldn't be bothered trudging down there with a watering can. Or so he told himself. Truth was, at that end of the property he was visible, much too visible to anyone wandering along the cliff path or in a boat out at sea. Someone with binoculars maybe. And then there was his only neighbour, Tom, who was something of a busybody.

Billy pretty much left the bottom of the land for Patch. He went down every couple of days to collect her poo. When he did, he wore dark sunglasses and a hat. She made her way down there now as he watched, pausing to sniff this and that, and trotting along happily. There was nothing to harm her in his walled yard, but he stayed outside anyway, on guard with the morning sun on his face and the ocean breeze blowing back his hair, pressing his T-shirt to his chest.

The peace didn't last long. Something had disturbed Tom's dog Penny. A visitor? A bird? Billy was hardly going to stand on a chair and peer over the wall to find out. Penny was apt to bark at anything for no reason. The very worst kind of guard dog. A hound, really. That breed was a hunting dog. Patch didn't issue a reciprocal bark. She was the quietest dog he had ever come across, too quiet maybe. If there had been an intruder, would she have barked then? Or cowered?

Penny's barking stopped as abruptly as it began. Something and nothing then.

Tom's property was of a similar size to Billy's and a good fifty metres away to the south. They shared that small stretch of rocky headland, Billy's property situated above a small bay to the north. There was a beach of sorts down in the bay, although that, too, was rocky and no good for swimming. On the other side of the bay were the salt flats of Los Cocoteros. There were a few farms in the hinterland between the coast and the volcano. Not much went on in the fields. Billy had hardly ever encountered those farmers. The area was as remote as you could get while remaining in easy reach of everywhere. Access was via a gravel no-through road. Even in the height of the tourist season very rarely did a car come by. The location might not suit many but it suited Billy down to the ground.

Billy considered his neighbour Tom an interloper. Billy had got there first. He'd met with a stroke of good fortune in the first week of his new life on the island back in 1980, when he'd sat propping up the bar of a nightclub in the then tiny but burgeoning resort town of Puerto del Carmen. He was on the hunt for real estate, and he found himself sitting next to a down-on-his-luck Swede desperate to sell his half-built house after his daughter had died and his wife had left him. A chance encounter. They moved to a table and agreed a fair price over a bottle of Tequila. Billy went to inspect the place the next day. Torbjorn fell over himself with gratitude, it being near impossible to sell anything half-built. And, of course, there was no estate agent taking a cut. The guy even left Billy five pallets of concrete blocks and the phone numbers of a few expatriate tradespeople. Billy soon learned the local building ways that majored in rustic and cheap, and in basalt and concrete. Little to no wood. To build, you needed muscle more than skill and back then, Billy had plenty.

Good fortune had shone on Billy as he slid into his new life after witness protection. He'd even left his old London life with what amounted to a tidy sum in Spain. An only child, he'd inherited his parents' – originally his maternal grandparents' – large semi-detached house in a sought-after part of Plumstead in London's southeast. A recent property boom thanks to Margaret Thatcher encouraging a council-house selloff meant he then sold his family home for over forty-thousand pounds. In pesetas, that was an enormous amount. He was able to pay Torbjorn in cash and, aiming to capitalise on the looming tourism boom, for the next decade he bought, renovated, and on-sold properties for a healthy profit and ended up with a good bank balance. Eventually he held on to three properties to rent out as holiday lets. He'd been living off the income those properties generated ever since. Living in hiding meant he never wanted anyone to know anything about him. To that end, he paid his cleaner Maria a generous rate in return for her silence. And his booking agent Marisol was the soul of discretion.

There was a period early in his home renovations phase when he was forced to get by on his savings, a period in which he got involved in another sort of business. Observing Patch sniffing about down at the bottom of the terraces, he fought against remembering that time. Up until Natasha's death, he had never thought about the early 1980s. He had just about erased all that from his mind. Sealed it off. Now cracks appeared. Maybe that dream was not a harbinger but an echo of a memory.

The ocean, shimmering a deep sapphire, rose and fell on the swell. It was mid-March, and the morning sun began baking the rock that was Lanzarote. Patch came trotting up the path and he ushered her inside and closed the sliding door on the freshening wind.

Patch went to her water bowl and Billy headed to his home gym for a workout. Usually he played music – Billy Joel was his favourite – but the nightmare had left him disconcerted for no good reason and he needed silence. To hear. It was Thursday and on Thursdays he did a much longer gym session and focused on his upper body. It was a lengthy routine, but he had nothing else on. And for the whole of that time, he listened and listened hard for any out-of-the-ordinary sounds.

Over the decades he had become a creature of habit. More so since he'd lost Natasha. Acclimatising himself to his life of solitude, he'd carved up his week and allotted different activities for each day. On Mondays he cleaned the house, did the washing, and went grocery shopping. Tuesdays he drove to Arrecife for lunch. Wednesdays and Saturdays were golf days. Fridays he did nothing. Sundays he drove to a village market or to some other tourist location just because he could. At home he had his jigsaws and his gym room and Patch.

Two hours of punishing lateral raises and shoulder presses and bench presses later, he spent fifteen minutes stretching and then took a much-needed shower.

With Patch pitter patting behind him on the terracotta-tiled floor, he went to the kitchen and made one of his deluxe coffees from the organic coffee beans he ordered in from Colombia and ground himself. The local coffee was bitter and tasteless by comparison. He took his coffee and his book – he was reading *Talking to GOATs* by Jim Gray and finding it entertaining enough – out to the front patio where, over by the drago tree in the corner beside the house, shielded from the sun and wind, he'd built a seating area from concrete blocks comprising a corner seat, a low table and two more seats to complete the setting. The table and seats he'd rendered and painted white as was the custom. He'd had a bunch of foam seat pads made. Natasha had covered the seat pads in brightly coloured fabric and decorated the setting with an array of cushions. It was comfortable if a bit dated. The whole place had a vintage 1970s feel, the result, obviously, of its age.

He was four pages into the chapter on Tiger Woods when he heard a car engine in the distance. He paused and looked up, waiting. The sound grew closer. Patch looked up as well, a sure indication that the car was heading their way. He left his book, face down on his seat, and went over to the gates. He watched through the grille as a white Mazda drove past Tom's, kicking up dust in its wake. He waited. There was a brief moment of stillness while the engine idled. The tourists, they had to be tourists, had reached the road's end. Then, as anticipated, the engine revved a few times then issued a steady thrum. On its way by, the car moved at a crawl. The driver was male and young, as was the female passenger. They were craning their necks looking every which way, pointing, and stabbing the air. Seemed to be having an argument. Typical tourists. No doubt lost. He wasn't about to open the gates and help with directions. Satisfied they presented no danger, he left them to it and went back to his coffee and his book.

What mattered to Billy Mackenzie each and every day even after forty years in hiding was not only not being seen much but not being recognised ever. Sometimes he missed the old days, the action, the thrills. But he'd learned to keep his head down after those escapades on the island early on had nearly landed him in a lot of trouble. If wistful thoughts crept in, thoughts of a life that was anything other than humdrum, he reminded himself that he was more than lucky to be alive – in fact, it was something of a miracle.

He took a gulp of his coffee and settled back with Tiger Woods.

It wasn't until lunchtime that his thoughts touched on what he'd been trying to avoid all morning. Something about the slice of beetroot that shot of out the side of his sandwich as he cut it in half. Truth be known, he'd been avoiding the same thoughts all week.

Alvaro was dead.

That was bad enough.

But Alvaro was not only dead. He'd been murdered.

Which came as no surprise. But when he dwelt on it, he was catapulted back to his old life in London, to his other kids, the ones he'd had to leave behind. And to Marjorie, who'd made it all happen and saved his life.

3

ON THE BEAT, SOUTHEAST LONDON, JANUARY 1979

EITHER NOTHING HAPPENS OR ALL HELL BREAKS LOOSE. THAT WAS how it was in uniform, and I'd never much liked it. From the moment I joined the force in 1977 I held on tight to my wish to get out of uniform and into plain clothes. The CID was where I belonged. I, Marjorie Pierce, was a detective through and through. Even though I was only twenty-four and it could hardly be said that I knew my own mind, I was emphatic about what I didn't want, and that helped shape my future.

Walking the beat was not for me. The night shift was not for me either, mostly thanks to my neighbour, a stay-at-home mum who insisted on playing 'Bridge Over Troubled Water' loud, over and over again while hubby was at work – maybe it was the only song that got her child off to sleep, but I could hear it through the party wall and it had the opposite effect on me.

One morning, after an especially tiring Friday night shift, I was kept awake by the same neighbours digging up a tree in their front garden. I relocated to the back bedroom only to be disturbed again when the neighbours brought the tree around the back for replanting.

Then there were the door-to-door salesmen who rang the doorbell at any hour of the day, and, in summer, when the wind direction was just right, the smell of fish and chips from the café down the street wafting in through an open window.

The last straw came when I was driving around in a panda car one Sunday afternoon. The light was getting low, and I wasn't expecting anything to happen when someone jumped out into the road, waving for me to stop. 'There's been a terrible accident,' the distressed woman cried. She pointed at a shop. She was frantic. I walked in to find a middle-aged man standing there blackened from head to foot and missing the front of his shirt. His eyebrows and the front of his hair were singed. He was still standing, I had no idea how, and he seemed in shock. Although it was only me who was shaking. I could scarcely look at him and the stench of singed hair and flesh made me reel.

You needed to be prepared for such events. Able to steel yourself. And it was down to me as the officer in attendance to take down all the details. Making matters worse, it was my first major incident. I could scarcely hold my notebook steady enough to write down what the man said in response to my questions.

He'd been using a crowbar to dig a hole in the pavement outside and he'd hit the main electricity line, sending 240 Volts through him.

The woman hovered near the shop entrance, making me self-conscious. I turned to her and said, 'Did you call an ambulance?'

Before she answered we heard the siren. The woman hurried out of the shop, leaving me alone with the singed man who had started to whimper and looked about to buckle. I had never been more relieved to see a paramedic. I stood back and waited until they'd loaded the man in the ambulance. It was as the ambulance was driving off that I realised I had no idea how to get to the hospital they were taking the singed man to, and I had to head to the nearest police station and suffer the humiliation of asking for directions. The whole experience left me keen as mustard to get off the beat and into the Criminal Investigation Department (CID), where, I thought, detectives would spend their days sleuthing. They were not first responders dealing with varying degrees of carnage.

A week later, I had to return to Hendon for my final exams. It was while I was there that my sergeant saw an advert for the CID. He knew how eager I was, and he managed to delay the deadline for applications a whole week to give me time to apply. When I discovered what he had done, my faith in the constabulary rocketed. I felt a profound sense of belonging. I was cared for. The other officers looked out for me. Sure, I had to tolerate their smutty camaraderie, but they meant well.

Back at the station after my exams, I was determined to put in a good application. I took advice from the detectives upstairs when it came to composing the details. The next week I was interviewed by a panel of five. Once I got news I was accepted, the on-the-job training began. I was posted to Woolwich and became a rookie sleuth. Not that I did much sleuthing. I tagged along to interviews both in the station and out and about. I observed the admin involved in the job. I listened and absorbed. I did a little detecting of my own, mostly low-key crimes committed by third-rate criminals. Nothing violent, nothing organised, nothing that put my life in danger. Yet again, I felt cared for and protected, affirming I was in the right job with a promising, life-long career ahead of me.

REGIONAL CRIME SQUAD, GREENWICH AREA, 1979

I was only at Woolwich six months when out of the blue I got phoned up on a Friday afternoon with an offer I couldn't refuse. I was to join the Regional Crime Squad set up to nab a notorious London gang. I was to start with the squad the following Monday.

I found out later that I had two people to thank for my rapid ascent to the squad: a superintendent and a typist. Although it wasn't so much an ascent as a couple of sideways steps from uniformed copper to trainee detective to a constable-level member of a major crime squad. But this was a role I relished. To be part of a team nailing a notorious criminal gang known for violence and murder.

What luck!

Really, it wasn't luck at all; it was my gender.

When the squad was formed, Detective Superintendent Drinkwater asked the local squad members if they knew of anyone suitable for an obs assignment in a block of flats. Had to be female because women didn't stand out as coppers and the flats in question housed the rough and ready, the sorts of residents who would spot a male copper at a hundred paces. The team already had three women for the obs and needed a fourth. A typist who had already been seconded to the squad from my old station put my name forward. When DS Drinkwater heard the name Marjorie Pierce, he remembered me. He'd been on my interview board when I applied to join the CID. He had also been in charge when I'd been assigned to two autopsies, one a nine-month-old baby, the other a twenty-year-old male. He saw how I handled those autopsies. I'd had a little more experience by then. And knowing I was not dealing with a living subject like the singed man but a cadaver, meant I didn't faint, and I didn't throw up. I didn't even quiver, let alone blink or look away. DS Drinkwater had no idea that after I left that day, I took off to the Shooter's Hill nick to tuck into a liver and bacon lunch, but if he had, it would have helped clinch things, no doubt. Funny how dead bodies never fazed me.

That weekend I celebrated with a couple of work buddies over a few pints and a curry at the Taj Mahal. On Sunday I didn't care when my neighbour turned the volume up on 'Bridge Over Troubled Water'. I drowned out her Simon and Garfunkel with my vacuum cleaner. I couldn't settle to much, so I used the surplus energy to spring clean the house.

When I joined the force, I bought a mid-terrace house in Welling thanks to my savings and a small loan from my parents which paid for the deposit. The house was narrow and the party walls thin, but it was mine, if mainly also the bank's. Home ownership was something my parents, a fireman and a teacher, were emphatic about. The Pierces were all about social betterment. They didn't much like the area I had chosen to buy into, but my budget meant choice was limited. Besides, the house was conveniently situated a stone's throw from the main drag, a dead straight Roman road taking me all the way to Blackheath. From there it was about a mile to Greenwich, which meant I could be at the headquarters of the squad in under half an hour.

Or so I thought.

That first Monday, I got caught in a traffic jam thanks to the bottleneck on the approach to the Blackwall Tunnel and arrived twenty minutes late. Not off to a good start. I bolted into the station and rushed up the stairs to where I was told the offices of the squad were situated. Bright red and panting, I walked in on a meeting being held in a cramped and smoky room filled with men sitting on chairs, on desks, or standing. The room went silent as the door swung shut behind me.

'Sorry I'm late, sir,' I said to DS Drinkwater who was standing in front of the others.

'Traffic jam?' he asked.

Someone laughed.

'There's always a traffic jam around here, love,' said a guy seated at the front.

The man sitting beside him gave up his seat and joined the others at the back. I quickly saw that the men outnumbered the women six to one.

'Maybe leave a bit earlier next time.'

DS Drinkwater – a tall and imposing man with strong features and a commanding voice – caught my eye and gave me a friendly wink. I discovered I wasn't overly late when he carried on explaining to the room why Operation Rancho had been formed.

We'd all heard of the Rotherhithe Tunnel job. A bunch of armed robbers had held up an armoured security van and made off with over a million pounds. It was the same gang, DS Drinkwater said, that had held up another security van in Deptford last year. Word had it they were planning another job.

The squad had been formed thanks to information received from one of the gang's hired help, now a guest of Her Majesty's Service doing a long stretch for money laundering. Most in the room were from local divisions – five sergeants each with his own constable, plus the four women on the obs. Others had been seconded from Essex, Thames Valley, West Midlands and as far away as Yorkshire. Those seconded from elsewhere were only on the squad for six months. There was even someone from Scotland Yard's secret service.

The detectives in the room listened with varying degrees of interest – it was same old same old to them – but I was almost on the edge of my seat. Even if all I got to do was sharpen pencils and make the tea, I was thrilled to be part of this squad.

The meeting didn't last long. I had no idea what each detective was assigned to do, but I guessed that was none of my business. DS Drinkwater signalled to us women to wait. He left the room and the men all wandered off. Then Detective Inspector Brace came over. I'd met him once before. A charmer of a man sporting a moustache and long sideburns. Garbed that morning in a leather jacket over a wide-collar body shirt and flared trousers, he looked like he'd stepped out of Starsky and Hutch. I hadn't expected plain clothes to appear so fancy. Us women all paid attention as he spoke.

'There's a block of flats in Bow overlooking a car yard on the other side of the A12. Your job is to photograph all who come and chat with this geezer.' He handed me a photograph. I took in the tall, square-jawed beefcake of a man bursting out of a shabby brown suit and handed the photo to the woman on my left who had a quick look and passed it on.

'Fred Timms of Timm's Cars,' Brace said. 'He was the getaway driver for the tunnel job.'

'A fairly unmistakable character, that one,' I said.

'You could say that.'

There was a ripple of laughter. The inspector talked us through the essentials. We were to work in pairs and take shifts. When we saw a car going into Timm's yard, we were to take a photo of the car and the registration number. We were to photograph anyone seen talking with Timms. We were told to keep no records, only the photos. A photographer was coming in to show us the tricks of the camera. With a quick sweep of our faces to make sure we all understood, he left us to get to know one another.

'I'm Liz,' said the woman beside me. 'You must be Marj.'

Marjorie, I thought, but I wasn't going to correct her. Everyone on the force called me Marj.

'And this is Marion and Julie.'

The two women smiled a hello. Liz explained she was paired with me on the morning shift. She was a good-looking woman who chose trousers over skirts and had a close-cut hairstyle that lent an androgynous aspect to her appearance. I liked her. She seemed unpretentious and friendly. We went down to the canteen for a cup of tea, leaving the other two women to their own devices.

The following morning, Liz and I met at the station and took her car over the river to Bow. The council flat was situated upstairs at the end of the building closest to the main road. Access to the estate was off a side street. There was a parking area out the front.

It was the sort of housing estate my parents brought me up to be wary of. They never wanted me to have anything to do with the school kids who came off of the council housing estates in my area, not because they had anything against people living in that sort of accommodation per se, just that they were dead set keen that I would aim for better things. They didn't want other influences affecting my decisions growing up. I didn't want my parents' negative judgements. Which meant I kept my school friends at school and socialised with my home friends at home. It was a form of compartmentalising which would later stand me in good stead when I met Jess.

The flat – notably spacious and airy and much nicer in layout than my narrow little terrace house – was rented by two women. One was retired and the other worked as a police typist. They were more than happy to let us hijack the main bedroom upstairs for as long as we needed to because while we were there the police paid all their rent and bills.

Two tripods were already set up by the window, one holding a pair of binoculars, the other a camera. The binoculars were preset and the camera focused. The police photographer had done a good job. The window had a clear view of Timm's car yard across the multi-laned road. Liz sat behind the binoculars, and I positioned a chair beside the camera and sat down on the bed. We would take turns by the window,

Sing Like a Canary

observing and photographing. And that was the extent of our physical activity on shift.

It was in that upstairs bedroom doing the vital work of evidence gathering that I learned how boring being a detective could be. We sat there – or lay there as was the case with Liz if she'd been up late on the booze the night before – six days a week for six whole months, watching the season change from winter through spring to summer. And one of us had to stay focused and alert. Staring out that window at a car yard for six hours straight was mind-numbingly dull. Mind you, we did manage to clock all of the getaway driver's known associates and among them were the gang members. Result. And it wasn't all bad. The women downstairs made us countless cups of tea and with each cup came a large slice of cake. Liz and I both put on a whole dress size. There were funny moments, too. Smoking was frowned on and banned inside the flat, and Liz was a smoker. One time she was having a fag out the toilet window and when she finished, she dropped the butt and let it fall to the ground without realising the women of the house were out on the patio below having a cuppa. The fag butt landed in the mother's coffee.

The best outcome of that obs was Liz and I became good pals. She was DC Liz Meyer but she was always just Liz to me. We ended up knowing each other inside out.

To celebrate getting through each week of boredom, on Saturday nights we went out to the pub.

One Saturday about four months into the obs, I found myself sitting in a corner of the Ship and Anchor with Detective Sergeant Graham Spence from my CID days in Woolwich, Liz having got caught in a heated exchange with an old boyfriend at the bar. She'd had a few too many gin and tonics. Seeing the guy was in no particular danger as he copped her wrath, I left them to it.

Spence knew I was with Operation Rancho, but he didn't

probe me for details. He was a good copper, solid and reliable. In the short time that I had known him, I found him decent. Not for him the bawdy banter and crude innuendoes. He confided in me once that his wife would lock him out of the house if he came home late from the pub. But I didn't need to thank her for moulding Spence into any sort of subservience. He was gentle by nature and happy to oblige her demands.

Spence explained he was moving out of the area. 'Valerie's mother is getting on. You know how it goes. So, I've asked for a transfer.'

'They'll miss you at the station.'

'I doubt it.'

Spence spotted a mean-looking guy leaning near the back wall and tilted his head in acknowledgement. The Ship and Anchor was known as a coppers' watering hole, which made it an okay place for a certain kind of local to have a drink. Retired cops, informers, local businessmen keen to keep in with the law. And occasionally, someone new to the area who had no idea what sort of hostelry they'd stepped into.

We both finished our drinks and Spence went to the bar. I glanced over at Liz who had calmed down and was having a laugh with some of the other members of the squad. I was about to visit the Ladies when a scruffy-looking guy walked in and went straight over to Spence. They chatted while Spence was waiting to be served. Curious, I decided my pee could wait.

Spence came back with three drinks and the guy in tow. The man seated himself down next to Spence. The pub had started to fill. The smell of frying scampi and chips which half the pub seemed to be enjoying made my tummy rumble. I hadn't eaten since lunchtime as I was trying to lose that dress size from all the cake on the obs. Scampi and chips wouldn't help the diet. When Billy lit up a cigarette, even though I'd never enjoyed passively inhaling smoke, I was relieved as it masked the cooking smells.

I took a sip of my vodka and orange.

'Marjorie, this is Billy.'

'Wotcha,' he said and half-raised his pint. He sported a full beard in need of a trim, and the side parting of his wiry red hair did his appearance no favours. Neither did the ponytail. His beady blue eyes observed me beneath low eyebrows. I didn't enjoy being sized up. What was his game?

We chatted about sport, the weather. That summer of '79 was a cool one. And dry. The days never seemed to warm up. But that week, a mini heatwave saw temperatures up in the nineties. The pub had thrown open all its windows and propped open the door, but the interior remained stuffy and much too warm. With both Spence and Billy facing me and leaning over their drinks, I felt claustrophobic. I would have left them and joined Liz at the bar, but it would have been rude. Instead, I made an effort to get to know Billy, although he didn't make that easy. He evaded every question I asked about his work, his life, his interests. In the end I stuck to sport.

When Billy drained his pint, said his goodbyes and left the pub, Spence said, 'I thought you two should meet. I've handled Billy for years. He's a good contact to cultivate.'

He told me Billy's background. He was a milkman by trade and a getaway driver after hours. And a snitch. Divorced, couple of kids.

'He seems a nice enough bloke,' I lied. 'Not that chatty.'

'You want me to set you up with him?'

'Sure.'

Seemed too good an offer to pass up even if the man was a little repugnant. I had no idea what use Billy would be to me on the squad, but you never knew.

'Watch what you say to him, mind. Don't get too friendly with him. And don't tell anyone you have a snout.'

I took note of the advice. The bell for last orders rang and

Spence finished his drink. 'I better get going if I want to sleep in my own bed tonight.'

We both laughed. I stood with him and went and joined Liz at the bar.

4

GUATIZA, LANZAROTE, THURSDAY 14 MARCH 2019

Guatiza was a mile or two south of Mala. In the centre of the village, I made a left. After crawling down the narrow lane that zigzagged past the church, I made another left at the next intersection and pulled up in the designated parking area in the gravel, the front garden being wall-to-wall gravel marked out with large stones each sporting a smear of white paint. No one had thought to lay any sort of path to the front door or even a few stepping stones. Rustic. The garden – if that patch of some ten-by-twenty metres could be called a garden – contained a few large cacti and some spiny-leafed plants. No flowers, but the low stone walls were capped with white-painted concrete and the cacti lent a sculptural element. They were nothing like the chaotic array of leaves of the prickly pear in the fields all around. Instead, giant spiny shafts reached skywards. One cactus was an enormous furry-looking blob. Deceptively furry. I wasn't about to stroke it. There was a fleshy-leaved groundcover, too. Didn't cover much ground but I supposed it would spread.

I had no idea what any of those plants were called. I'd never been a gardener. That was Jess's forte. I had always been happy to leave her to it.

My heart clenched in the remembering. Dear Jess, poor Jess, my beloved Jess. I never thought at my age I would grieve so hard.

I crunched my way to the front door, cursing my sandals that served as gravel catchers, the gravel digging into the soles of my feet. Never mind the damage the gravel was doing to my brand-new sandals. I had to empty them on the doorstep, which was no easy feat as I had my tote in one hand and my keys in the other and my brain didn't think to collate the two before I reached down to pull the ankle strap off my left foot. I felt clumsy and stupid and old and about to topple over onto that depth of sharp black gravel. I ended up dropping my keys. And, of course, when I shoved my foot back in the sandal, I managed to ferry in more gravel with it. I knew this island was proud of its gravel – they used the stuff everywhere to remarkable effect – but it was really beginning to annoy me, and I found myself craving lawn. I stopped short of texting a complaint to the owner of the holiday let as that would only draw attention to myself, and I didn't want to be known here, any more than Billy did.

I tried not to let the door slam on my way in, as it tended to do due to the through breeze if I left the kitchen window open, which I had. It wasn't until I had made a cup of black tea – strong and sweet – that I could properly think about that letter to Alvaro. Clarissa must have found it in the village during the weekend she was trapped there. And she'd taken it, hidden it away, come to Lanzarote to read it. I regretted not having the front to inquire about the letter when I'd had the chance. Then again, I had the woman's phone number. I would get in touch, maybe even confide a bit more. Um, maybe not. But I would make sure I found a way of reading that letter.

On second thoughts, from the perspective of the bigger picture of Billy's life, the letter would probably not yield much. It was written in 1989. Odd that Alvaro had hung on to it all those years. Must have meant a lot to him. And dads don't generally write letters to their kids unless they are access dads post the divorce. Somehow, I couldn't picture Billy as a father, although I knew he'd left behind his two kids from his first marriage when he came here. That must have hurt.

I'd heard on the grapevine that he'd had another kid. It was the last bit of news that had filtered through from Lanzarote via my old sergeant Graham Spence's new informer. The weak link since he knew Billy's whereabouts – I'd hammered it home to Billy in the safe house that he wasn't to tell a soul, but the temptation or the need must have been too great – or he would have been if he was still alive. Spence's informer became part of an M25 bridge pier after crossing the Mavers gang in the mid-1980s. Spence himself would never have breathed a word about Billy to anyone but me. That, I was sure of.

With cup in hand, I grabbed the newssheet I'd bought in Playa Blanca and went out onto the patio that faced Las Calderetas. As ever, the view held my attention. There was something compelling about having a volcano rising up on the other side of your backyard, a couple of hundred metres away and from this angle nothing more than a wide cone-shaped hill, its flattened crest jagged here and there indicating the crater within. Appearances were deceptive. I'd consulted a map. Las Calderetas comprised triple craters, a low monster of a volcano spewing most of its wrath eastwards towards the coast. Well and truly extinct, the eruption of all that fiery molten rock in the distant past.

As were the events that brought me to the island, relatively speaking. The repercussions of those events, though, were far from extinct.

I opened the newssheet and read the article in full.

When he was slaughtered, Alvaro had only just got out of prison for smashing a fellow surfer over the head in a violent rage. Nice. Fancy smashing someone over the head with a surfboard. Billy had spawned a right rotter, by the sound of it. Not surprising. I studied the photo, more a mugshot, and found he had a face to match his demeanour, with that hallmark underbite. At least Billy had had the sense to hide his with a beard, the sort of full beard that made the lips hard to spot. The article said that Alvaro's body was yet to be found. Police had mounted a search of the whole length of coastline down on Fuerteventura's southern tip to no avail. No funeral then. A memorial service? Maybe. Not likely, if it was up to Billy. But there would be a court case. Likely as not Billy would show his face then. Although I would have a long time to wait for a trial. Forget that.

As things stood, I would need all my old copper wiles to track Billy down.

That night after I'd booked the trip, I dreamt the plane had landed and there he was on the tarmac waiting for me with a bunch of flowers and a grovelling apology. As if. There had never been an apology. He didn't have it in him to apologise. He would never think he'd done anything to warrant it. Whereas I did. I wanted that apology big time. I had waited forty years to pluck up the courage to go chase it. An apology, or? Come to think of it, an apology was the last thing I wanted from Billy Mackenzie. It was the *or* that interested me. He owed me. And there were many ways to settle a score.

My phone rang as I set down the newssheet. I was on edge in an instant. Who was it? What did they want? No one called me because there was no one to call me now that Jess was gone. No kids, because we never got round to that, and no parents, which I was glad of because both of mine went peacefully with no fuss and no care homes, and I didn't have a raft of friends. Those I did have never phoned, they texted.

I scrambled in my pocket, extracted the device, and squinted at the screen. It was my old work-colleague Clive. Detective Sergeant Clive Plant as he was then. Perfect timing, Clive.

On my way inside the house, I tapped the green button on the last bar of Bruno Mars' Finesse. People assume because you're nearing seventy you must be into Max Bygraves or Frank Sinatra or The Beatles, depending on who is doing the judging. It's a small pleasure of mine, proving them wrong.

'Settling in?' Clive said, so loud he must have had his mouth pressed up against his microphone. I pulled my sound level down to half.

'Is that why you called?'

It definitely wasn't. Clive only called when he had something pressing to pass on which was practically never. It had been forty years since I worked in the force. He only had my phone number because a couple of decades back our old superintendent Philip Drinkwater had died, and he wondered if I wanted to attend the funeral. He knew we'd been close.

It was a poor connection, and his voice went weird. I asked him to repeat what he'd just said.

'Word is Mick Maloney is getting out next week.'

'Wow, they didn't think to stagger the releases, then.' His brother was getting out, too.

'Different prison.'

That day at the trial when the Maloney brothers both got banged to rights would have been a highwater mark in my career if I hadn't already left the force. I'd taken a day off my new job and sat incognito, or so I'd thought, at the back of the courtroom doing my best not to grin.

'Pity they didn't die there,' I said.

'True. Anyway, I thought you should know. I reckon with them both out, there's a good chance they'll be booking a holiday in the sun before too long.'

Apprehension flickered through me. What was it Clive wasn't telling me?

'Billy won't be happy.'

'I doubt he knows. He's probably left the island by now, anyway.'

I said I hoped so. I was the only one out of the squad who knew where Billy had relocated to back in 1980 and I planned on keeping it that way.

'He'll know they're getting out, surely.'

'Maybe, but not about their travel plans. Doubt he knows he's got company either, if he's still there.'

'You mean me?'

'I mean Oscar. And no one but no one is going to tip that toerag off.'

'He's here?' The island felt suddenly small. Miniscule.

Oscar Cribbs was the Maloney boys' muscleman. He had been charged with looking after Eric's wife Sally while Eric was inside. I guess almost twenty years was a long time to keep your legs crossed and fly zipped up, but Oscar and Sally had taken one hell of a risk.

'I've no idea what Sally plans to do about it,' Clive said. 'What excuses she'll come up with, how she'll try to deny it, or even if she plans to stick around, but the moment he heard the news of Eric's release, Oscar took off to Lanzarote.'

How long had Clive known all this? It wasn't worth asking. I wouldn't get the truth.

'Should have kept it in his pants,' I said.

'He probably thought Eric would rot in prison.'

We all thought Eric would rot in prison.

There was a sound of something shuffling on Clive's end. Then a high-pitched whine.

'You cooking or something?'

'Something.' There was a short pause. 'You sure picked a

choice time to go holidaying in the Canaries.' He sounded concerned for my welfare.

'I needed to get away. Seemed like a good idea to come here.'

'You be careful.'

'You can count on it.'

'Crims have long memories, Marj. I mean it.'

'They don't know I'm here though.'

I thanked him for letting me know and hung up.

It suddenly seemed providential that I had reinvented myself as Edna Banks. Because Clive was right. The Maloney boys would be on my tail if they spotted me. Two birds and all that. Although I needed a disguise to go with the alias. Wrinkles and sagging aside, I still had that English rose face, those innocent brown eyes and that pert mouth. My hair was grey, but the curls remained. There was no way I could look Spanish, for a start. A hat? A headscarf? Large sunglasses? All of the above. I needed to rethink my image. Buy some hippy clothes, maybe. Everyone ignored a hippy.

Clive's tip-off about Eric Maloney's release and how he would be gunning for Oscar caused my grudge against Billy to resurface. The Maloney boys were busted for armed robbery in 1979, along with some of their hired help. Oscar, charged with wielding the chainsaw – he used it to cut into the side of security vans – did his stretch and got out on parole for good behaviour. That, and his secret role as a grass. Both Mick and Eric were stupid. First, they both tried to escape, a plot that extended their time by quite some years. Then Eric murdered a prison guard, and Mick was caught running a drug syndicate. What would have been twenty years max had turned into about forty. The boys were by now eligible for the aged pension. But that didn't make them any less dangerous. If anything, life inside would have hardened them and deepened their desire for retribution. Payback would be exacted as number one on the to-do list. No parole officer on the planet would be able to stop them. I didn't rate Oscar's chances no matter where he fled to. As for Billy and me, our safety was anyone's guess, but forewarned is forearmed and I'd be kitting myself out first thing.

Good old Clive. Then again, if it hadn't been for Clive texting me about Eric's release, I would probably not have come. I would have gone somewhere else after losing Jess. But the old humiliations stirred, and I thought tracking down Billy would give me something to do while I recovered from my loss. Keep my mind occupied. Stop me dwelling. The idea of Lanzarote had grown big fat legs after another squad member, Jim Ackland, the guy I was meant to meet in Playa Blanca, had contacted me through Clive to say that Billy had been bragging and mouthing off about me. In Lanzarote, of all places. He said he'd spotted Billy – unmistakable with the same bushy beard and that grating nasal timbre to his voice – at a golf course's 19th hole and he wanted to tell me to my face what Billy had said. I'd booked the flights and the holiday let that same afternoon.

I went and filled the kettle for another cup of tea and sent Jim Ackland a text while I waited for it to boil.

5

COSTA TEGUISE GOLF COURSE, SATURDAY 16 MARCH 2019

Eggs and bacon were the order of the day before a round of golf. Something about being out in the fresh air all morning gave Billy a hearty appetite. Although on this particular morning he wasn't that hungry and had to force himself to carry through on his ritual, flipping his eggs and sliding three rashers of bacon onto his warmed plate. He couldn't put his finger on why, exactly, but since that nightmare the other day he'd felt uneasy, and his do-nothing Friday had not done him any good. But a routine was important, especially now he was grieving, and he would never let down a friend.

Ben, known to most as Benjamin Caruthers, a retired banker, had taken a liking to the man he knew as Eddy Banks, not only because they both enjoyed a round of golf but also because they were both avid puzzlers.

In the modern era of smartphones and online gaming, jigsaw puzzles felt like a relic of the past and there'd been a resurgence of interest in some quarters, a backlash against technology. Such a similarity of interest – retro as it was – might have been the only real basis for a friendship between a man of high social standing and someone of Billy's ilk. Although Ben only knew Eddy as a retired milkman. He never questioned how this Eddy came to be living on the island. Billy suspected Ben had secrets of his own.

Ben made Billy feel respectable. Through his friend, he'd been introduced to an array of expatriates over the years, most of whom he chose not to get along with. There was nothing wrong with any of them other than the complaining and the strong opinions about every little thing, it was just that the fewer people who knew him the better. Ben found his odd friend's taciturn manner entertaining. It was something else that united them, the refusal to suffer the great unwashed.

Billy worked his way through his eggs and bacon, mopping up the last of his second yolk with what was left of his toast before taking his plate to the sink. Then he went and brushed his teeth and combed his hair. He liked to look smart for golf. He even ironed his T-shirt so that a neat crease ran down the arms. Even a bearded man could splash on some cologne and Billy did. He liked to make an effort for Ben. Made him feel almost posh. Usually at this point Billy would be feeling buoyant and enthusiastic. Golf was the highlight of his week. Instead, he gave himself a rueful look in the bathroom mirror.

Life goes on, Billy boy.

It was no use giving himself a pep talk. He wasn't convincing enough.

The golf course was no place for Patch who seemed to know what day it was. The golf caddy parked near the front door was a dead giveaway, and she was slumped on her daybed in the living room. Eyeing Billy as he walked back and forth getting ready, she seemed almost morose.

'Later,' he said, roughing up her fur before wheeling the caddy outside. He often thought of storing the caddy in the garage, but there wasn't much room, and his clubs were better protected in the house. Everything was better protected in the house.

As Billy reversed out his car, he saw his neighbour Tom standing with a garden hose watering his succulents outside the entrance to his property. A stupid hour of a sunny day to water plants. A ruse? Tom waved, put down the hose and started walking over. Billy instantly felt trapped. He had no choice but to entertain the old man; he needed to close his gates. In the time it took to do that, Tom would be upon him. It was as though he'd been lying in wait.

'Hey, so glad I caught you, Eddy. How's it going? I wanted to ask if you've shopped in the little supermarket lately. I bought some salami there last week and I am certain it gave me the trots. I was going to go in and complain. Anyway, I thought I better warn you in case you are a salami man. Do you like salami? Penny wouldn't touch it. Not that I would give salami to a dog. But I let her have a sniff and she turned her nose up good and proper. I should have paid attention. Maybe I should call environmental health. What do you think? Do they even have an environmental health officer on the island? Maybe the position is centralised in Las Palmas. Who knows? You heading off, are you? Of course you are. It's Saturday. Silly me. Well, I'll keep an eye open for any snoops or thieves. I know you would do the same for me. Excellent guard dog, Penny. How's your Patch?'

'Good.'

'Good? Excellent. Well, I won't hold you up any longer. I can see you are keen to get going. See you later.'

Not if I can help it, he thought but didn't say.

'Have a good day.' Billy grinned and waved as he pulled away.

The drive to the Costa Teguise golf course took all of ten minutes. A slow stretch of dirt road around the southern side of Montaña Tinamala took him to the main road and on into

Tahiche. From there he headed towards Arrecife, turning left at the next roundabout, and making for Costa Teguise from the south. It was a bit of a loop but saved him crawling through the tourist strip of Costa Teguise itself. The golf course was on the right a couple of kilometres down the road and backing onto the island's prison.

Ben's Mazda was parked beneath the car park's shade canopy. He pulled up beside it.

As he unloaded his caddy, he saw Ben chatting to Aaron Tyler from Location! Location! estate agents in Costa Teguise. For the second time that day, Billy had to quell an urge to bolt in another direction or cower and hide. He told himself he was being ridiculous. You can't escape irritating people. It was a different sort of person he needed to be worried about. It was no use. As he closed the boot, he steeled himself for the encounter and made for the concourse. Ten paces on and Ben noticed Billy and waved. Billy kept walking, hoping they were not about to make a threesome.

'Ah, here he is now,' Aaron said breezily, and Billy's insides sank.

'Ever the early bird, Aaron,' said a cheery voice, and Billy turned to see a deeply tanned man in a white polo shirt and shorts right behind him. Where did he come from?

There was a brief exchange of greetings and very welcome goodbyes. Aaron and his friend were having a late breakfast before teeing off.

'See you on the fairway.' There was that breezy attitude again. And then Aaron made off with that cheesy seller grin smeared across his face and Billy felt himself relax.

'Unbearable man,' Ben said when they were out of earshot, as though reading Billy's mind. Billy laughed in agreement, inwardly relishing the moment.

They headed straight through the club house foyer and on out to the terrace. There were a few other golfers standing around chatting. After nods and smiles to various acquaintances, they set off for the first tee.

The course was designed in 1978 and enjoyed a tremendous view of the ocean and the nearby volcano. There were eighteen holes, many with doglegs. The grassy fairways were lush and green and neatly mown and lined with palm trees. On a desert island, that always felt incongruous at best, but golf was golf. How else was anyone to play it.

They had to wait while a grey-haired couple who'd got there before them teed off.

'I found a fabulous vintage puzzle depicting a group of fine dogs the other day, and I thought of you,' Ben said, passing the time.

'Condition?'

'Good, but only five-hundred pieces. Too small for you, Eddy, I'd say.'

'Ravensburger?'

'Liberty.'

'Hmm.'

'I have my eye on a Van Gogh.'

'Oh, yes?'

'A Clementoni.'

'Impressive.'

They watched as the man tried to help the woman putt the ball and she shrugged him off. Took a few goes before they both collected their balls and walked off up the fairway.

'It'll be a triple bogey by the look of it,' Ben said.

They both laughed.

'We should give them a head start.'

'Do you think?'

Ben bent down and positioned a ball in his tee holder. He waited until the couple were off the green before settling into his stroke. His ball landed squarely at the top end of the fairway. Satisfied, he stood back and watched.

'I might not be on good form today,' Billy said when it was his turn. 'I'll probably lob the ball into the sixth hole.'

'Never.'

The sixth hole was situated on the other side of the rough on the first fairway.

'Something troubling you?' Ben said.

'Nothing fresh air won't cure.'

'That's the spirit.'

Billy managed to slice his ball which landed, as anticipated, in the rough.

'Self-fulfilling prophecy, I must say,' Ben said in mocking judgement. 'Might I suggest you apply some positive thinking to the game from this point on?'

'You're right, I know.'

'It's a psychological thing.'

'You lent me the book.'

'So I did.'

Billy got lucky on his next stroke and managed to land the ball on the green. One putt each and they walked across to the second tee. The couple ahead of them were nowhere in sight. Billy looked around and spotted them walking up to the third hole's green. Cheats. People like that should stick to minigolf.

The various fairways and greens were separated by areas of black volcanic gravel and the gritty, rocky land of Lanzarote. And the ingenious designer had left patches of that barren land between the various fairways on each hole. The second hole with its three patches of green was a case in point. This was not a golf course for amateurs. There were few opportunities for a hole in one. Billy had managed it on the sixth and they had both succeeded on the fifteenth. For some reason, the twelfth, while short and seemingly straightforward, eluded them.

They wended their way from hole to hole. It wasn't until they'd reached the fourteenth that the prison came into full view. A long and low complex positioned between the golf course and Tahiche and benefiting from the same impressive views of the ocean and volcanoes. Billy had never driven down the dead-end access road for a closer look, the prison a reminder of his own destination had he not opened up and told all. He'd had to overcome considerable inner resistance when he first took up golf and realised the prison's close proximity, not keen to have to confront that particular trigger twice a week every time he reached the fourteenth hole. He'd taken a leaf out of Ben's book of stoicism and avoided looking in the prison's direction. It was that or he would have had to forego golf.

Billy stood back as Ben took his shot. In a moment of weakness, he found himself unable to prevent his gaze sliding past his friend and homing in on the high fence and the low grey roof not two-hundred metres from where he stood. He was reminded of his own six-month stretch inside for stealing money out of the till at a garage in Catford. He was only eighteen at the time, but it was hardly his first offence and the judge had shown no mercy. There was a tough-on-crime stance in the government of the day. But that wasn't the reason Billy was sent to jail. He was sent to jail because out of the gang of ruffians he had got involved with, he was the only one who was readily recognisable. And that was because he had red hair. Through his teenage years of petty crime in his gang of ne'er-do-wells, he was always the one who got identified thanks to his hair. It was a curse, he found, and it wasn't long before the cops in his area all knew him. They called him carrot top. Before that theft in Catford, he'd been up before a judge a few times for fighting and petty theft, and he was always let off. His luck ran out that day of the garage job.

In prison he had time to think things through. He realised he needed to either dye his hair, shave it off or go straight since otherwise he would always be singled out and caught. The trouble was, going straight was not part of Billy's makeup. He came from good criminal stock, and he didn't want to disappoint his forbears, and besides, he profited nicely along the way. How could he marry his deviant instincts and lead some sort of normal life? By then, he'd got to know a bunch of coppers and his fellow inmates were forever complaining about one snitch or other who was the cause of their incarceration. The snitches were the most hated group of shady characters there ever was. But something about snitching appealed to Billy. He thought of MI5 and spies. He thought of the revenge he could exact on all his old gang mates who got away with everything all the time. He made up his mind. He would turn informer when he got out. He thought it would be a nice little earner.

There was only one complication. His cellmate was Eric Maloney, serving two years for grievous bodily harm. Billy had enough nous to realise he needed to keep Eric sweet, but his efforts proved so successful Eric made him a kind of honorary mate. Knowing what he had planned for his own future, Billy felt uneasy. Yet the Maloney boys were big fish and Billy thought informing on them would carry a good fee. Definitely worth the risk.

Back then, he wasn't to know where the association would lead. If he had to blame a single factor in the unfolding of his own shady life from then until now, it was his stupid thinking during his time in Brixton prison.

Ben was waiting patiently by his caddy. Billy peeled his eyes away from the Tahiche prison and tried to pretend it didn't exist as he positioned his ball. As he swung back his club, he wondered yet again why those who built the golf course chose this particular spot beside the prison. He also wondered, but not too hard, how they managed to keep the greens so lush on this desert island. Must cost a fortune, but he was not about to question it. Golf was his one luxury. He felt safe on the course, away from the marauding hordes. Away from any retired criminal turned tourist. He felt an honourable part of Lanzarote society, largely thanks to Ben. And as his ball sailed all the way to the green at the other end of the fairway and he walked off up the rise between the stout palm trees, triumph pushed all those memories and fears away.

Four holes later and, seeing Aaron walk out of the clubhouse restaurant, Billy suggested to Ben they head into Costa Teguise for lunch.

'I know a place that does a good steak.'

'Bit of a change will do us good.'

Ben had seen Aaron too.

THE RESTAURANT'S outdoor seating area was crowded. Billy went inside and made a beeline for a table at the back. 'Quieter,' he said as Ben sat down.

The menus came. Billy used his as cover while he assessed the other diners. It was a habit. He'd never had cause for concern, but this time felt different. He felt different. It was that dream again, disturbing his mind, putting him on edge now he was outside the relative safety of the golf course.

Lucky he was cautious, as a guy four tables away making to leave made his blood run cold. Wasn't that one of Marjorie's old cronies from the squad? Jim Ackland? Couldn't be, surely? Or was it? Same height. Same round face. And that conk of his was unmistakable. He'd seen him in the pub many times when he met up with his old handler Graham Spence. Judging by his manner, the guy hadn't clocked him, not this time, but Billy was sure he'd seen him at the clubhouse a week or so back wearing the same blue hat. That was the night Billy had let Ben buy him one too many martinis. He kept his eye on Ackland until he'd left the restaurant and disappeared. He was as confident as he could be that Ackland hadn't noticed him. He certainly hadn't looked his way.

'You're missing Natasha. Am I right?' Ben said and Billy put down his menu.

'I've never known you to be wrong, Ben.'

A waiter came and they ordered steak and beer. Ben was in a chatty mood and entertained him with funny stories from his past. Billy laughed in all the right places, but his laughter was fake. What was meant to be a pleasant lunch proved an ordeal. In the end he couldn't pay the bill fast enough.

Leaving Ben with a cheery, 'See you Wednesday,' Billy drove north to Teguise to visit the cemetery. He needed to clear his head. Spotting Ackland had unnerved him. Sure, Lanzarote had become a popular holiday destination but what were the chances? Then again, if Ackland had chosen to holiday in a hotel in Costa Teguise, which was as likely as not, then it stood to reason he would dine here, dine here in the vicinity. If Billy never wanted to risk encountering anyone from his past, he shouldn't go out. But then his home might as well be a prison. It was a one-off, he told himself. It was just a one-off.

He pulled up in the parking area outside the cemetery. There was no one about. As he got out of the car, he realised he had no flowers. He'd failed her.

The wind whipped across the plain. He turned his back on it and his hair blew in his face. The afternoon sun carried a bit of sting. Should have brought a hat. Flowers, and a hat. He wouldn't stay long.

Walking inside the high white walls the wind dropped, the heat rose, and an air of despondency soughed through him. It had been a year, almost to the day since he lost Natasha. He was supposed to be over his grieving – wasn't that what the advice books said – but life would never be the same without her.

As he walked towards her niche, he was taken back to the day they first met. It was after Alvaro's mother Ramona had left him, and he'd needed to find a replacement Spanish tutor. He'd given up on the idea of finding one through an agency after his single spectacular if salacious failure with Ramona. He had no idea where to look, but then his lucky star shone the night he met Natasha in a bar. She was dressed in high-waisted jeans and a flattering white top that showed off her tan. They'd hit it off straight away after she complimented his red hair. No one had ever done that before and he was flattered beyond measure. She was petite and pretty and came from Telde in Gran Canaria. He knew nothing about Telde. He still knew nothing about Telde. She never spoke of her past. She focused all her attention on him. He had to invent quite a story to keep her satisfied. More challenging still, he had to remember it. As a result, and under her tutelage, his Spanish improved dramatically. Within a year they were living together. She didn't want children which suited him after Alvaro. Best of all, she was nothing like Ramona. Natasha was perfect. They'd spent thirty-seven happy years together. Then he lost her to cancer.

Standing in front of her niche, he felt hollow inside, and he couldn't help thinking of the other family he had lost. His parents, his sisters, their children. His ex-wife Moraig – they'd split up long before he came to the island – and the two girls Emily and Sophie that he'd fathered with her. Never really meant never and he had only once risked a breach. Death would be on the other side if he took that risk again. He knew it.

He stood there a while, contemplating his past with the sun cooking his face. Eventually he roused himself. He needed to shake off this maudlin state of mind or he'd die of sunstroke. You have Patch. Remember. And the poor dog needs a walk.

He drove home via the sprawling and uninteresting village of Teseguite. The authorities had allowed too many subdivisions. There were too many houses popping up, some with front gardens overflowing with exotic plants, replete with elaborate bird baths and gnomes, a kind of expatriate regeneration of the land, plot by plot. Whereas the Spanish went for walled patios and balconies and loggias, lots of concrete and paving with planters and perhaps a cascade of bougainvillea or jasmine, all of it hidden away. You could tell who wasn't a local or Spanish by the type of garden, or the apparent lack thereof to the onlooker passing by. Billy found it amusing. It was something Natasha would make fun of, the Brits and the Germans and their gardens, a little criticism they shared. The walled patio of his own home suited the climate, Billy's love and need for privacy, and Natasha's tastes perfectly.

Patch was waiting for him at the door when he stepped inside, her tail wagging enthusiastically. He downed a glass of orange juice, put on his walking shoes, grabbed a hat and the dog leash, and they headed off.

When they reached the fork in the dirt track, Billy let Patch lead him down past the old saltworks. She knew the way. All the doggie smells along there were either hers or Penny's. He walked behind her, concentrating on not twisting an ankle on the rough track, not taking much notice of the surroundings, feeling himself more at peace. There was not much to see up ahead. Just a load of marked-out squares where salt used to be. Half a kilometre on, they passed the functional saltworks that did contain shades of salt, and then they entered the village of Los Cocoteros. Billy could never make much sense of the locality. A couple of hundred houses and no shop. Did have a few plazas and they'd walled a tiny inlet and created a fake beach, providing residents with a safe place to swim. Clever. And the area was a long way away from the tourist enclaves and inhabited mostly by locals. He never felt he needed to avoid being seen here.

As he entered the village, Billy put Patch on the leash. There was always the risk of an off-leash dog wandering aimlessly about the streets and Patch was safer beside him. Patch didn't mind. She was too busy enjoying herself, sniffing and inspecting and giving the occasional spot a bit of a water. He usually turned back about now but Patch was enthusiastic, so he decided to keep going. Once clear of the village, he let her off the leash again and she enjoyed trotting along beside him on the uneven and undulating cliff path.

And Billy felt safe.

They had the ocean on one side and inland, the terrain was divided up into small fields edged with low rock walls, fields long ago abandoned by farmers chasing the tourist dollar. Although not all the fields were abandoned. Farmers did still farm. Billy found their presence impressive and comforting. He'd never fancied trying his hand at growing anything in such a windy climate. As it was, the wind buffeted him, making the walk more of an effort, especially on the uphill stretches.

The rocky path meandered, as did the cliff, from time to time the two meeting, and Billy got a clear view of the ocean surging against the rocks below.

He skirted by the holiday let of Buen Retiro and carried on past the water cave with Patch now trailing behind. From here, the going got tougher, the path hugging the cliff edge, the walled fields giving way to basalt scree. After a short stretch he thought of turning back. Besides, not long and he'd be at Charco del Palo, and he tended to avoid the naturists.

A few more strides and he turned and retraced his steps. The wind was now behind him, pushing him along as his eyes searched for Patch.

A sudden rush of anxiety as he realised that she'd disappeared. He called her. No reply. His pace quickened.

As he neared the water cave, he heard barking up ahead. He called and called again but she wouldn't come.

Strange.

He thought it must be another dog. He left the path and drew closer to the water cave.

Known locally as a jameo and formed out of a sunken

section of lava, the cave's depths were open to the ocean, the water in the pool rising and then falling on the swell.

He saw there was some jetsam on the rocks on the far side. Must have washed up over the cave's outer rim.

A few more paces in that direction and he saw it wasn't jetsam.

It was a body.

On the near side of the cave, Patch was giving it her all. He took hold of her collar and clipped on her leash and told her to stay. Then he picked his way around the perimeter of pool to where the body lay face down, keeping an eye on the water surging and spurting into the cave which, thanks to the strong wind and the ocean swell, resembled the insides of a washing machine.

Close up, he saw it was the smell of blood that had alerted Patch.

The man had been stabbed many times. The blood was fresh. The body felt tepid. Didn't seem like it had been here that long. Now he was close, he doubted it had been washed up by the waves; the cave's outer rim was too high. The man had been killed right here.

What a location to end up dead in.

Billy looked around. There was the cave, the path, the rocks and the ocean, the tips of the volcanoes in the background. Not another human in sight.

He knew he should leave the body alone and waste no time heading back to his place, no matter who it was. But temptation took hold and he pulled hard on an arm and the body flopped over onto its back.

He stared into the dead man's face, frozen with disbelief, his old life crashing into the new as if the last four decades had been an aberration.

It was the Maloney boys' muscleman Oscar Cribbs. What

the hell was he doing in Lanzarote? More's the point, who killed him?

Paranoia stiffened his bones. He could hardly breathe, let alone walk. But he needed to get away from there, fast.

He scrambled back around the perimeter of the water cave, making sure not to slip and tumble into the churning water below. Patch eyed him anxiously as a sudden upsurge doused him in spray. On unsteady legs, he went and picked up her leash and led her back to the path and away from the scene.

He might have called in at the holiday let on his way by, but he didn't.

He might have knocked on some doors in Los Cocoteros to report what he had found, but he didn't do that either.

He might have waited until he had phone reception and reported the body to the police, but there was not a chance in hell he was going to do that.

Instead, he made a beeline for his place, breathing a sigh of relief as he closed his high metal gates, realising as he did that his legs were still trembling.

What were the chances of Oscar Cribbs turning up dead not two kilometres up the coast?

Once he'd seen to Patch's water bowl, Billy opened his laptop and searched the internet for information on the Maloney boys. Last he'd heard, they were still in prison, but they would be due out around now. He soon found that both Eric and Mick had been released.

And his island paradise hidey-hole was compromised.

First Ackland. Now Cribbs.

What the hell was going on?

The coincidence was weighted. Behind it lay intent. He had no idea why either Mick or Eric would want Oscar dead, but there was no doubt in Billy's mind that they were behind the killing.

The trouble was, if the Maloney boys were behind this, that meant they were on Lanzarote, too.

Did they know he was living here on the island?

They couldn't, could they?

If they did, would they be after him as well?

Of course they would.

But what was the risk?

He paused.

Ackland. He was the risk.

Ackland would have known who he was back when he met up with Graham Spence.

Or guessed.

And he would no doubt have clocked him that night at golf club.

The night he'd made a spectacle of himself.

The one and only night he'd ever got drunk in public.

Idiot!

His guts churned. His mind raced. Protection. Supplies. Disguise. He would need to lie low, only go out when he had to. Maybe buy some hair dye. He eyed Patch lapping water from her bowl and went to the fridge for a beer.

6

ARRECIFE, LANZAROTE, SUNDAY 17 MARCH 2019

I was due to meet Jim Ackland in Arrecife at two. He'd suggested a café in a side street off Plaza de las Palmas, down near the waterfront. A little after one, I stepped outside and closed the farmhouse door and paused to take in the fields of prickly pear and the neat cuboid dwellings and the soft curves of the mountains. Such a contrast to any scene I was used to. And my attire was also beyond anything I was used to. As I crunched my way across the gravel to the car, the wind blew my silk scarf every which way and it was a real battle keeping the thing around my neck. The fabric was thin and light and the pattern not at all to my liking. Paisley, and it was purple and pink.

After a fruitless and exhausting Friday shopping in Puerto del Rosario, I'd managed to source the scarf along with two pairs of flowing patterned pants at the arts and crafts market in Haría on Saturday, and at the Teguise market this morning I scored three loose and brightly coloured blouses that clashed with the pants and the scarf in typical 1970s hippy style. I also purchased a pair of sunglasses that practically covered my face, and some cheap patchouli perfume. I never was one for half measures. I looked ridiculous but very much the part and, thanks to the patchouli, I stank. But there was no sign of Marjorie Pierce inside the apparel. No sign of Edna Banks for that matter. And not a chance Eric and Mick Maloney would recognise this old copper. Neither would Oscar or Billy. Or even Jess. No, that wasn't true. Jess was my beloved, my consort, my only love. She would have seen through my disguise straight away. She would have laughed until her sides split and then teased me ruthlessly.

My campaign to discover Billy's whereabouts had so far yielded no results but I felt in no particular rush. Early days. That's what I told myself. Besides, I'd been too busy kitting myself out to concentrate on sleuthing. The delay meant I was yet to puzzle out the sort of haunts Billy might visit other than that golf course Ackland had mentioned. There were two on the island and until I met him, I wouldn't know which one. I could have just texted him and asked, but that would be giving too much away. I didn't want all and sundry knowing why I was here.

Not wanting to be late, I swept up the wafting silk of my scarf and bundled myself into the car. I knew I would find the narrow one-way streets of the capital a challenge. In the older part of the city closer to the coast, the streets were narrower, more crowded, and laid out higgledy-piggledy. And there was no avoiding them.

Having allowed ample time to get lost in, I was early. I enjoyed a clear run in and then got lucky, finding a parking space in Avenida Coll directly opposite the old fort.

The turquoise ocean pulled me, and I strolled along the promenade on that sunny and warm afternoon, soaking in the atmosphere, enjoying the slow pace of life, the sense of being far from anywhere. An outpost, yet also, to a degree, cosmopolitan, Arrecife had a lot to offer. The capital of a lovely sunny island full of cacti and palm trees and gravel and rock. Such a lot of gravel and rock. It was the sense of being almost in the tropics without the sticky heat. Although, the island was not for everyone. You had to be into barren landscapes and volcanoes. After a few days here, I got to thinking expatriates would be hankering for rolling green. Which was probably why the local councils planted so many stout Canary palms. That, and for the shade. And all the doors and windows of the inland villages were painted green, which helped.

The café was situated in a lane off the main drag and offered a vibrant if dimly lit contrast to outdoors. Coming in from all that light and white, my eyes took some time to adjust. There were about ten tables in the space, many of them occupied. I sat down at a table for two near the bar, choosing the seat by the wall so I could keep an eye on the room, and was promptly presented with a menu. My Spanish wasn't up to explaining I was waiting for someone, so I ordered a coffee.

Before it came, Jim Ackland entered, peering into the gloom, his sunglasses in one hand, a newspaper in the other. He saw me and I removed my sunglasses and smiled, but his gaze slid from my face. I had to stand up and wave. He still didn't recognise me. I left my table and walked towards him as he was heading out the door.

'Jim.'

He looked startled then confused, and then he broke out in a deep belly laugh.

'What on earth?'

'It's my disguise.'

'What do you need a disguise for?'

'You heard Cribbs is on the island?' I said, keeping my voice low. 'Clive thinks it won't be long before the Maloney boys are here as well. Hence the outfit.'

He gave me a critical look, screwed up his face and sniffed. 'Well, it works.'

I laughed. I felt reassured. Although I made a mental note to toss that patchouli perfume in the bin.

We sat down and when the waiter came with my coffee, Jim ordered the same. He was a tall open-faced man, distinctive with that schnoz of a nose, and he sported a deep tan.

'Enjoying your holiday?'

He grunted. He went on to tell me in an even tone what he thought of Lanzarote, which wasn't that favourable. He preferred Greece. Italy. The south of France. I had no idea where I preferred and kept quiet. We didn't choose to meet to discuss the ins and outs of favourite holiday destinations.

The arrival of his coffee changed the course of the conversation.

'I heard about your loss.' He gave me a sympathetic look as he stirred in some sugar, rattling on about how hard it was to lose someone.

My, how news travels. Out of all my old police contacts I had only told Clive.

Although Jim and I had worked together on the squad, we'd never been close. I would go so far as to say I didn't much like him or trust him. With good reason. Besides, I didn't want to discuss my private life with an old colleague, especially one from the 1970s. Times had moved on, but I had no idea if Jim had, and lesbians used to be the number one topic of ridicule when it came to the treatment of female members of the constabulary. Back then, you were either a whore or a lesbian. Or, as Liz, who found herself plonked in the first bracket, told me once, you were deemed to be a nun, pure as the driven snow, an exemplar of saintly perfection. As if.

I took a sip of my coffee and glanced around the room. The tendrils of a straggly plant hung in a basket near the door. The walls were decorated with expressive paintings of the island.

The other diners in the room were occupied with each other. No one looked our way. I leaned forward and sought Jim's gaze, coming straight to the point.

'What did you overhear Billy say?'

Jim paused as though preparing a reply.

'He was drunk,' he said, 'and slurring his speech. He didn't mention you by name, but I knew it was you he was talking about.'

'How?'

He seemed awkward. Evasive. 'There weren't too many women in the force back then,' he said. 'Who else could it have been? He managed to avoid telling the whole room he was a criminal and a snout, but anyone who knew anything about either would have twigged. He was raving on about how easily conned some coppers are, that most coppers, female coppers especially, would believe anything you tell them. That sort of thing. I'm a bit fuzzy in the recollecting, but I thought you should know. He's sailing close to the wind. People have long memories, and Lanzarote is full of Brits. Some say it could become the next Costa if you get my drift.'

I pondered Jim's account for a few moments. I didn't want him to think I was rattled by his tip-off.

'I still think he could have been talking about anyone.'

'I suppose.'

He looked doubtful. I offered him a smile, hoping to leave him with the impression that I was grateful.

'The main thing is you recognised him,' I said. 'Which means he's blowing his cover, the fool. Must think just because he's on holiday he can do what he likes.' I drank some more of my coffee and, as though changing the subject, I added, 'Where are you staying on the island?'

'Costa Teguise.'

That would be the golf course then. Handy. Nice and close. I thought I might scope the terrain on my way back to Guatiza.

'What about you?' he said.

'Playa Blanca.'

'Any good?'

'I like it. A much-needed getaway.'

'I'm sure it is.'

I was relieved when he left it there and we fell into silence. I drained my cup. Jim did the same. Then he mumbled, 'Excuse me,' and took himself off to the bathroom. I wanted to leave the café right then, but it would have been impolite. Instead, I paid the bill. And then I waited but Jim didn't reappear. What was he doing in there? Was there a queue? Impatient, I pulled his newspaper towards me and leafed through the pages. An announcement of a local murder on the third page caught my eye. Police had found the body of an Englishman in a water cave near Los Cocoteros. It was the victim's name that got me. Oscar Cribbs.

Would that be the same Oscar Cribbs? It was not a common name. He was on holiday, the article said, and he'd been stabbed multiple times.

Unease rippled through me. Had Jim seen this? Must have done if he'd read the paper and the paper looked read. Why didn't he mention it? Was that why he made that comment about the island becoming the next Costa Crime? I didn't care for the implications. Either the Maloney boys really were on the island, or they'd sent someone to do their dirty work. Whichever it was, I needed to get to Billy before he made his presence here screamingly obvious, shooting his mouth off in bars. It wasn't any kind of protective instinct at play in me. A dead Billy couldn't explain himself, couldn't apologise, couldn't atone.

I caught movement in my side vision and hurried the newspaper back over to Jim's side of the table. There was no point bringing the killing up with Jim. No point dredging up the past. Besides, Jim was of no use to me; he was leaving the island the next day. I didn't want to pack him off with yet more gossip. Better he thought I knew nothing. Protected by innocence? I thought not. I was feeling peeved that he hadn't bothered to mention there were more people than Billy Mackenzie that I needed to keep my eye out for. Killers. People who would just as likely want me dead.

As Jim neared our table, I stood and thanked him for his time and said my goodbyes in as casual a tone as I could muster.

7

THE COCK AND BULL, CHARLTON, LONDON, SEPTEMBER 1979

SEE ALL, HEAR ALL, SAY NAUGHT.

That was the advice my old sergeant told me when I was still in uniform. I took his comment to heart and made sure I kept my eyes and ears open, and my mouth shut. It stood me well in the squad. But it wouldn't be enough to protect me from the likes of Billy Mackenzie. I didn't have enough life experience in my mid-twenties to figure out who not to trust. Besides, Billy had come highly recommended, and I had no reason not to trust Spence or his judgement. I couldn't say I exactly liked Billy Mackenzie. He had a shifty nature. He was a snitch, after all. But I was eager to impress my bosses, eager to make an impression, eager to be recognised and respected as a good detective. As a female copper I had to work twice, no three times as hard as a bloke to get noticed, for my contribution to be valued. And so, I did. I was ambitious. The one thing I did not want to happen was a return to uniform. Ever. It would have felt like I'd been stripped of a stripe. I knew I could never deal with the humiliation.

Life in the CID was never dull. There was always another job, always another tip-off. How else did the police find out what was afoot? And Billy and I had a regular haunt. Not the Ship and Anchor, but an out of the way pub in Charlton, the Cock and Bull.

I never liked entering that dingy old local stinking of beer and fags. I kept a change of clothes at the nick for those days when we met. In a public toilet block in a nearby park, I removed the clothes I wore to work – knee length A-line skirt, blouse, and leather jacket – and put on flared jeans and a loose top and denim jacket. Even in that garb, I didn't fit in with the regular clientele and heads always turned on my way in.

One Thursday lunchtime in September, about a month after the car yard obs had finished, I pushed open the pub door and confronted the flock wallpaper that clashed hideously with the swirl pattern of the deep-red and near threadbare carpet to find Billy tucked in a quiet corner hunched over a pint. I went straight to the bar and ordered a half of bitter.

I knew he'd seen me in the backbar mirror. He gazed at me through beery eyes for a moment before looking away. I checked the time. It was only half past one in the afternoon, hardly a good time to be drunk.

I sat and drank my beer. When I had half a glass left, I slid off the bar stool and went out the back as though on my way to the Ladies. I waited in the hall. Billy joined me a few minutes later.

I asked him how he was. Got the usual story about his dwindling milk round and how he wasn't seeing enough of his kids. I told him I didn't have much time to make him stop complaining.

'What's news?'

'Not much. I might have something for you, though. Sounds

like the Maloney boys are up to their old tricks.'

My instinct was to lean forward and hunker in, all cloak and dagger, but then anyone walking by on their way to and from the toilets would prick up their ears.

An old man with a walking stick exited the Men's and passed by behind us as he returned to the bar. I stood back and kept my gaze pinned on Billy, offered him a bland smile as though he had said something mildly witty and said, 'And?'

'They're planning a job on a security van.'

'I need specifics, Billy. You know that.'

'That I can't give you.' He paused and eyed me expectantly. I reached into my pocket and slipped him a tenner. He squirreled it away and said, 'Meet me here tomorrow.'

'Same time?'

I had to go back two more times to get enough info to convince the Super.

OBS, LEWISHAM

Epsom, Billy had said, the robbery to take place on a Tuesday.

'Well done, Marjorie,' DI Brace whispered to me as I took up a seat in the meeting room. I filled with pride. I was soon deflated as some of the sergeants threw doubt on the info.

There were plenty of murmurs. Where had the info come from? Who was the source? Can they be trusted?

DS Drinkwater and DI Brace shielded me but that also meant no one knew it was my informant. I was hungry for the glory, but the inspector warned me not to be too quick to grab it in case something went wrong. Besides, my tip-off was bundled in with all the other information the squad had on the gang. I mustn't get too big for my boots.

Instead of finding myself the centre of attention, I was back on another obs. This time Liz and I were told to watch a telephone box in a quiet street in Lewisham. Mrs Timms, the wife of the getaway driver, used that telephone rather than her own as she knew hers was tapped.

We were to sit in the front bedroom of a terraced house across the street and quite some distance from the phone box. We were to wait in that bedroom for Mrs Timms to leave her house thirty yards away, cross the road and enter the phone box. Should she appear, we were to notify via the two-way radio our colleague parked nearby who would then drive by the phone box to check it was her. If that was confirmed, he was to notify British Telecom to do a trace and find out who she'd called. That was the plan.

We soon found the obs lacked the buzz and the convenience of the car yard obs.

We took it in turns to sit behind thick net curtains in the bay window, the binoculars and camera discreetly situated at the level of the windowsill, poking out of small gaps in a row of ornaments. The owner of the house, a police secretary, was out at work all day. No tea and no cake. And no activity beyond the net curtains. Instead, an empty street and a house whose front door never opened. But our time in that bedroom wasn't quiet. Someone next door to us spent all day playing an electric guitar, badly. A teenager, we decided. Should have been at school.

Although we were much better off than our squad member stuck in the car below. The stiffness, the muscle cramps, the urgent desire to get up and walk about, or, worse still, pee, must have been horrendous. At least Liz and I had each other, and we could talk. Mostly we listened to the radio to drown out next door and took turns to either read or play patience or doze. And Liz had had the presence of mind to pack flasks of coffee and sandwiches.

It was nearing two in the afternoon of the Friday of that first week when Liz stretched, and I yawned.

'Mint?'

I peeled back some of the tight wrapping and levered her out a Polo. She popped it in her mouth and sucked.

'I think she's on to us.'

'They're parked so far away though.'

'She hasn't left the house.'

'True.'

'Not once. I find that dead weird. Don't you?'

She was right.

Even so, all the next week we watched that house as well. We had no real idea if she knew we were watching her, but Mrs Timms didn't approach the phone box once. Back at the station, Brace decided she had in fact clocked the car parked in the street much too close to where we were, just as Liz suspected.

OTHER SQUAD MEMBERS had set up more surveillance, but it wasn't enough to prevent the robbery. While we were busy observing and questioning our sources, the gang were plotting and scheming. And since they had the advantage of knowing exactly what they were doing, right down to the day, date, time, and place, while we were groping around in the half-light, of course they pulled it off.

We got news of the robbery the next day. Brace held a briefing, and, amidst much groaning and growling, he announced the gang had held up a Securicor van near Tadworth, Surrey. Not exactly Epsom, but the day, Tuesday, was right. And it was the same MO. The gang had staged a car accident under a narrow bridge, effectively creating a roadblock. After the van came to a halt, they shot the tyres and terrorised the driver and his mate, while one of the gang used a chainsaw to cut a hole in the side. They'd even taken the car keys off drivers approaching the scene, after threatening the drivers with guns. Those extra vehicles completely blocked the road. The robbers had then taken off in a getaway car. All we knew was that the car had headed south.

We were hamstrung. All the squad could do was sit and wait for another tip-off. Any officer with an informer was out the station door putting the pressure on. No news came in, other than that the robbers had been very clever when it came to forensics. Not a fingerprint to be found. Descriptions from the witnesses were useless as the gang had all worn balaclavas.

The daily briefings were getting that little bit more depressing as the days went by. It was enormously frustrating to know exactly who the gang members were and not be able to find them let alone make arrests. Someone must know something, but who?

I MET Billy in the Cock and Bull at the regular time the following Thursday. On entering the pub, I nearly didn't recognise him. He'd trimmed his beard and had a haircut and even had on a clean shirt. Must have a date, I thought. I was pleased for him.

Billy seemed to me a lonely guy, withdrawn, careworn and fighting off a hard-done-by attitude. There was never anything cheery in his manner, no banter, no wit. And there were few topics of interest we shared, which made conversing with him a chore. I supposed it also meant I needed to waste little time cutting to the chase. I went to the bar and ordered a drink. Orange juice this time.

He was nursing a pint of bitter. I waited, toying with the stem of my glass. There was always that moment of uncertainty before I slipped out on my way to the Ladies.

He soon joined me, and we made small talk. Impatience grew as I waited for him to divulge what he had. He liked to make me wait. Eventually he said, 'Two of the robbers are holed up in a caravan park.'

'Any idea who?'

'Not the Maloney boys. They're long gone. Oscar Cribbs and the getaway driver.'

'Fred Timms?'

'Yeah, him.'

'And this caravan park...'

'Littlehampton. On the river.' He went on to describe the location. It was as though he'd been there himself. Maybe he had.

'How reliable is this, Billy? I mean, where did you get this info?'

'A snitch never reveals his sources, Marjorie.' He paused, stroked his beard with grubby fingers. Then he met my gaze. 'It's a dead cert. You can count on that.'

I slipped him a tenner and took myself back to the station and straight to the DI's office.

'You reckon this is kosher?' Brace looked doubtful as he leaned back in his seat, arms on the armrests, fingertips pressed together. I stood there on the other side of his big desk. It was covered in paperwork. I refused to look down at that mess and I refused to look away even as his eyes bored into me. I felt myself blushing.

'The last tip-off proved right.'

'Didn't get us anywhere though, did it? We needed more detail.'

'This time he's given us all we need, sir. Names and a location.'

'And you trust this guy?'

'I have no reason not to.'

'Alright, leave it with me.'

'Thank you, sir.'

On my way out of his office, he added, 'Cup of tea would be

nice.'

I went to the tea station like an obedient pup. Milk, two sugars, slightly stewed. Before I'd had a chance to take it to him, he'd rounded up the squad.

'Some information has come to light,' he said, and I felt instantly diminished. Was I going to be excluded from the action as well? I stood there holding his tea. He went on. 'We've been told Timms and Cribbs are hiding out in a caravan park in Littlehampton.'

'Which one?'

'There's only one. It's on the river. There's a boat house next door. And a container yard.'

'Not Butlin's then.'

'No, not Butlin's. Not a holiday park at all, in fact.'

'I get the picture.'

As a salve for my hurt pride, Brace teamed me up with Detective Sergeant Clive Plant, one of the few officers on the squad from my area, a tall man, his curly blond hair framing a mean-looking face with sharp blue eyes and a stern set to the mouth. His favourite colour was black. Black pants, black shirt, black everything. But I didn't hold his appearance against him. He was kind to me, and that was what mattered.

The squad wasted no time organising a raid. The local police were notified within the hour. Guns were procured. A plan was made. Roles assigned. The only difficulty we faced was ascertaining which of the fifty caravans on site contained Timms and Cribbs. A call to the site manager didn't provide us with a definite caravan as most of the vans housed men in various numbers, among them workers in the boatyard and nearby factories, ex-cons and addicts and alcoholics. Not the sort of caravan park to take a family. Which I thought was a good thing, considering what was about to happen. The site manager did help narrow it down to a list of three.

. . .

It was a cool and bleak late-September afternoon as we made our way in a small convoy to Littlehampton. A weak autumn sun hung in a milky sky and clouds banked on the horizon to the north threatened rain. Anticipation had the adrenaline pumping and I was pleased to find DS Plant good company, keeping me entertained with stories from his old days in uniform and distracting me from the butterflies dancing in my belly.

We arrived in Littlehampton a little after four. While Brace, along with Detective Sergeant Jim Ackland, visited the site to pinpoint the exact location of the caravan, the rest of us congregated in a café down the road, one of those local cafés selling stewed tea and bacon butties. None of us were about to order anything else, although a couple went for a spam fritter. The café manager seemed to know better than to ask questions after getting fobbed off by Plant with a curt, 'Out of town,' when he asked where we were from. I was pretty sure the café manager knew who we were, but he said nothing despite the curiosity shining out of watchful eyes.

Brace and Ackland burst into the café as most of us were draining our cups. Heads turned. We kept the conversation general until we were outside. A sudden burst of excitement filled the air. After almost seven months we were finally about to nab two of the gang. Brace took command and divvied out the roles. I was disappointed not to be allotted any sort of backup role. Instead, I was told to stand by the caravan park entrance and send any approaching vehicle on their way.

'Can't the local cops do that?'

No answer. Peeved, I stood by the gates in the cold and the wind and waited.

The caravans were lined up in three rows, most on bitumen. Not a blade of grass in sight except right at the back by the river. Behind me, on the other side of the lane, containers were stacked cheek by jowl. A smell of diesel hung in the air. I began to hope no one approached as I wasn't sure I wanted to get up close to anyone who lurked around here. What sort of copper was I?

The squad had taken up their positions and had the caravan surrounded. Brace crept forward, gun to the ready. Just when I thought I would miss all the action, a panda car pulled up and a local constable appeared.

I thought fast. 'Where have you been?' That threw him. Before he could reply I said, 'Just wait here and stop anyone from coming in.' Then I hurried closer, choosing a spot two caravans away from the action, watching.

There was a loud bang as Plant booted in the caravan door. He disappeared into the van with Brace and a couple of the others. I pulled back and waited. Then I heard a commotion of shouts and thuds. No shot was fired. Just when I thought it was all over, I heard someone panting and hurried steps coming my way. How close? Not far. I saw a pair of legs approaching the side of the caravan. I stepped out and stuck out my foot. Great timing. Whoever it was landed flat on their face. Then Plant was ready with the handcuffs.

'Well done, Marj.'

Other than from Brace, Plant's praise was the first bit of real endorsement I had received from anyone on the squad so far and I was ecstatic. I was especially thrilled that it was due to me and my informer that we'd nabbed Timms and Cribbs.

Although Brace had forbidden me from mentioning it, I couldn't help dropping that little bit of truth into the conversation with Plant on the way back to the station, and instantly regretted it. He congratulated me but I sensed he was not too happy that a rookie, not even a fully-fledged detective, had been the cause of the arrests and the recovery of some of the loot.

'And who is this snout?'

'You know I can't tell you that.'

'That's okay. I already know. Spence never could keep his trap shut. And I've seen you outside the Cock and Bull. That's where you meet, right?'

'When have you ever seen me at the Cock and Bull?'

'Walls have eyes.'

'Don't you mean ears.'

He laughed.

'You be careful, Marj. There's plenty on the squad who'll stab you in the back.'

'I will.'

'And whatever you do, don't let Ackland find out. He's a blabbermouth and a shit-stirrer who'd like nothing more than to bring down a wannabe like you.'

It was good advice, and I made a mental note to remember it. Yet again, I felt protected, I felt that benevolence of older wiser coppers looking after their own.

Back at the station, the interrogating began. I played no part in the interviews. It was Plant who told me the rest of the gang had gone to ground, but because Cribbs and Timms had turned supergrasses to lessen their sentences, nailing the gang was starting to look promising.

The rest of the squad thought so, too. A fresh optimism pervaded the air. Optimism reinforced when DS Drinkwater came down to congratulate us.

The capture was an outstanding success, even though most of the gang and the loot from the robbery had got away. I remained frustrated not to find myself at the centre of the praise and all the cheers, but I knew I had to let that go. My ego took a further battering now I was off obs, and Brace had assigned me to do the photocopying and make the tea. Twenty-eight mugs of tea each time there was a meeting and somehow, I was to know who had milk, who had sugar and how much. I told myself I was the most highly paid tea maker in history, but it did nothing to diminish my resentment.

8

LOS COCOTEROS, LANZAROTE, SUNDAY 17 MARCH 2019

BILLY PACED THE LENGTH OF HIS LIVING ROOM. HE NEEDED A plan, but he couldn't think straight. Should he flee the island or hunker down and hope? He couldn't decide. It was Sunday, not twenty-four hours after discovering Oscar's corpse. He was on the verge of packing a suitcase when his phone rang. His stomach tightened as he glanced at the screen.

Her.

He groaned. This was not what he needed. Not now. Not at any time. Not Ramona.

As he swiped to decline the call, he realised the bad feeling he'd been harbouring could be traced back to when he found out from Ramona that Alvaro was getting out of prison.

She'd been urging him to visit ever since Alvaro was convicted for grievous bodily harm. The prison was only in Tahiche, about a ten-minute drive she'd said in that reproachful tone she put on. But he never went. Maybe if he had, Alvaro would still be alive. He doubted it, he never had much influence over his son, but that was what Ramona thought. Maybe now Alvaro was gone she would stop harassing him. How likely was that? Billy paused. No chance. He'd been murdered, after all, and there was all the distress that came with that. Or at least, not until after the court case could he expect to be free of her demands. Assuming there would be one.

As sure as eggs is eggs, his phone sprang to life again and Her appeared on the screen. This time he hit the green button.

'Ramona.'

'You following the news?'

Not even a "How are you?"

'Of course,' he lied.

'The police have not found any sign of Alvaro anywhere. They say without a body it will be very hard to convict anyone of his murder. Eddy, you have to do something.'

Eddy, short for Edwin, his alter ego.

'What the hell can I do?'

'Think. You of all people must know how to find a missing body.'

'Ask your father.'

'Don't bring my father into this.'

'I know nothing about missing bodies.'

It wasn't true. He knew plenty of ways to dispose of a body. It wasn't hard. Deep ocean, bury in concrete…

'Wait a minute. Wait a minute.' There was a long pause. He picked up the sound of a radio or television in the background. Then, in a moment of high drama, she breathed, 'Oh. My. God. I don't believe I'm hearing this. Eddy.'

'Tell me.'

'They say forensics may have found something in Villa Winter.'

Plausible. He'd never been down to Cofete – not having a

head for heights he couldn't face the cliff road – but he'd seen the documentary of Villa Winter, and he always thought the incinerator built in the basement kitchen could have been used to burn bodies. What else would it have been for? He didn't mention his grim musings to Ramona. She'd freak. Instead, he dropped a not-so-subtle hint.

'Ash, I bet.'

'Ash?'

'Never mind.'

That set her off.

'You don't sound like you care. Why don't you care? What's the matter with you, Edwin Banks? No, don't answer that. I know what the matter with you is. And you will have to carry the guilt of the death of your son to your own grave.'

He let her rave on for a bit and then told her he had another call coming in and hung up.

Ramona was the cross Billy was forced to bear. Old familiar emotions rose up in him, the frustration, the injustice, the inability to fix it. And he rued the wrong turn he took when he first came to the island, all because he wanted to blend in, and to do that he needed to learn Spanish.

OLD SALT WORKS, LOS COCOTEROS, LANZAROTE, JUNE 1980

Billy hadn't anticipated the hard work ahead of him when he bought the half-finished house from Torbjorn. He was a mere thirty-five years of age, yet as he hefted another two concrete blocks, one in each hand, and carried them over to where he'd got to with the perimeter wall, he sure as hell felt the weight pulling on his muscles. He worked as fast as he could. His mortar mix was starting to go off in the wheelbarrow, thanks to the scorching summer sun.

Five blocks later and he could bear the burning of his skin

no longer. What fool thought it a good idea to build a high concrete block wall in the Lanzarote summer sun without a shirt on? This fool. He'd seen too many brickies in London on hot summer days in a singlet and pants or wearing no shirt at all. He could understand why, but when it came to following suit, he needed to think twice. He'd only been on the island a few months and he was still getting used to the way of things, and he needed to adjust fast, or he'd have no skin left.

Every morning since he came to the island, he pinched himself. He didn't miss filthy old London town with all of the scams and the dangers of his gang-centred life there, not one bit. He had found paradise, even if it was a bit rustic. A bit? Very rustic, then. But he liked that. The landscape had charm. The place was not overrun. The roads were empty most of the time. Sure, things happened slowly, if at all, and the locals were a closed shop, but so far, he had managed to find his way.

Thank you, Marjorie, he said to himself, cleaning out the wheelbarrow with a watering can and a rag and pouring the slurry on the land beyond his block's perimeter. He pictured a kind of shrine with her photo as the centrepiece and smiled to himself. She was far too nice to be a copper. Far too trusting. Gullible, even. Believed whatever bullshit he fed her. Although it hadn't been bullshit. You can't be an informer and pass on a pack of lies. He owed her his life. That is what he knew. And he would never forget it.

It was after he turned supergrass that he was put in witness protection. Those were the rules. And the role wasn't hard. He had enough information on a whole chorus of gangsters to satisfy the force. And so, one miserable Sunday in December, he was whisked away. No more milk round, no more access visits with the kids, no more eyes and ears on every little matter. His whole life as he'd known it, no more.

SAFE HOUSE, WALTHAMSTOW, FEBRUARY 1980

He did not feel safe here at all. And the place was dismal. A sparsely furnished two-bedroom terrace in a narrow street of identical houses. Only the front room downstairs had a bay window. The carpet was threadbare and smelled faintly musty. The kitchen sported its original cabinetry and cooker. Sections of wallpaper in the back room were torn. Scummy didn't cover it. He needed out and he had enough funds stashed away in the bank thanks to his inheritance to make a clean escape. He just needed to choose where. Marjorie had swung by with provisions and to help him plot his next move. She'd also brought maps, bless her. He poured over them, indecisive. She finger-stabbed the dining table.

'You better hurry up and choose somewhere, Billy.'

'You need to call me Edwin. Or Eddy.'

'Eddy suits you better.'

'I quite like Edwin.'

He grinned at her, but she didn't reciprocate. She seemed stressed. Between them was a map of Europe. On the radio, Debbie Harry was telling the world she was not the kind of girl who gives up just like that.

The tide was high for Billy Mackenzie. That was plain as day.

Why on earth Marjorie had got so involved she was prepared to help him escape the country, he never could fathom. He'd vetoed Spain the moment she put her finger on Costa del Sol. All the villains in Britain had already retired there on their proceeds of crime. The last place on earth a dodgy grass wanted to find himself was mingling with his own kind.

She'd brought the *Let's Go* guidebook with her. She sat back and flicked through it, reeling off countries. The Iron Curtain pretty much ruled out Eastern Europe. Nowhere cold held any appeal so they agreed anywhere north of the Alps was out. There was Greece, which had tempted him for about ten minutes. Then he found out how hot it got there in summer. Brutal. Italy sounded okay if he went north, but then he'd be up in the mountains, and he vetoed mountains. He wanted somewhere at sea level more or less. Hilly was fine but nothing spectacular. His nerves couldn't take it. There was France. Marjorie did a hard sell on France. But he remained unconvinced. He couldn't see himself tackling the language and he had an irrational aversion to, well, the French.

'There's nowhere left,' she cried, 'unless you head to Africa.' She pointed with her pencil vaguely in the direction of Morocco, but the nib ended up in the ocean nearby. They both peered at the map.

'Tenerife?'

'The Canary Islands.'

'Hang on.' She read up about the islands, reading out snippets and one by one Billy turned them all down. All bar one.

'Lanzarote?'

A volcanic desert island with a population of about forty thousand that still retained its traditional ways. Sounded like the back of beyond.

'Why not?' he said, taking the book and dogearing the page.

Marjorie went to a travel agent and booked his ticket. He was on the plane two days later.

OLD SALT WORKS, LOS COCOTEROS, LANZAROTE, JUNE 1980

Inside, his new house was coming along well. There was nothing to do except for the finishes and the painting. Torbjorn had already completed the kitchen and bathrooms. Had the power connected. No need for mains water. The cistern under the patio would be ample for his needs. Runoff when it rained helped keep the cistern full. If he ran low, he could truck some in. He opened the front door and waited for his eyes to adjust to the subdued light as he went in.

Every time he entered the house, he gained an immense sense of pride. It was a cavernous space far in excess of anything he was used to. Straight ahead was the living area looking out through large windows at the ocean view. An ocean view! And that ocean was pretty much always sapphire. Not murky brown or gunmetal. Sapphire! Never in his wildest dreams. That windowed wall had a bit of a curve to it, too, in the style of local artist César Manrique. Torbjorn had got quite ambitious. Pity he never got to live in his dream home. What was misfortune for Torbjorn was great for Billy née Edwin. Or Eddy.

On the south side of the living room was a guest bedroom which Billy was using for storage, and a small bathroom. Immediately to the left of the entrance was the long kitchen with a curved island bench and space for a dining table in front. Torbjorn had even thought to put in a small utility room behind the kitchen with access to the front patio. The roof was flat, with deep concrete eaves for shade. The design had a modern, late-1970s feel. And Billy loved it.

Beyond the kitchen and dining areas was the hall leading to three more bedrooms in the north wing – two with ocean views, the other and the bathroom facing west – and then the main bedroom at the end, also enjoying that ocean view. There, he found an old, long-sleeved T-shirt and a hat. Time to take his sunburn a lot more seriously.

Time he took his remedial Spanish more seriously, too. He'd never been one for languages. But if he wanted a life here, wanted to blend in, he needed to not be that Englishman who only knew Gracias and Buenos días. Only, he wasn't going to risk joining a language class. He wasn't even sure there were any going on the island. He needed a private tutor. Someone to come to his home. How was he going to find one if he couldn't ask around?

He managed to learn *Necesito una profesora de español*, but every time he resolved to ask in the local supermarket, he lost his nerve, knowing whoever he spoke to would speak back in Spanish and he wouldn't understand a word.

After a few weeks of indecision, on his way back from the bank in Arrecife one afternoon he got lost in the warren of one-way streets and ended up outside an English language school for children. The door to the small building was open and he decided to risk it.

Entering a cool dimly lit foyer, he could hear through a partition wall a teacher saying a short phrase and her class responding. He looked around. At the far end of the foyer, a woman seated behind a wooden office desk – a receptionist, possibly the owner – greeted him in perfect if heavily accented English, and he was instantly optimistic. He made his inquiry.

'Private classes? Where? In your home?'

'Unless you have a better idea.'

The woman thought for a moment.

'My teachers are English natives. But I know Ramona is looking for work. She's a Spanish language teacher.'

'Does she speak English?'

'Of course. Here's her number. I will let her know to expect your call.' She handed him a square of paper. 'But you should meet her in a café, first. Introduce yourself. You understand. I cannot send teachers to the homes of strange men.'

It took him another week to muster the courage to make the call.

He met Ramona in a café on Calle León y Castillo near the waterfront. He spotted her on entry, the only woman occupying a table by herself decked out in a figure-hugging dress. She had long and thick black hair, and bow-shaped lips painted a lurid red. Her dark eyes lit when she saw him. Must be short-sighted or there was some Adonis standing right behind him, he thought. Billy knew he wasn't the most attractive man on the planet. Still, the beard hid his underbite, and he was tanned and muscly thanks to the build. Maybe she lusted after Anglo blood. Who knew? He went over and introduced himself. Ordered a beer and offered her the same. She stuck with her coffee and lit a cigarette.

'You are living on the island, Eddy?' she asked, taking a drag and inhaling sharply, breaking the awkwardness that hung between them.

He almost looked behind him, so strange it was to hear himself as anything other than Billy.

'I have a place up near Guatiza.'

'Nice.' She sounded doubtful. 'You like it up there? I prefer to live here in Arrecife,' she remarked, tapping her ash in the ashtray containing her previous cigarette, the end of its filter coated with lipstick. 'More life.' She paused, sipped her coffee. 'What brings you to the island?'

'What brings you to the island?' There was no way she was born and bred here. She had cosmopolitan chic stamped all over her.

She threw her head back and issued him a mocking laugh.

'I wanted time to think about my future. My family are from Valencia, but they moved to Fuerteventura. Do you know it?'

'Never been.'

'Don't bother. There's nothing there.' She sounded dismissive, resentful almost. There was a brief pause. Then she said, 'It is good you want to learn Spanish.'

'I'm no good with languages,' he said, taking a slug of his beer.

'I'm no good with bad students.'

Her smile was brazen. He picked up an extra-curricular subtext and something stirred in him down below. They chatted for a while longer before arranging a weekly lesson at his place starting on Saturday morning. On the way home he wondered if he'd been reckless letting her know where he lived.

He spent the rest of the week finishing the last section of the front patio wall and painting the living room. Couldn't have a woman like Ramona walking onto a building site. On Saturday, he dashed around cleaning and tidying, realising as he stripped his sheets that he needed to lift his game if he was going to impress any member of the opposite sex let alone a glamour-puss like Ramona. Women liked a man who was housetrained, not a slob. And he'd let himself go since he arrived on the island, there being no one to pass an eye over his mess. An hour before she was due to arrive, he took the trouble to trim his beard. Eyeing himself in the mirror, he decided next week he would even risk the local barber and have a haircut.

She pulled up in a VW Polo a little after three in the afternoon. Hearing a car heading down the gravel track, he'd gone out onto the patio in anticipation, ready to open the gates. He watched her slither out of the driver's seat, long silky tanned legs, the delectable curve of her hips accentuated by a figure-hugging skirt that reached mid-thigh, the top half, that deep cleavage, held suggestively inside a bright red blouse. He gulped.

She greeted him with a customary kiss on both cheeks. Sweating inside his shirt and hoping it wouldn't show, he led her across the patio.

The moment she stepped inside the house, her eyes scanned about, taking note of every detail, pausing to drink in the ocean view across a patio that was very much a work in progress, her approving manner confirming for him his clean-up effort had been worth it.

'Drink?'

He'd sourced some lemonade at the local supermarket. Added a splash of bitters for a bit of a kick. Ice. They sat down at either end of the couch. As the condensation built on their glasses, Ramona spoke simple words and phrases in Spanish and made him repeat after her. Listening as he soaked her in was akin to mental torture. He did his best to concentrate. She remained oblivious to the impact she was having on him, or so it appeared. She corrected his pronunciation, taught him to roll his Rs and get guttural with the J. Then she pointed to objects in the room and named them: el vaso, el suelo, la pared, la ventana. He got to grips with the masculine and feminine. With I and You and He and She and We and Them. An hour later, his brain felt fried.

She'd brought with her some workbooks created for children and told him to use them.

'They will help. You have to be a child again, Eddy. You think you can do that?'

He told her yes in a voice unexpectedly husky.

'You must say Sí.'

'Sí.'

She gave him a coquettish smile. 'And you'll be a good boy for your teacher, yes?' Beneath her simmering gaze, he almost knocked over his lemonade.

How long had it been since he last got laid? Far too long. Should he risk it?

He sidled over and reached out. He hesitated, watching her intently, his hand hovering over her knee. Did she want this? She answered him with a small movement in his direction.

Thank goodness he'd changed his sheets.

BILLY MACKENZIE AKA EDDY BANKS, at the tender age of thirty-five, fell hopelessly in lust. In bed, Ramona was every bit as he'd hoped she would be. No woman had ever devoured him the way she did. Her sexual appetite was formidable. After that first instalment, he lay on his back gazing up at the ceiling with her lying naked beside him. He was stunned, a little sore and depleted, and deliriously happy. She was vocal too, and he was pleased his place was in the middle of nowhere, her moans and yells drowned out by the ocean. He would have felt a touch embarrassed had there been a party wall.

As it was, two weeks into their love fest, he had to repair a section of the plaster on the wall above the bed, where his bedhead landed blow after blow after blow. He pulled the bed further into the room after that.

Was it her Spanish blood that made her so energetically sexual, so insatiable? He didn't want to stereotype. Besides, he had never had much luck with women. He found them demanding and uptight, and, up until Ramona, unresponsive in the intimacy department. He had obviously attracted or sought out the wrong sort of woman. With Ramona, he underwent a kind of sexual awakening, managing to keep up with her demands for more, although only just.

Desire eclipsed all thoughts of Eric and Mick Maloney. The likes of chainsaw wielding Oscar Cribbs never entered his mind. He had a new life now, a satisfying life. He'd been born again, his reward for snitching, and Ramona even made up for all the losses that came with that absolute separation from his past.

Lust meant the pace of the build slowed, the perimeter wall taking twice, three, no four times as long as it might have done without Ramona. Especially as, the day after he repaired the bedroom wall, she moved in.

He managed an intense spurt of progress one week in the middle of the year when she went to visit her parents in Fuerteventura. He wanted to impress her and distract himself from his unexpected longing. It worked, but she returned with a bigger distraction, announcing to him what she had already told her mum and dad: she was pregnant.

They were in the kitchen, and he was making dinner when

she told him the news. He'd made a salad and had the steaks seasoned and ready to fry. He'd uncorked a bottle of dry white: her favourite. Her words seeped into him, knocking him sideways. He scrambled to offer her a positive reaction. Truth was, he felt nothing of the sort.

She stood with her back to the island bench, gazing at him with the same lustful smoulder in her eyes, waiting for a response. He hovered by the fridge. Her blouse was unbuttoned revealing her fulsome cleavage and she did that wriggle she always did when she wanted to take him to bed. He looked at her with something like horror on his face.

'Don't worry. You can't hurt the baby. Sex is good for pregnancy. Strengthens the muscles, you know.'

He wasn't convinced, but when she sashayed his way and reached down her hand and fondled his balls through his pants, that other part of him responded in an instant and they were back in his bed in a tangle of sheets.

It was midnight before they started on the steaks.

He spent the next few days and weeks contemplating fatherhood. Would a kid help replace in his heart the two he would never see again? He didn't feel ready to find out, but he guessed no man really did feel ready, whatever the circumstances. He supposed it would be a sort of crowning glory of his new life in the sun, making up for all the family and friends he was forced to leave behind forever. Suddenly, his future felt sealed. He hadn't met her parents but assumed he would soon enough. Although he wasn't overly keen, knowing something of their background. He didn't want to mingle with his own kind.

It was only as her belly grew that his desire for her waned. It wasn't her shape putting him off – she was a very voluptuous pregnant woman – it was the dramatic change in her personality. He supposed the tendencies had always been there, but he had been happy to ignore them while his dick was being so handsomely serviced. She became restless and demanding. She nagged him, bossed him, ordered him about, issued him with a list of needs and wants, started to exercise the sort of control he would never tolerate. He told her that money was tight. It wasn't. He had plans, he said, a vision – he'd buy three more properties cheap, do them up and let them out – and he wasn't about to squander his savings on frivolities. She had a job; she could pay for the nappies. That remark did not go down well at all.

Then, one day out of the blue she announced she wanted him to move with her to Fuerteventura. There was no way he was doing that.

That was when the big rows started.

That was when she took to hurling whatever was to hand.

And unlike those films in which flared tempers give way to passionate embraces, Billy would dish Ramona the silent treatment and focus all of his anger and dismay on finishing the perimeter wall down by the cliff.

Progress was rapid. He'd started on the render. Then, one morning as he was about to start another mix in the wheelbarrow, Ramona came out of the house yelling for him to drive her to the hospital. He dropped his trowel and raced inside for his car keys, slipping on a large puddle of water by the dining table on his way by.

Alvaro came into this world a wrinkled, bluish-coloured screaming runt with curly black hair – the curls came from Billy, the colour Ramona – and he was the ugliest baby Billy had ever seen. Not that he had seen many. Ramona might have seen loads more. All he knew was she felt as he did, slightly appalled at what they had produced between them.

Alvaro had trouble latching on to Ramona's nipples due to his already pronounced underbite and she got engorged and then ill with milk fever. If pregnancy hadn't suited her temperament, nursing an infant suited her less. She did her best to foist the little beast onto its father. Alvaro spent the first few months of his life being ignored in his pram by a parent filthy with concrete dust and sweat rendering a long and high concrete wall that seemed to go on and on for miles, while its mother mooched about inside the house, listless and thoroughly fed up.

One spring day as Billy applied the last of the render and was steeling himself for the paint job to follow – the whole lot, inside and out, was to be painted white – Ramona took Alvaro to visit his grandparents in Fuerteventura. Grandparents who never once came to Lanzarote to visit their grandson and meet the father for the first time. He might have noted that fact as a sign.

She never came back.

LOS COCOTEROS, LANZAROTE, SUNDAY 17 MARCH 2019

What still got to Billy was the way Ramona blamed him for how Alvaro had turned out. The absent father. Never mind her temper. Never mind it was Ramona who had left the family home with Alvaro when he was only six months old and taken off to Fuerteventura to be with her parents. She'd thought Alvaro would be better off close to her family. Billy thought now as he always had, that Alvaro would have been better off staying with his father even though he fell far short of being any good in the role. His mind flooded with images of all those drives down to Playa Blanca to catch the ferry to Corralejo. He'd done that about once a month. Then it was every two months, then twice a year, then yearly and then not at all. Why? Because every time he made the effort Ramona hit him for cash. There were clothes and shoes and then school fees and the rest. Enough cash in total, he'd decided in the end, for a backyard swimming pool.

He swilled his mouth with water and fixed himself a ham sandwich and took it to the dining table. Patch watched him eat with half-interest. She knew it was unlikely she'd get a crumb of his lunch. Nothing worse than a begging dog. He had her well-trained and look how well she'd turned out. A rescue dog held in the pound for months, transformed into an obedient affectionate companion in lockstep with his daily routine. They were made for each other. He made a good parent, of a dog.

When was the last time he'd seen his son? He thought back. Must have been about twenty years ago. By then, Alvaro had left school and fallen in with a bad crowd. His eyes, bloodshot and half open, had been hard to look at, and he stank. Like his mother, he wanted not love but money. What was Billy? A bank?

But he didn't cut off his son because he had his hand out. He did it for Natasha.

Losing his appetite, he straightened his back and folded his hands behind his head. The stretch felt good. But not for long. Try as he might to push it all away, Alvaro's death merged with Natasha's and Billy was left floating in an ocean of loss. Bemused and numb. The only way he knew how to deal with that loss was to block it out, just as he had successfully blocked out his old life before he moved to the island. What was the point of dwelling on children, an ex-wife, siblings and nephews and old school friends when he couldn't see any of them again, ever?

The curse of the new identity. The old one gets dumped.

And he did feel remorse. He thought it was remorse. Not a feeling he recognised but that uneasy queasy heavy feeling must be it. Even though they had been estranged, Alvaro was still his son. And no father wishes his son murdered. Only, he should have felt hollowed out, but he didn't. Grieving for a wastrel was not in Billy's DNA. At the forefront of his mind was the knowledge that he'd fathered a prick of a man and his

Spanish wife couldn't educate that prick-ness out of her son no matter how much she tried. And Ramona did try. He had to give her that. The way Alvaro had turned out was a combination of things. Bad seed. And this island back in the 1980s was no place to bring up a mongrel of a kid with a bad attitude who had the worst of both cultures embedded in him. Billy had managed to pass on his hard-nut London ways, and Ramona her shady Valencian traits, her family relocating to Fuerteventura for pretty much the same reasons Billy had left for Lanzarote. The local schools were not the issue – Ramona didn't want her boy mingling with the natives – but the international school he attended instead was haunted by the offspring of timeshare agents hoping to get rich out of the new boom in tourism. Money was their god. The whole situation had made for a sort of cultural desert.

Billy eyed Patch asleep on the rug in the living room. Mongrels could turn out well if the mix was right. He wondered, as he often did, what breed had caused that white patch over her eye. Judging by her temperament and size, he'd ruled out the hairy giants like the husky, as well as the bulldog, Pitbull, and Staffordshire terriers. She didn't have poodle in her either. Which left the cuties, like the Pomeranian and the Pekingese. No way. Not in Patch. He decided on either the Scottish Highland terrier or the Maltese. It was impossible to imagine a Maltese mating with a Labrador, so he decided there had to be a third breed in the mix. A border collie or a spaniel. Probably a spaniel. What he did know was he felt much better about life in general and recent events in particular when he concentrated his attention on Patch.

She knew how to make him feel at ease.

As soon as he stopped dwelling on Ramona and their son, he thought of Natasha, and as soon as he managed to divert his attention, it went straight to Oscar Cribbs. There was nowhere to turn. His reality had become a living nightmare.

He couldn't function with his thoughts going round and round and round. He couldn't make a decision. There was nothing for it. He gave Patch a quick pat then headed down the hall to the puzzle room, with the pitter patter of small feet trailing behind him.

9

WATER CAVE, LANZAROTE, MONDAY 18 MARCH 2019

It was a risk, but what sort of copper doesn't visit the crime scene. And the newspaper had given away the location by mentioning the water cave. Finding Billy could wait. Such were my musings over breakfast out on the patio.

A quick Internet search yielded only one water cave near Los Cocoteros, and it wasn't far from Guatiza. When I studied the map, I discovered that the only access by road was a dirt track that came out in my very street. The close proximity made my blood curdle. In choosing the holiday let, I had put myself right in the thick of things. Since I had arrived on the island, I could have been spotted by those brothers any time I walked out my front door. Worse, what if they were also renting a place in the village. I tried to reassure myself. Maybe they chose the spot for a specific reason that had nothing to do with where they were staying. And the killers could have taken the coastal path, although knowing the Maloney boys, that seemed unlikely. But why commit the murder in that particular spot?

Could they have spotted Oscar and given chase and that's where they all ended up? Thinking on it, that was the most plausible scenario.

I donned my disguise, minus the patchouli perfume, and headed off.

Once out of Guatiza, Calle Amor Indiano made a beeline for the coast, cutting a path between a patchwork of small fields. At the end was a holiday let comprising three buildings arranged in a walled compound. I parked away from the entrance and took the cliff path north.

I hadn't walked more than a hundred metres when I arrived at the cave. I had the place to myself. The ocean was calm, the water within the cave still and a lovely shade of turquoise. The area had not been taped off and I had no idea exactly where the body was found. I picked my way across the gnarly rock until I was closer to the pool. The gentle whisper of water beyond the cave gave the pool a strange ethereal feel. Jess would have loved this place. And it was a secluded location for a murder. Out of sight of anyone on or offshore. If Oscar had been chased here, he could not have picked a worse place to run to. Maybe he simply got lost. Blind panic will do that. Whatever happened, it was done, and I had no means of finding out more.

The terrain was rough and uneven, and I didn't rate my chances of not falling or twisting an ankle, so I headed back.

I was halfway to my car when my phone beeped. It was a text from that woman from Fuerteventura. Clarissa. She said she would like to meet for lunch if I was free. I texted back that I was, and we arranged a time and place.

I couldn't decide if I liked Clarissa, but she was my only link to Billy other than the golf course. I would need to think of a way to raise the topic of that letter Billy wrote to Alvaro. Would she have it on her this time? Doubtful. But I couldn't very well ask her to bring it. That would seem strange, and I would have to reveal too much.

The lunch date meant I would need to forgo scoping the golf course. Another day wasted. I should have gone there straight after meeting Ackland but I'd felt too preoccupied with his revelations and the death of Oscar Cribbs. I needed to think, prepare, plan, before I set off to the one place I was likely not only to encounter Billy but the Maloney boys as well.

LOS ALJIBES RESTAURANT, TAHICHE

Clarissa was already seated in the restaurant's outdoor area when I arrived. A pleasing arrangement of chunky wooden tables out on a large patio enclosed by high basalt walls, each table sporting a wide umbrella. I strode right up to where she was sitting, all smart in a tailored blouse of royal blue and contrasting tan capris, her wavy grey hair defying the wind. I had to speak to her before she cottoned on to who I was.

'Interesting get up, Edna,' she said as I sat down. 'Who are you hiding from?'

I did a double take then realised I had to get used to my new name as well as my new get-up. I'd never make a spy. I laughed lightly and offered no reply. I wasn't about to explain the reason for my disguise and Clarissa made no more of it. She must have arrived early as she was halfway through her drink. She was having wine. When a waiter came by, I ordered the same and a refill for her.

'What are we celebrating?' I said. 'Not that I need an excuse.'

'Me neither.'

She smiled. It was a grim smile. Why invite me to lunch if she was not in the mood for levity? Was she that lonely?

It was then that I noticed the pendant hanging from a silver chain nestling above the last done up button of her blouse. It was large, circular, and I recognised the glyph of Capricorn only because Jess was a Capricorn, and she had a similar pendant necklace. Hers was gold. She bought me one of my own – I'm a Virgo – but I never wore it.

The waiter returned with our drinks and took our order. We both settled on the mixed grill with tiny potatoes and salad. As he walked away, I made a second attempt at conversation, the lunch suddenly feeling like a bad blind date.

'Do you come here often? To the island, I mean.'

'As much as I can. I visit an inmate in the prison here,' she said, finally opening up.

'You mentioned him before,' I said, dimly recalling our first conversation down in Playa Blanca. 'A guy wrongly imprisoned for murder.'

'His name is Trevor Moore. He's an author. The poor wretch does not belong inside. He receives no other visitors so it's down to me to keep him in good enough spirits.'

She filled me in on the details. Trevor had been convicted of murdering a priest and making off with a rucksack full of cash. Turned out it was some weird cult who were behind the killing, and Clarissa had given the police enough evidence to prove it. Alvaro's murder was connected. I took a keen interest in her potted account of her ordeal down at Villa Winter in the clutches of that cult the weekend before last for no other reason than since he was Billy's son, presumably Billy himself would be at least mildly interested if not eager for justice for Alvaro.

'When's the trial?'

'Early days. The police are still putting together a case.'

She looked careworn, and I could see the ordeal had taken its toll. Civilians were not used to the drama of crime. While we waited for our food, I lightened the mood with a funny little tale involving Billy's first ever tip-off, leaving out the bit about who Billy was.

'I received info that a delivery driver was selling wholesale goods to a third party somewhere between central London and the delivery point in Dover. It was going to be my first big bust. Can you imagine what it was like for a female copper back in the '70s?'

'Very hard to get taken seriously, I imagine.'

'It was. And I organised the whole operation. I arranged for six squad cars to follow the lorry, anticipating it would pull over in a layby and offload the goods. It didn't. When we got to the destination there was a long queue of lorries, and we were forced to hang back as we were too conspicuous. We ended up parking a mile or so up the road and when the lorry returned to London we followed.'

Her gaze drifted. She seemed preoccupied. Hoping to hold her attention, I pressed on.

'There are dos and don'ts with tailing a suspect. Keep your distance. No indicators. If you are forced to jump a light you have to tell the person behind you and you need to turn left, left, left, and let someone else take over. Takes a team of four or more cars to pull it off. At one point as we were driving through London the driver cottoned-on to being followed. That was when I was doing the tailing.'

'What did you do?' she said with polite interest. I could have ended the story there, but I felt obliged to answer her question. Besides, I hadn't got to the punchline.

'I had to go around a roundabout and leave someone else to pick up the tail. We managed to intercept the lorry as it was entering the depot, expecting the goods to still be onboard. There were twelve coppers involved in that operation. Can you imagine us all gathered around as we got the driver to open the rear of his lorry? Eleven experienced coppers and me, the instigator of the job. Instead of finding the lorry full of the undelivered goods we anticipated, all we found were a bunch of out-of-date tea bags. The driver had managed to offload the merchandise to a third party at the destination itself and I looked like a right idiot.'

Clarissa laughed lightly and I laughed along with her but now that I had come to the end of the tale, a tale I could scarcely recall ever having told anyone before, not even Jess, it began to sink in that Billy had, even that very first time, passed on information that was rather lacking. Had he known the drop-off point was at the destination and not en route?

He had a knack for passing on not only incomplete but downright false information, as I later found out to my cost. I should have severed ties with him after the tea bag fiasco. Not stayed loyal. But I was too wet behind the ears. Besides, DS Spence had recommended him, and I trusted Spence's judgement. I could have had no idea back then where it was all leading.

Watching Clarissa drink her wine, I thought I shouldn't have brought it up with this stranger, a story like that. Only other coppers knew the rigmarole involved, the thrill of the pursuit, the anticipation, and then the let down and humiliation, what with six squad cars involved. I almost blushed in the recollection.

Food was a welcome distraction. I tucked into the meat on my plate, hot and juicy and full of flavour, as though I hadn't eaten in a week. We made small talk, commented on the weather – it was fine for the time of year – and sipped our wine. It was as I was forking the last of the tiny salty potatoes on my plate that I broached the topic at the forefront of my mind.

'That letter you had on you last time we met.'

She hesitated, a loaded fork midway to her mouth.

'What about it?'

'I couldn't help noticing the Dear Alvaro. The man who was murdered in Cofete.'

'Very astute of you.'

'Always a copper, I suppose.'

She set down her fork and reached for her wine.

'The letter was written in 1989,' I said. 'That was the only other thing I noticed.' I paused, and then asked a question I already knew the answer to. 'Who wrote it, do you know?'

'His father.'

'What did it say?'

'Not a lot. Just a big, long sob story about how he should have been a better father but the visits on the ferry had become too much, and his mother kept hitting him for money.'

'Was she Spanish? I mean, Alvaro is a Spanish name if I'm not mistaken.'

'Ramona, so I suppose she was Spanish.'

I tried to picture Billy with a Spanish partner or girlfriend, tried to imagine what she would have seen in him. It was a struggle.

'Where did you find it? The letter, I mean.'

'In a car, his car in Cofete. In the glove compartment. I should have left it there, but at the time I was gathering clues.'

'And was it one?'

'Not really. Except that I got the impression this father was not a nice man. People who issue a string of excuses for their poor behaviour rarely are.'

'True,' I said, thinking of all the criminals I had encountered over the years. It was thinking that brought me straight back to the scene at the water cave.

She picked up her fork. Taking her cue, I continued eating, sending away images of Oscar Cribb's body with every bite.

We finished our meal and when the waiter came to take our plates, she asked for the bill and insisted on paying.

Returning the favour, I drove her to the bus stop. I did think about taking her into Arrecife, but I wasn't too confident navigating my way to the bus station. Even after driving in to meet Jim, I still hadn't got my bearings. Driving on the other side of the road made it even harder. Or maybe I was just getting old. I waited with her until her bus came and we made a date for lunch again next week.

Jess joined me on the drive home. I saw her there in the passenger seat beside me, all hale and hearty. Then I saw a scrawny Jess, pale, lost in her clothes, on that awful last drive back to the hospital. My heart squeezed in my chest. We'd lived together for almost forty years, falling madly in love the moment we met. A Leeds gal through and through. Oh Jess!

In my anguished state I blamed Clarissa for the necklace, the association, the trigger. But I knew it was no use blaming. Anyone or anything could have brought up my grief. It was still much too soon to expect anything less.

Gradually, as I drove north through open country, memories of Jess gave way to the landscape. Pulling up in the drive of the Guatiza farmhouse my life felt surreal as though the agony of the recent past had never happened. Here, with the fresh ocean wind, the sunshine, the strangeness of the volcanic terrain, it was as though I had moved my life to another planet where my past never existed. At least, that was how it felt at first as I entered the house and wandered around the sparsely furnished rooms and sat out on the sheltered patio with my feet up. Somehow, nothing could touch me here, no harm could come to me. I was hidden, secreted away, protected.

It was an illusion, I knew. The moment I began putting myself about, started snooping and sleuthing, I would attract danger. Part of me didn't care if the Maloney boys did see me, recognise me, decide to kill me. There would be some relief in that. And I was back to missing Jess again. And the elixir that was Lanzarote struggled to make itself felt.

I reminded myself that I had come to the island to be a copper. I had to keep focused on my mission. Billy Mackenzie owed me, and I was finally going to make him pay his debt. It would be a release. Maybe it would even set me free from the one burden I had carried with me all these decades, that I had failed as a copper.

Later, I downed a sleeping pill and forced myself to have an early night in preparation for my golf course watch in the morning. But my mind drifted back to Billy, to how it all began, and I spent half the night reliving the past.

10

THE COCK AND BULL, LONDON, 1979

I walked into the Cock and Bull at ten one Friday morning to find Billy in his usual spot. He sat hunched over his pint and as I sat down at the bar with an orange juice, I saw via the back bar mirror that he had a wary look about him. Instead of the usual brief repartee outside the toilets, he launched straight into his info.

'Two of the gang are in Southampton,' he said, muttering beneath his breath, his eyes darting every which way. I leaned forward. He went on. 'Not the Maloney boys.'

'Who, then?'

'Pete Stokes and Gary Trent. They staged the roadblock, then terrorised all those who arrived at the hold up and took all the car keys.'

'The details?'

'They'll be in the Fox and Hound in Hythe at lunchtime today. You better leave now,' he said with a grim laugh.

'What's the matter? You seem on edge.'

He looked at me intently. 'Next time, we'll meet somewhere else.'

He'd been clocked by someone, that much was clear, and it had put the fear of God into him.

I raced back to the station and straight to DI Brace's office, barely pausing after my knock before I opened the door. He was alone. I told him in hurried sentences what Billy had said.

Brace frowned. 'Funny neither Cribbs nor Timms has mentioned this.'

'They are both locked up though, sir.'

'And you're sure about this?'

'My informer was right about the caravan park.'

He thought for a moment, then reached for the two-way radio on his desk. He turned to me and said, 'Go and get Plant.'

I went out to the main office. Heads turned. I made straight for Plant who was at his desk on the other side of the room doing some paperwork. Not wanting to draw any more attention to myself, I leaned towards him and said softly that Brace wanted to see him. Plant nodded then carried on with whatever he was writing up. 'Now,' I hissed. He put down his pen and stood.

'What is it?'

I raced back to Brace's office with Plant on my tail.

In his rushed explanation, the inspector let it slip that the tip-off was down to me. Pride sparked in me, but it didn't have a chance to take hold. By then, we were all pumped with adrenaline, ready to make the arrests. And I was also carrying a gnawing apprehension. What if Billy had got it wrong? I was beginning to understand why DI Brace avoided telling people where these tip-offs came from.

Ackland and Jones walked into the main office about ten minutes later. I realised word of my tip-off had already spread through the squad when Jones gave me an appraising look. Instead of approval in his eyes, or even appreciation, there was something else, something dark. Jones saw me as competition. That, and I sensed he wasn't overly keen on female coppers. There were a few like Jones in the squad.

But there was no time to dwell on personal matters. Plant and Ackland retrieved their gun holsters from their lockers while I fetched my handbag. Things became real and surreal all at once. We went downstairs to the front desk and showed our warrant cards. Plant told the desk sergeant we wanted guns and the station officer came out from behind the high counter as a couple came in off the street. Needing privacy, he led us through to a small annex where Plant and Ackland signed for the guns and the bullets. In minutes we were out the door and in car park.

'We'll meet at the local nick in Hythe,' Plant said to Ackland.

Once we were off, making our way through south London to Richmond to pick up the main road to Southampton, Plant glanced at me and said, 'So this is your tip-off, again.'

I didn't know how to answer, except to say yes.

'Piece of advice, Marj, if you don't mind.'

'Am I doing something wrong?'

'Not wrong exactly. More naïve. You're still new here. There are guys in the squad hungry to prove themselves. After promotion.'

'And?'

'Just keep your head down.'

There was little chance of that if the DI shot his mouth off. I felt instantly undermined. Being a female copper was a minefield at the best of times but in the squad, it was on a whole different level. Something to do with the sense of superiority, specialness, elitism seemed to bring out the best and the worst in people.

In the Hythe nick, I found myself standing beside Ackland.

Plant's words of caution were reinforced when Ackland said, 'You're a bit of a dark horse.'

'What do you mean?'

'Since when does a trainee DC have an informant?'

I scrambled for a reply. 'It all happened by accident,' was the best I could come up with.

'Yeah, right.'

Plant looked over and caught my gaze. A told-you-so expression appeared in his face. 'Ready?' he said and made for the door.

The Fox and Hound was located across the road from the station. On the left, a long wooden jetty stretched out into the Solent. Southampton formed a low sprawl on the other riverbank in the mid-distance.

Plant and Ackland went first, assessing the pub, entering through the main door. I was told to wait outside. Jones went around the back. They hadn't made it far into the pub when muffled screams broke out. A few patrons spilled out onto the street. Thinking that the gang members had bolted out the back door, I ran around the side of the pub.

I spotted Stokes and Trent running towards the water. Pedestrians wandering along the waterfront scrambled to get out of the way. Pub patrons came out to watch, pints in hand. Plant and Ackland gave chase with Jones not far behind. I tried to keep up. Stokes and Trent mounted first one low fence and then another. I heard a shot. A young woman screamed. When I reached the second fence, Ackland and Jones were panting. I stared out at the Solent. Plant was waist deep in the water below.

'There they are,' I said, pointing downstream.

'The bastards.'

They'd taken advantage of the current. There was no way any of us would have jumped in to catch them, not garbed in jeans and woollen jumpers and leather jackets. We each had enough weight on our torsos to sink a ship.

Ackland and Jones took off back to London, leaving me waiting in the station while Plant was given some dry clothes. The attempt at an arrest had failed but my info was spot on. That, I reminded myself, was what mattered.

We took our time driving back. Plant forwent the M3 in favour of the slow route. After turning onto the A31 at Winchester he turned up the car's heating and ten minutes later I was forced to unbutton my jacket. We chatted and laughed all the way to Guilford. Major road works at a set of traffic lights caused a long tailback and we inched our way along through the town's main street. It was then, as Plant was talking about how his wife didn't understand him, that his hand slid from the steering wheel and landed on my thigh. I froze. He gave my flesh a squeeze and then started to bring his hand up towards my crotch. I grabbed his hand and put it back on the steering wheel, my face bright red. There was a long and awkward silence. After that he didn't say much. I never suspected not even for a second that Plant was that sort of guy.

Back at the Greenwich nick, I pushed open the office door to find Brace wearing a broad grin. Heads turned. There was no sign of Ackland or Jones. They must have stopped off somewhere. Thought we would as well. They were wrong.

Brace kept grinning, holding something back. I said nothing.

'We lost them,' Plant said, deflated.

'Not quite.'

'Nah, they got away.'

'Yeah, but a short while later the goons flagged down a passing motorist. Must have been the fact that they were both soaking wet that led him to drive them straight to Hythe nick.'

'You mean, we got 'em!'

Plant fisted the air.

A cheer broke out. We now had four of the gang either under arrest or charged. And those arrests were all down to me. Heeding Plant's advice and noting the reactions I had got from Ackland and Jones, I swallowed a childish urge to brag, even to Liz. I also knew Operation Rancho would not be deemed a success until we nailed Eric and Mick Maloney. The other arrests were just window dressing. Those guys were easily replaced. We needed the organisers, the brains behind the robberies, if we were ever to stop them happening again. The trouble was, the Maloney boys had gone to ground.

Ackland and Jones wandered back in after the excitement had died down. Plant told them what had happened while I sat quietly at my desk. Eyes flashed my way, but I avoided meeting anyone's gaze. There was a brief discussion of possible leads. Then Brace walked back in with DS Drinkwater who said the chief super had authorised a reward.

'Put it about among your contacts that there's ten grand on offer for information leading to an arrest.'

I realised in that moment that not only was I just as ambitious and just as eager to prove myself as the rest of the squad, I was more so. I was a woman. And I wanted to belong to the CID more than anything. I never, ever wanted to find myself back in uniform.

Which was why I told Billy about the reward the moment I had a chance.

Three days later, I got a call from Billy asking me to meet him in the lane behind the Cock and Bull. He was standing by a cluster of dustbins when I arrived. More hunched over than ever, hands in pockets, the hood of his jacket hiding his flaming red hair. On my approach he shifted, shot me a quick look, then turned away, not from me, but from the road behind me.

'What have you got?'

'I'll tell you where Mick Maloney is but you gotta make sure it is me that gets the reward.'

'If the information comes from you, of course you'll get the reward. What do you take me for?'

He waited. I waited, too, but I knew what he wanted. I handed him the tenner I had ready in my pocket. I was beginning to resent parting with my own money and regretted the day I first proffered the amount. From then on, Billy expected the same each time he had something to tell me. I found out from Liz that it wasn't customary to pay an informant, not unless it was sanctioned from on high. But by then it was too late, the habit was set.

Pocketing the money, Billy said, 'Mick Maloney is hiding in a caravan park on the Isle of Sheppey.'

He filled me in on the details.

'Thanks, Billy.'

'No worries.'

He left me in the lane and hurried off.

His behaviour was nothing like the Billy I had come to know over the months. Something was wrong. He was in some kind of danger. Maybe someone was on to him. Couldn't be easy being a grass.

I was quick to leave the lane as well. It was no place for a young woman. My badge wouldn't protect me, not in a place like that.

Risking further disapproval from the others, this time, I made sure the squad knew it was my tip-off. I walked straight into the office and interrupted Brace and Plant with a quick, 'Excuse me, sir.' And then told them both in a voice loud enough for half the room to hear that I had information crucial to the case. Brace steered me into his office. He didn't remonstrate with me. I thought he might even have admired my pluck. Plant, though, was right behind me and his attitude was anything but positive.

'This informer of yours sure is coming up trumps,' Brace said. 'What is it this time?'

Sing Like a Canary

I explained what Billy had said about Mick Maloney hiding out on the Isle of Sheppey. 'Someone down there spotted him. The caravan park owner, I think.'

'You better nip home and grab an overnight bag, then, Marj. You too, Plant. I'll come down as well.'

'It'll need more than the three of us to nab Maloney, sir.'

'First let's make sure it is Maloney. Get your skates on.'

It was back downstairs for the guns. Then I raced home and packed. Brace picked me up an hour later. Plant was in the passenger seat, so I hopped in the back. The drive to Sheppey on that fine November afternoon would have been pleasant had it not been for Plant's smouldering resentment. Did he want to be the one to come up with the leads? The one to get the glory. The promotion. It never occurred to me that Plant was ambitious. I was shocked. Or was he still stewing over my rejection?

When we stopped for petrol and Brace went to pay, Plant turned around and glared at me and said, 'You shouldn't have done that.'

'What?'

'Shot your mouth off.'

'I didn't shoot my mouth off.'

'Then what would you call broadcasting your tip-off to the whole nick, then?'

'Not the whole nick. Just the squad.'

'You really don't get it, do you.'

'Get what.'

He inhaled sharply.

'You'll come down to earth with a thump, believe me.'

I said nothing. Plant continued to sulk, and Brace wasn't in a talkative mood. We drove the rest of the way in silence, arriving in Leysdown-on-Sea a little after seven, and pulling up by the caravan park entrance. The site manager came out of a small and scruffy-looking office and introduced himself as

Brian. He handed Brace the keys, marked the location of our caravan on a site map and told us to park our car beside the door. The idea was to watch, wait, then act when the time was right.

The caravan was freezing. Brace had booked us into one of the larger, family-sized caravans, but that only meant a pull-down double bed at one end and a narrow bench seat that doubled as a single bed opposite the door. A small kitchen area. No toilet. We had to use the communal facilities. But there was power. I flicked on a light then quickly drew the curtains. Plant figured out how to use the small wall heater. I claimed the single bed with my shoulder bag, vowing to sleep fully clothed if it came to it.

I couldn't believe anyone would want to book themselves into a caravan in the middle of November, but when we went back to the office to find out where Maloney was holding up, Brian said there were a few occupied. He pointed out the caravan in question and we headed in that direction, stopping a good distance away. There was a car parked beside it. I took down the number plate and back at our caravan Plant radioed through a plate check. A short while later the message came through that the car was registered to Mick Maloney. There was an exchange of triumphant glances. We had him. Almost...

When we went back to make the arrest, there was no sign of the car, and the caravan, it appeared, was empty.

Plant shook his head in disbelief. 'We've been spotted, and he's bolted.'

'You reckon?' Brace said. 'Marj, go and ask the site manager. See if he knows anything.' And the two men trudged back to our van.

A few minutes later, I faced two inquiring and downcast faces and was tempted to come up with some tall tale just to wind them up. Instead, ever honest, I said, 'They'll be in the pub.'

'They?'

'He's here with his wife and kid.'

Brace let out a long sigh. There was nothing to do but wait.

And wait we did. Four whole hours we waited, taking it in turns to lie flat on our stomachs in the long grass near the caravan, getting increasingly cold and damp while the Maloney family sat in a cosy pub and ate and drank their fill. Eventually, a little after pub closing time when it was me and Plant on our bellies, we heard a car approach. The brake lights lit up and then the engine died. Doors closed. Hushed voices. Maybe the kid was asleep. The creak of the caravan door opening.

I crawled over to Plant. We needed to confirm it really was Maloney and the only way to do that was to clock him. After a short discussion it was agreed that I had the better memory when it came to faces.

I crept around, keeping a safe distance from the caravan, hoping Maloney would appear in one of the windows. I didn't have long to wait. A light went on in what I took to be the kitchen area. And there he stood in nothing but a singlet, brushing his teeth. He had the same build, the same haircut, the same colouring. It was Maloney. I was certain of it.

I rejoined Plant, and we went back to our caravan.

'Is it him?'

'It's him.'

Brace radioed for back up. We needed a SWAT team, but they were on another job on the other side of Kent. Instead, the whole squad was summoned, along with the dog handler.

We had an hour or so to kill before they got here. A pack of playing cards would have been handy. I poked around for a kettle. I found one in the cupboard above the two-ringed cooker but there were no tea bags, no sugar, no milk. Not one of us had thought to bring a flask. About ten minutes later I heard a sudden fizz and Plant proffered a can of Coke. We took small sips and passed on the can until the contents were empty.

Plant then lay down on the bed. Brace took the other side. An hour and a half later, Brace's handset crackled. He sat up and swung off the bed.

'They're here.'

We went and met the others on the road. The squad huddled round Brace for instructions. The mood was tense. Charged. No one wanted the arrest to go wrong. We all wanted Maloney, alive.

Everyone crept off to take up a position. We formed a circle around the caravan, some twelve feet away. Brace went back to his car for the loud hailer. He then strode up to the caravan, breaching the circle and stopping about five paces from the door. I was standing behind him, between Plant and Jones.

'Come out with your hands up.' His voice echoed. Then silence. There was a long pause. Those occupying the other caravans stirred. Lights when on, faces appeared in windows. Who were these people, renting caravans off-season in Leydown-by-the-Sea? I couldn't fathom it.

'Come out, Maloney. We've got you surrounded.'

Another pause.

'Get your arse out here, now!'

The caravan door opened. A man matching Maloney's description appeared and yelled, 'Fuck off.' The door slammed shut.

'Shoot the bastard,' someone yelled. I thought it was Ackland.

It wasn't a bad idea. But then again, given our positions, I wasn't comfortable with shots being fired. The circle idea now that Brace was in the middle of it with the loud hailer, was not the smartest arrangement. He stood right in the firing line. The reality was a stray bullet could hit any one of us. What had seemed sensible out on the road suddenly seemed ridiculous. I wondered if anyone else was realising this.

Things moved quickly when Brace ordered the dog handler forward.

'Come out,' he yelled again.

Plant took the initiative and went and yanked open the door and the handler unleashed the dog which bounded inside. There was a loud cry and a lot of growling. It took a few seconds to handcuff Maloney who staggered out of the van, blood dripping from his forearm. Dog bite. The woman inside the van was screaming. No one took much notice of her. All eyes were on Maloney. We'd got him.

Only, we hadn't. We'd got someone, but the moment this Maloney was standing on the ground surrounded by a crowd of officers, I knew we had the wrong man. He looked just like Maloney, at least from a distance, through glass, in the dark, but he was at least four inches too short.

And he was livid.

I had no choice but to approach Brace with the news.

'Are you sure,' he hissed.

'I'm sorry, sir. It isn't him.'

I was glad we were all standing around in the dark as my face flushed red.

Brace was now as livid as the guy who'd just had his arm bitten by a police dog. He wouldn't let it go, apologise, walk away. He went right up to the guy and yelled into his face, 'How come you're driving a car registered to a Mr Maloney? Did you pinch it? Is that what you did?'

'I borrowed it off a geezer in a pub last week. Mine conked out, and I'd booked this bleeding holiday for the wife.'

'Some frigging holiday,' she yelled through her tears. She stood in the doorway, hugging herself. The kid was behind her, bawling.

Plant told me to go and comfort them. Calm them down. I beheld that hard-faced woman with her dishevelled peroxide blonde hair and heavy eye makeup streaming down her cheeks. The kid was in blue pyjamas. As I made my approach, he looked at me through cold eyes and whined and tugged at his mother's skirt. 'Get off,' she said and yanked the fabric back and he started bawling even louder. She picked him up, stared at me, and said, 'See what you've done.'

'There's been a mistake,' I said apologetically, even as I felt like slapping her for being so rude. 'I'm really sorry.' I wasn't. 'It'll be alright.' I damned well hoped so. 'Your husband, he's not in any trouble.'

'Then uncuff him,' the woman shrieked.

She was right. We should uncuff him. I went out and suggested the very same to a still irate Brace. Only, I soon discovered that wasn't so easy. We had brought down the handcuffs but no key. Not one of us had a handcuff key.

I thought twice before going back to the woman and her kid, choosing instead to leave that pair to their own devices while I joined Brace and Plant and the others crowded round the Maloney lookalike.

'We could try the local nick,' Jones said.

'No good,' said Brace. 'They'll have a different key.'

'I'll radio through,' said Plant. 'See if I can get someone to drive one down.'

'I'll do it,' Brace said. 'Marjorie, go get the handset.'

Ever the fetcher and carrier. Still, it was good to be active, busy. Better than standing around like a lemon.

Brace met me on the way back to the others. I stood nearby as he radioed through. When he explained what had happened, instead of sending someone down with a key, we heard, 'What right do you have to take handcuffs out of the area without permission...'

Brace hung up. He handed me back the radio and then yelled to Ackland to head off to the local nick for a pair of bolt cutters. We went to join the others.

'I feel like a Keystone Cop,' he said to me under his breath, and I suppressed a laugh. 'Thank heavens the SWAT team were on another job.'

'I'll take the blame for the handcuffs, sir,' Plant said.

'And I don't mind copping the mistaken identity, sir,' I said, hoping I was not about to cop the blame for the whole fiasco, given it was my tip-off.

We were all anticipating a formal complaint, even getting sued. Thankfully, nothing came of any of it. Seemed the guy was relieved just to get the cuffs off his wrists and get back to his wife and kid. A guy holidaying in a caravan park on the Isle of Sheppey in November who just happened to have Maloney's old car in his possession was most likely guilty of all sorts.

No one said anything, but on the way back to London in the thick of the night, going around and around in my head was the knowledge that Billy had given me a bad tip-off. Now Brace would be less likely to trust my information and the squad would no doubt have a good laugh behind my back. First the teabags, then a partial and fairly useless tip-off about the robbery, and now a mistaken identity. Still, his last two tip-offs proved good. Swings and roundabouts, Liz said later when I explained what had happened, reassuring me that my intelligence had led to the arrest of four criminals. Police work goes like that, she said. You have to take the rough with the smooth. None of her platitudes made any kind of impression on me. Brace decided after that to appoint me chief tea-maker whenever there was a briefing. Which was daily. Which made Liz happy as she was shunted across to the photocopier.

11

GOLF COURSE, COSTA TEGUISE, TUESDAY 19 MARCH 2019

The sun crowned the volcano, gifting the patio a sudden flood of light, the cool of the early morning giving way to spring warmth. Already the sun had a kick to it, and I pulled my chair into the shade of the high wall to the north. The sleeping pill I took the night before had left me a touch groggy, but the sensation faded as the coffee did its work, and I grew hungry.

I took my near-empty cup into the dim of the house to prepare a cooked breakfast. I had a big day ahead of me. As I fried my eggs, I had to push aside the misgivings I felt knowing Oscar Cribb's murderer might still be on the island. I had to, or I would never find Billy.

Not for forty years had I done an obs. Back then I had the benefit of a companion, Liz, and the security of being part of a squad. The protection of a badge along with the various rights that come with all that. This time, I was a spy. I had no permission, no special access, nothing. I could even be accused of loitering. Worse, stalking. And the one thing I did not want to have to do was buy a membership, hire some golf clubs, and spend all day trying to pot balls.

I had no aptitude for golf. Jess did try to teach me, and there was that year she won an annual membership in a lucky draw and dragged me along for company. She had quite a swing and what appeared to me to be a natural talent. Her balls landed on the fairway or the green. Mine ended up in the rough.

The humiliation I endured that year was exacerbated by the mirth Jess extracted from my ineptitude and might have cost us our relationship, had it not been for my own sense of humour. I was not so precious that I had to be good at everything I did. My mother had instilled in me the attitude that it was okay to be no good at some things. Or a lot of things. That was what made life rich and interesting. We were all different. She had acquired that belief through her teaching career and no doubt tried to instil the same attitude in all of her students. With me, to a large degree, her efforts paid off, and I was grateful, for it lent me a level of tolerance and self-acceptance I might not otherwise have had.

Once I was on the road, I had little time to prepare myself for the ordeal ahead of me; the drive to the golf course took all of ten minutes. Despite the steady stream of traffic coming down from the north, there was no congestion and wherever you looked there were volcanoes and mountains, a refreshing change from the high rises, the grey concrete and steel of an urban view. But it was a strange place to be sleuthing. Too exposed.

A Londoner by birth and having lived all my life in the heart of cities, I never had the chance to appreciate open country. At least, not before Jess. She was the one who would drag me along to visit stately homes or insist on long rambles through woods. Coastal walks. Then there was that walking trip along The Pennine Way. Thankfully not the whole stretch. But she made me do Cross Fell. And I had to admit the scenery was spectacular. She liked to discover places few visited, which was hard in the UK and near impossible on Lanzarote, but I still suspected she would have loved this island. She'd never mentioned a desire to visit. Then again, she'd never mentioned a wish to leave her homeland even for a holiday. She loved Britain. Bless her.

Oh, Jess.

The car park was half full when I arrived, pulling up in the shade of an awning. I got out and went around clocking every vehicle. Old habits. But there was no point writing down number plates. What would I do with the information? Didn't stop me scrutinising every car, eyeballing everyone I saw. I was wearing a wide-brimmed hat this time, along with the full hippy garb including the paisley scarf and the sunglasses that covered much of my face. Which meant, I realised as I wandered over to the entrance and felt every pair of eyes on me, that my disguise was not the best attire for the golf course. Too late now. I steeled myself and kept right on walking.

Inside, the club house was spacious and cool. A shop set to one side sold an array of golfing attire. Handy. Opposite, on the other side of the foyer, was the restaurant. I went and hovered by the entrance and surveyed the tables and found it empty. Not surprising, as it appeared formal, all white linen and elegant chairs, although also rather plain, almost functional in décor. Expensive? Probably.

The foyer led out onto a shaded terrace. Beyond the paved area, a path cut through neatly laid out gardens leading to the first hole. Not keen to hover where all eyes could see me, I wandered over to a palm tree surrounded by succulents which provided some good cover and hid me from the clubhouse. From there I could more or less see almost all the holes of half the course. I took out my binoculars and had a good look at the holes further away, marvelling at the immaculate green lawns of the fairways. Incongruous, with all the rock around. I got a

Sing Like a Canary

good look at most of the holes. Couldn't spot anyone who looked anything like Billy. The trouble was, I needed a second pair of eyes on the other side of the terrace to view the other half of the course. Not ideal. Impatience got me. I decided I was approaching the situation all wrong. There had to be somewhere from which to view the whole course.

I went back through the clubhouse to my car and drove around the northern perimeter of the golf course and discovered that the prison where Trevor was incarcerated had a panoramic view of the holes. Pity there was not a way to enlist his help.

The location proved no good. Standing outside a prison with a pair of binoculars was sure to arouse suspicion. And there was nothing beyond the prison buildings. The road came to a dead end.

I drove back around the course to survey the perimeter to the southeast.

At that end, a small housing estate was being built along a road with numerous cul-de-sac offshoots. I drove to the end of a cul-de-sac of vacant lots and saw that the perimeter of the golf course was fenced off. Clearly, trespassers were not welcome. From there, I could survey the first half of the course as I had from the terrace gardens, but not the second half. There was nowhere I could get high enough to see the whole course. Really, I needed a small army for the surveillance. At least a team of two. Two pairs of eyes were always all the better. Ideally six, three teams of two. I was thinking like a cop again. Wishful thinking. All that left me with was frustration. My best bet was the car park itself. I drove back, not looking forward to many hours seated behind the wheel practically cooking in the heat if not the sun.

I pulled up in the same spot as before. Then I whittled down the amount of time I would spend there by trying to decide when Billy would likely appear. He'd been a milkman for much of his previous life, which made him a morning person. Although for all I knew, he'd hated those early shifts and had taken to lying in ever since. A round of golf took how long? Three, four hours? You would aim for finishing at lunch, afternoon tea or dinner. That was how my mind worked. Were golfers like that too? Billy? My only hope was to find him coming or going in the morning tea and before lunch slots. I'd never go the distance beyond that.

I decided to stay as long as I could and break up the tedious activity with short walks in whatever shade I could find. As the morning wore on, the breeze picked up and began to blow hard through my open window, whipping up my scarf and threatening to lift my hat whenever I stretched my legs. After three hours and no sign of Billy, I got fed up and drove back to Guatiza.

12

OLD SALT WORKS, LOS COCOTEROS, LANZAROTE, TUESDAY 19 MARCH 2019

TUESDAY WAS WHEN BILLY WENT FOR LUNCH IN ARRECIFE, treating himself to a table for one at the best establishments the little city had to offer. But after last Saturday every day had turned into a do-nothing day normally reserved for Fridays. Since discovering Oscar Cribb's body, there were moments when Billy was almost beside himself with paranoia. Times when his stress levels reached such a pitch, he was immobilised. He knew a run or a swim or some heavy lifting in his home gym would do him good but on that warm and sunny Tuesday some other part of his mind led him to the one room in the house where he was always calm, always centred, always focussed: the puzzle room.

Billy was not a self-reflective kind of guy, but if he had been, he would have named this part of himself his inner puzzler. All he knew was that the best way to funnel his anger or his paranoia was by tackling a hard puzzle. The harder, the better.

On the go, he had: a 2,000-piece puzzle of some yachts

sailing into harbour – the preponderance of blue was the challenge; one of a German castle, the stonework and the moat presenting the greater difficulty, as did the cloudy sky; another of a Swiss snow scene with the obvious difficulties that went with so much snow; and an antique and curios shop, which he thought might have proven less challenging due to all the variations of detail, but he'd only just upturned all the pieces and was already finding the border hard.

Each puzzle was laid out on its own table and there was ample room to walk around and sit down at whichever side of whichever table took his fancy. The only other furniture in the room was a custom-built floor to ceiling cabinet to store his puzzles and a long shelf containing an array of trays. The tables were of equal size and able to accommodate a 2,000-piece puzzle with enough room around the puzzle border to lay out an assortment of pieces. No food or drink was ever brought into the room. Natural light was favoured, supplemented with sconce lighting. Overhead light caused glare.

He'd been puzzling for over twenty years. His hobby began when he purchased a second-hand puzzle at the Teguise market because he liked the picture on the box and felt sorry for the woman behind the stall who'd told another browser standing beside him that she was selling up everything she owned before moving back to Cornwall to care for her ailing mother. Could have been a tall tale, the array of household items stolen from some holiday let, but he doubted it. The woman looked sincere and very sad to be leaving the island. He handed over the pesetas marked on the box and tucked the puzzle under his arm thinking he'd done a good deed, if nothing else.

When he brought the puzzle home and set it down on the kitchen bench, Natasha had giggled and asked him if he had bought it for her niece. That gentle ridicule led him to forgo the dining table in preference to a folding card table which he set up in one of the spare rooms. Up until then, that room was used for storage, or rather, overflow, namely, bags of unwanted clothes and boxes of assorted items Natasha didn't want cluttering the house. It quickly became apparent the card table was much too small for the puzzle. He only had to read the dimensions on the lid to realise that, but he'd already tried to assemble the frame and found he needed considerably more space. That week, determined to have a go at finishing the puzzle in defiance of Natasha's gentle ridicule, he bought a second-hand dining table. Moving that table into the spare room marked the beginning of Billy's new hobby.

Natasha stopped teasing him when she saw how serious he was, and instead she began to appreciate the time and freedom she had to do whatever she wanted while he sat bent over jigsaw puzzles, and she no longer needed to worry about him when she was at work. In many ways, his decision to start puzzling saved their relationship from that kind of quiet decay that sets in when two individuals are not gainfully occupied doing their own activities and start getting on top of one another.

Natasha rarely entered the puzzle room, but these days whenever he was puzzling, he felt her presence, sensed her in other parts of the house, how she would potter in the kitchen, play music and dance in the living room, sit out on the back patio to enjoy the cooling breeze, or sit out on the front patio to get away from it.

His heart ached in the remembering.

He had to remind himself he was lucky she'd stayed true to him all those years. Scrawny old him with his red hair and bushy beard. Not exactly a lady killer. That a woman as beautiful as her should fall in love with a man as unattractive as him had always been a source of amazement.

He glanced down at Patch sunning herself by the window. The momentary diversion was all it took for him to find the last remaining piece of one edge of the antique and curios puzzle, his focus primarily on the pattern as depicted on the lid. When it came to a scale of difficulty, this one ranked extreme.

He moved on to the yachts, hoping to have better luck with the water in the harbour. He spent the next hour separating all the tones and shades of blue, placing them into trays. It was methodical work, painstaking and necessary. He managed to insert five pieces along the way, mostly pertaining to a section above the waterline.

He soon tired of the process and moved on to the Swiss snow scene. He only had about a hundred pieces left. Whenever he was down to the last hundred, always of the most difficult sections of a puzzle, he would forgo his tone and shade method in favour of collating the pieces by shape and laying them out in columns. The task from there was mechanical. All he needed to do was look out for the puzzle-piece gaps that had two edges both requiring a socket or a loop. Sometimes, he thought the method felt like cheating, but when a puzzler is that close to finishing, those fine judgements of pattern-matching and colour discrimination go out the window.

It took one hour to finish the snow scene, and he stood back to admire it. Then he took a photo and forwarded it to Ben who replied moments later with a smiley face emoji and a thumbs up.

A brief pause in which to admire his handiwork and then he broke the puzzle up and returned the pieces to their box.

Billy wondered which puzzle to tackle next. Generally, the puzzles would take Billy about a week to complete if he really got stuck in, but after putting himself into lockdown, he found he could whip through a puzzle in four days. How long would he need to keep up this home-isolation lifestyle? Fortunately, he'd recently purchased ten vintage puzzles from an online auction site majoring in deceased estates. They were all hard puzzles – what self-respecting puzzler would want an easy puzzle – and he'd been assured by the vendor that all of the pieces were present and intact. They had better be. He'd paid a handsome sum on the strength of that guarantee. He opened the cabinet and made his selection, going for a painting by Paul Cézanne: Still Life with Skull. He could see straight away that the shades of black background would be the challenge. But then, when it came to puzzles, it was generally the background that was the hardest. Although not always. He lifted the lid and started separating the outside pieces from the rest, turning the puzzle pieces onto their backs, and collating them by tone into trays.

The day wore on. He realised he'd been sitting bent over puzzles for too long when a crick in his neck shot a sharp dart of pain through his skull. Thinking a break long overdue, he went to the kitchen to fix a late lunch. The fridge contained a carton of UHT milk, a pack of butter and another of cheese, a selection of tired-looking vegetables and the remains of the previous night's meatball bolognaise. And he was out of bread. He should have gone shopping the day before, but he wouldn't risk it, not after his encounter with the very dead Oscar. Part of him also regretted relinquishing his usual Sunday outing and cancelling his Wednesday round of golf. He needed to come up with a good excuse for Ben as he had no intention of playing golf this coming Saturday either. He made a commitment in his mind to play golf on the following Wednesday, out of fear Ben would find another golf buddy to replace him if he had too many days off. It was a question of balancing one fear against another, and the golf clubs won. Besides, surely whoever had killed Oscar would have left the island by then. He wished there was a way of finding out for certain. He had to go shopping soon or he'd starve.

In the meantime, Patch was the only reason Billy risked leaving the house. A dog needed a walk. After downing a bowl of cold leftovers, Billy donned a bucket hat and sunglasses and grabbed Patch's leash hanging from a hook in the laundry. Even with a hat and glasses, he suspected he would be readily recognisable from a short distance. Everyone had a gait. Everyone gave off some essence of who they were, no matter the disguise. Those were his paranoid thoughts. It was the only time in all of the forty years he had lived on the island that he wished for some thick woods. Shrubbery. The place was too exposed. And the site of Oscar's dead body was much, much too close to his home.

Patch had heard the jingle of her leash and was waiting expectantly by the front door. Billy reached for her collar and secured the snap lock. Then he led her outside.

It was hot for March. The early afternoon heat hit him like a punch, the patio glare strong even behind his sunglasses. What was he doing going out at this time of day? Dog walking was for early mornings and evenings, not the middle of the day. Then again, who says? Better to perform habitual tasks at a time when they would be least expected. That was the rational thing to do under the circumstances.

He unlocked the gates, stepped out onto the barren rocky plain, closed and locked the gates after a quick scan around, and then took the cliff path up towards the salt works, turning off after about fifty metres and taking the narrow footpath down the low cliff to the little beach beside his place. It was not a spot he visited often but it was tucked out of sight.

The beach was rocky, the shoreline plastered with basalt reefs and no good for swimming. At one time, the old salt works reached right to the cliff base. All that remained were rectangles of flat land demarcated by the remains of dry-stone walls. He let Patch off the leash and together they crossed the orange-coloured grit.

He stood and watched the waves splash on the rocks while Patch sniffed about and did her business. Then he strolled along beside the dry-stone walls up to the southern end of the beach where the cliff arced towards the ocean. From there, his gaze traced the exterior wall of his property.

He supposed if someone was keen, they could scale up the cliff and climb over the wall and enter one of the patios, but it would be one hell of a way to go about breaking in. He needed to stop thinking like that. The next thing he'd be out in the dead of night cementing in shards of glass as a wall topper. Ridiculous.

The wind cooled things down and made up for the lack of shade. He hung about, waiting for Patch, and when he thought she might have had enough, he called her over. She trotted obediently up to him, and he reattached her leash. He took his time climbing the path, not wanting to get out of breath. As they neared the top he paused and scanned about. There was no sign of anyone, let alone anyone suspicious, no car parked up, nothing. He headed home.

As he cornered the front of his place, he saw that the gates were open to his neighbour Tom's property. Tom's blue Saab nosed out, creeping slowly, and turning into the road. Tom didn't like to kick up too much dust. His gates closed automatically. Billy scrambled in his pocket for his keys, hoping to make it inside before Tom drove by, but he needn't have rushed. The Saab just sat there. The engine idled. He thought he saw Tom wave. He raised a friendly hand in response and then unlocked and opened his gates. Patch trotted in and headed straight for her water bowl. All was well. All was normal.

Billy caught the sound of a second car engine on the wind. Could be one of the local farmers. Explained why Tom wasn't moving. The track was a single lane, and he wouldn't risk damaging his car. Plus, there was the dust.

Billy hurried in, locked the gates, and waited, peering through the grille. A car appeared. It was white and looked like a rental. The car came to a halt in front of Tom's. There was a long pause. Billy held his breath, his heart thumping in his chest. Then the car did a three-point turn and headed back the way it had come. Tom followed a good distance behind.

Billy rubbed his sweaty hands on the thighs of his jeans before heading inside. He needed to get a grip. Forty years of exile had turned him into a coward. He went back to the puzzle room and sat for a while before the antiques and curios store, attempting a second side of the border.

It took him some time to regain his equanimity. Then his phone burst into life and sent a bolt of shock through him.

It was Ramona.

'Hey,' he said and waited.

'Did you know your son's killers have been charged with his murder?'

'I did not.'

'And they are denied bail, the whole lot of them.'

'Good.'

'I thought you would be pleased.'

'I am.'

There was a long pause. He heard Ramona inhale.

'Eddy, I don't like to have to call you like this but any chance you can cover the costs of the funeral?'

'What funeral?'

'Alvaro's.'

'But how can you bury a non-existent corpse?'

'He is not being buried. We are having a memorial service on Sunday.'

'Then pay for it yourselves.'

'You are the father.'

'And you are the mother. For once in your life, Ramona, do the right thing and stop hitting me for cash.'

'Then I can tell you right now that you won't be coming.'

'That, Ramona, is certain. You want a funeral, you have a funeral, and you damn well pay for a funeral. Got it?'

He didn't know where this sudden assertiveness came from.

Maybe it was the stress. Whatever it was, it worked. She hung up. He turned back to his puzzle and found five more pieces in quick succession.

Before the day got away from him, he sent his golf buddy Ben a text saying he couldn't make golf on Saturday as he had caught a bug that had set in for the duration. But he would be right for the following Wednesday. Ben replied with a thumbs up and a See you then.

He took himself to the kitchen and was about to turn on the kettle when the phone rang again. No bolt of shock this time but he eyed his phone warily. It was the agent who took care of his holiday let bookings, and he should have been expecting the call. Marisol always phoned late on a Tuesday afternoon with any news. He swiped the accept button and wandered into the living room.

He listened as she ran through the updates on each property – the Arrieta property was booked solid for the foreseeable and the apartment in Costa Teguise needed some minor repairs after the last booking. Billy agreed to let Marisol arrange for the agency's handyman to do the work. And there was an issue with the Tiagua farmhouse. The booking was originally for two weeks, but now the guests wanted to book another fortnight. Only the next booking came a day later and, if Eddy remembered, Marisol had suggested getting the handyman in to paint one of the rooms and the plumber to fix the shower taps. 'It won't give the workmen much time to do the jobs. Shall I tell these guests to book somewhere else?'

'Sounds like a good idea.'

She phoned back ten minutes later.

'Maybe we can delay the painting and the plumber?' she said.

'Whatever you think is best.' He really didn't care.

'I think it's best. Señor Maloney has offered to pay double for those next two weeks.'

There was a brief pause as Billy succumbed to disbelief.

'Who did you say?'

'Señor Maloney.'

It couldn't be? Surely?

'Did he give you his first name?'

'Eric, I think he said. Eric and Mick.'

His world crashed in on him. The danger he was in had just gone exponential. He struggled to gather his thoughts.

'Are you still there?'

'Sorry.'

'Well?'

'Tell him they can stay. But do not mention my name.'

'I would never do that, Señor Banks.' She sounded a touch indignant.

He realised he needn't have mentioned that at all. The Maloney boys knew nothing of Eddie Banks. It was the one bit of security he had. Here on this island where there were no trees to hide behind, no dark alleys, where the bright and sunny days tended to reveal and never conceal, he at least had his fake name. It was all he had to hold on to.

That day Marjorie insisted he chose himself a bland name had been his best insurance against discovery. He had a lot to thank her for. As he stood there staring out the living room window with the phone still in his hand, unable to take in the glorious ocean view, unable to move or blink or even breathe properly, he filled with gratitude for the one copper who had made the last forty years possible.

He had always had a soft spot for Marjorie. He'd never forgotten the day he met her for the first time in the Ship and Anchor, how fresh-faced and naïve she'd seemed, how eager to get on. She had a gullibility about her, and she never questioned his tip-offs. She made informing too easy. And he'd got brazen as a result. Although it wasn't her fault, it was his. And he'd never stopped feeling guilty about how things turned out.

Sing Like a Canary

Right to the very end she had been there for him. And look how he'd repaid her. Unintentional, of course. But then again, he might have thought twice. For all these years he had carried deep in his conscience a wish to atone, to absolve himself. Turning supergrass wasn't enough. He owed Marjorie his life and that was never more apparent than right now.

He put the phone down beside the sink and went and sat on the couch and gazed at the ocean. Maybe there was something he could do to make amends. He scrolled through his contacts, indecisive. Then he sent his lawyer a text.

As though sensing his state of mind, Patch trotted over and lay her head on his thigh. He stroked her and gave her a pat.

His attention was not diverted for long, and he was back worrying about his predicament. What had caused the Maloney boys to extend their stay? After all, they'd got their mark. Oscar Cribbs was dead.

A sudden realisation sent a chill through him. They really were after him as well. They somehow knew he was on the island and were bent on hunting him down. It was no longer a question of keeping out of sight just in case Cribb's killer chanced upon him. He was prey.

If the Maloney boys did know he was here, then who told them? The only detective other than Marjorie who could have known where he'd moved to was Graham Spence. And that was only if his old mate Terry had blabbed after the one time he'd risked all to check on his kids.

Not Graham, surely? He just couldn't imagine that copper betraying him.

More likely it was Ackland. He'd bumped into the brothers and told them he'd clocked Billy at the golf course.

Either way, the risk was grave if Eric and Mick Maloney knew he was here.

His thoughts were making his head spin. He needed to relax. Take stock of his options. It occurred to him he could stake out the farmhouse, beat them at their own game and bump them off first. Them. Two hardened criminals against one wizened little man in hiding. And he wasn't a killer. He didn't have it in him. He was a rabbit not a fox, burrowing down in his little palace of a house, hoping time would be on his side. Hoping eventually, they'd get fed up and leave.

Fresh paranoia brewed in him. He was immobilised by cowardice and raw fear. He stared out the window at the pale sky blue over the deep ocean blue without seeing any sort of colour at all. Only black.

That evening, he shunted strands of fettucine around his plate, his appetite poor. Oscar's death had started playing on his mind. He'd never cared for Oscar. He'd had the sort of good looks that made women fall at his feet and he had always enjoyed putting himself about. No doubt that todger of his had finally led to his demise. What other reason could there have been to murder the man? As far as Billy knew, Oscar was loyal and avoided scams that would leave him exposed. In marked contrast to that scoundrel Andres who he'd met not long after Natasha had moved in.

Billy rued the day he came across Andres.

And there Billy sat, all dour and resentful, stewing over yet another crim who had done him wrong. He was leapfrogging from one bad situation to another, roaming all over the terrain of his life on the hunt for betrayals and hurts and every kind of menace. He was thinking himself into a corner, making himself ill. He was seventy-five and needed to watch his blood pressure, his heart. He'd give himself a stroke. Was it his age that had rendered him a coward? Where was his courage?

As the evening wore on, he got stuck on Andres. Somehow it was easier to mull over that particular asshole than dwell on the Maloney boys and that sickening thought that Oscar had led them to the island and ultimately, potentially, to him.

Andres.

Natasha's distant cousin.

Although Billy never held what had happened with that crook against Natasha. How could he? She wasn't to know? Whereas he should have known better. Should have seen it coming. Bloody Andres.

13

OLD SALT WORKS, LOS COCOTEROS, LANZAROTE, FEBRUARY 1982

BILLY HAD GONE OFF DRINKING TEA. THERE WAS A TIME HE savoured a good strong brew with two sugars and full-cream milk. No more. Not since he discovered tea in Lanzarote was not up to the mark and the UHT milk sold on the island gave a brew a funny twang. Oh, for fresh milk.

Those moments when he fancied a lovely cup of tea, he found himself missing his old milk round. He would stare out at the shimmering sapphire of the ocean and reminisce.

The early morning round in the gloom, the snow, or the ice, the chink of glass, the brief and friendly doorstep chats, the sense he derived of belonging to the community, of leading a meaningful life. He wanted to grab that bit of his life back even as he knew the days of the milkman were numbered. People were buying their milk from the supermarket. Glass was being replaced with cardboard. Still, whenever he felt a craving for a nice cup of tea, he missed his old milk float more than his family. And he missed his kids, big time. The sacrifices he was forced to make. He hadn't anticipated there would be so many, and that they would be at the micro-level of life.

Tea was té in Spanish. Coffee café. With milk, con leche. He could order a café con leche in his rudimentary Spanish and expect a reasonable flavour despite the UHT milk. Or his tastebuds were adjusting. Natasha had introduced him to almond croissants and eggs with spicy sausage – her favourite breakfast dishes – and under her influence his diet had changed. He had to admit both options had become his favourites, too. They were far superior to cornflakes or a bog-standard fry up. Swings and roundabouts. Pluses and minuses. That was life, wasn't it.

That August morning, he sliced into his yolk and speared a round of sausage without his usual enthusiasm for Natasha's cooking. He spent long periods between mouthfuls staring out at the ocean. Behind him, Natasha pottered back and forth cleaning up in the kitchen. He really didn't like it when she was subdued.

Last night was the first time they'd ever argued. And it shouldn't have happened. He'd gone to Fuerteventura on the ferry to spend a couple of hours with Alvaro and managed to miss the ferry back. He'd arranged for Natasha to collect him, and she was forced to wait two hours for the next ferry. He welled with gratitude seeing her at the port and that gratitude spilled out of him right up until the moment she slapped him across the face in full view of the other foot passengers. Someone laughed. Everyone stared.

'Don't you ever do that to me again,' she growled when they were driving home.

There had been little point explaining that it was Ramona's fault. She'd left Alvaro in Billy's lap saying she needed to get something from a shop. Five minutes, she'd said. Cinco minutos. That five minutes turned into two hours, and the only proof Billy had that he was telling the truth was a stain on his jeans where Alvaro's nappy had leaked.

In the end, that stain soothed Natasha. Especially once they were indoors and she examined the stain and saw it was a thinnish brown streak. She burst out laughing picturing Billy sitting there getting the stink and the overspill from a full nappy. Her mirth didn't last long.

'Next time, I swear to God, either you come with me, or I'll make her come to Playa Blanca,' he'd said, hoping to appease.

Make? There was no chance of that. Instead, as he took his breakfast plate to the sink, he knew he would be seeing Alvaro less and less. He wasn't sure how he felt about that. The kid was almost one and not yet walking. He'd never harboured a strong paternal attachment to the boy. Maybe he wasn't cut out to be much of a father. Although with Sophie and Emily things had been different. They had both adored him. With Alvaro, he just didn't feel the same bond. Besides, yet again Ramona had hit him for money.

Natasha's mood lifted as the day wore on. It was fiesta week in Arrecife, and she was meeting a couple of girlfriends there. Billy didn't know if he would be welcome, especially after the day before, but around six o'clock, when the house was filled with perfume and hairspray and she emerged from the bedroom in a tight-fitting black dress that showed off the inviting curve of her hips, he thought he might have been forgiven. With her lips all glossy red and her thick black hair pinned up she looked like a goddess. When she said to him, 'You must come, too,' he almost did, just staring at her.

He was on his feet in an instant. Figuring he looked okay in his T-shirt and jeans, he made for his keys. She folded her arms across her chest and eyed him critically. He feared she was back to being cross with him. There was a moment of awkwardness. Then she turned on her heels and left the room, returning with his smartest summer shirt.

PROMENADE, ARRECIFE, LANZAROTE

The fiesta was taking place along the waterfront. There were food stalls unleashing rich garlicky aromas. Local music blared from hidden sources, and smartly dressed people were ambling about. No one looked British. Natasha threaded her arm through his and they strolled like couples strolled, pausing here and there for a small bite of something or to look at the water darkening in the setting sun or simply to inhale the warm night air and kiss.

Natasha's girlfriends were gathered in a tight huddle along with some others in an al fresco bar near the live music. At the centre of the huddle stood a man a whole head taller than the others. As Billy drew closer, he saw why. The man had that classic look of masculine beauty found among Canarian men, and fire shone out of his keen brown eyes. He wore a crisp white shirt and an engaging smile, and his voice rose above the crowd, enchanting those gathered around him, men and women alike. As Billy sized up this male creature, Natasha worked her way into the throng. Billy attempted to maintain a steadfast closeness, already sensing competition.

'Andres,' she said, beaming up into the man's face. '¿Que tal?'

Andres' smile widened as he reached down and kissed her on both of her cheeks.

Jealousy coiled itself around Billy's heart.

As Natasha stood back and introduced Billy, the two men sized each other up. Billy knew he came up short in the good-looks stakes, but he hoped his girlfriend had more about her than to be taken in by looks and charisma.

Everyone carried on chatting. Billy's attention travelled around the group. Andres was the focal point among six smartly turned-out men, all of them swarthy and short, and an equal number of women, in varying degrees dazzled by Andres.

It took Billy all of five seconds to realise Andres was high. The entire group was high.

Coke.

Billy had witnessed enough cocaine in his ill-spent youth to spot the bravado.

Tequila was being quaffed like water, which didn't help. Billy was immediately on guard. He recognised in these men the same attitude to life carried by the Maloney boys and their cronies, although this lot didn't seem quite so hard. This was Lanzarote, not London, after all. Even so, he didn't want to get mixed up in local crime. He was surprised at Natasha, too, who up until that point had been to him as pure as an angel.

Billy bought himself a beer and Natasha a tequila sunrise, and then he hovered on the side-line, his Spanish no match for the fast chatter that blurred into an incoherent babble beneath the music.

Billy had never been much of a party animal. And his ego was taking a battering watching Andres undress Natasha with his salacious eyes. The remnants of her anger over the ferry fiasco meant she was lapping up the attention. It occurred to him that was why she had dressed as a temptress. There he stood, propping up the bar, the only Anglo-Saxon in a sea of Latin blood, lacking the language, the looks, the bravado to compete. He felt emasculated.

And he smouldered.

As he slugged his beer his insides grew as fiery as his hair. Three beers later he was aflame, and no amount of alcohol could snuff out his jealousy. Fuelling his chagrin, he saw through narrowed eyes that, thanks to a slew of tequila shots, Natasha was drunk.

No one came to his side to engage him in conversation or invite him to dance or retreat to a private spot for a line of coke. He was a fixture at the bar. He paced his drinks, grateful to be ignored as the partying dragged on and on well into the small hours.

At last, he saw some of the others peel away. Natasha staggered over and he let his heart lift thinking they were about to go home, but it wasn't to be. Instead, it was back to Andres' place for more cocaine, more booze, and more partying.

ANDRES' HOUSE, GÜIME, LANZAROTE

Andres had a house in the tiny inland village of Güime, about a five-minute drive out of Arrecife. As he pulled up outside behind the car in front, Billy ground his teeth. Part of him would rather have gone home and left Natasha to partake in the drunken, coke-fuelled revelry, but the larger part of him felt like a guard dog poised for attack.

They went in, Natasha stumbling on her heels.

The house was built in traditional Canarian style around an enclosed courtyard and originally belonged to Andres' grandparents. After he inherited the property, he'd tarted it up a bit with fresh paint and pot plants, but he'd kept all the old features. The guests congregated in the courtyard before wandering into the sitting room where Andres unleashed more coke. He cut and drew the lines like an expert and one by one each guest took a turn with the rolled up one-hundred peseta bank note. Billy watched on as Natasha kneeled at Andres' feet and took her turn. As she sniffed the line of powder, Andres and Billy locked gazes.

'¿Y tú?'

Billy hesitated. He hadn't snorted coke in years. He didn't particularly want to now, especially so late in the night. He valued his sleep. But he suddenly saw it as a sort of initiation and if he was ever to be accepted by Natasha's friends, feel part of the group, he needed to participate. It wouldn't kill him.

As Natasha stood aside and Andres' gaze drifted to her buttocks, Billy went to take her place.

The coke was strong, much stronger than any he had tried before, and he was flooded with that exhilarating brilliance that only coke can provide. And, thanks to the fiery pit of jealous rage he'd been carrying inside him all night, he was horny as hell.

He wasn't the only one. Two of the women paired off with two of the men and disappeared. One woman, off her head on coke, had started grinding her hips into the man she was sitting on. Her boyfriend? Who knew? There was an uneven number of women to men. Before long only Andres, Natasha and Billy were left in the room. Billy didn't know what had got into Natasha and he began to fear she would end up in Andres' bed. Then another woman walked in, a woman Billy hadn't seen before. She was stunning and sexy in lurid pink, and she claimed Andres as hers with a covetous smile as she smoothed her hands down her hips. Andres took her hand and led her away, announcing to Natasha in perfect English that they could take the small room at the back of the house.

In a soft double bed, as distant groans and shrieks of pleasure echoed through the house, Natasha Gonzalez devoured Billy Mackenzie. With his rage firmly located in his loins he enjoyed a consuming release the likes of which he'd never experienced before. Maybe, just maybe the night had been worth it.

The following morning, Billy woke up in an otherwise empty bed. He was damp with sweat. Light poured in through a curtainless window. Natasha was nowhere to be seen. He got up and pulled on his shirt and jeans and left the room. He had only the vaguest recollection of the layout of the house. A few steps down a dark hall and he found a bathroom. Then he followed the smell of brewed coffee and found Natasha sitting on a kitchen bench with one of her girlfriends.

'Hola.'

Seeing Billy, Natasha slid down to her feet and approached him coyly and planted a sloppy kiss on his lips.

'Coffee?'

'Sure.'

He looked around for a glass and water. Seeing his search, Natasha found a glass and went out to the internal patio. He hovered awkwardly, not knowing what to say to Natasha's friend. Thankfully, she ignored him.

'Here,' Natasha said on her return, placing the glass in Billy's hand. 'It's pure filtered water.'

'Cheers.' He took a slug and then another. It was the best water he'd tasted in ages.

Her friend left the room with a coffee cup in each hand, winking at Billy on her way by. It was a playful wink, not coquettish, and he suddenly felt talked about.

Natasha poured his coffee, topping up her own cup as well.

'He wants to talk to you,' she said, sliding the cup his way.

'Andres? What about?'

'Business.'

'I gathered that.'

'I'll translate.'

'Is there any need?'

She looked offended. Then she laughed and said, 'Oh, that. He can't really speak English. That was rehearsed.'

Billy was instantly jealous again. It didn't sit well with him, finding himself on the outside and in the dark. He needed to learn the language, fast.

'And when is this talk to take place?'

'Later today, at his brother's restaurant.'

An antenna buzzed in Billy's mind. That felt a bit sudden. He slurped his coffee and they opened cupboards and the fridge in search of something to call breakfast.

CALLE LA INÉS, ARRECIFE

Billy found it hard to appreciate the small and shabby eatery situated on one of Arrecife's dusty lanes and sporting only six tables in one long row, but the smells wafting through from the kitchen did give the impression of good food. The dining area was empty, and no one came out with menus. Billy looked around. The tables were covered in squares of clear plastic over floral-printed fabric. A few framed photos hung askew on walls of flaking paint, along with a ghastly print between some shelves behind the counter. The floor tiles were in a terrible state. 'Andres says they're renovating,' Natasha said apologetically, adding, 'Soon,' as Billy scanned for evidence in the form of paint tins, ladders, tools, anything to indicate building works.

Andres was nowhere to be seen, but when Natasha and Billy sat down at the last table in the row, the Canarian burst in off the street through the suddenly wide-open door and hurried to greet them. No doubt hearing his voice above the sizzles in the kitchen, a man appeared in a chef's apron over a plain shirt and black pants. The brother? Although he looked nothing like Andres. There was a brief exchange. Natasha did not bother to translate. The brother disappeared. Then a woman came out with platters of tapas and three beers.

As Billy tucked in to meatballs, freshly grilled sardines, roasted aubergine and spicy chickpeas, Andres spoke, addressing Billy through Natasha who translated. He was raising funds for a little import/export operation he had planned, and he was looking for investors.

'How much?' Billy said doubtfully.

In pesetas the figure sounded phenomenal, but it amounted to five grand. Natasha took her role seriously, but Billy could see she wasn't completely at ease with the situation. And rightly so. When she turned to him and said, 'The investment is safe. Totally one hundred per cent guaranteed,' Billy could see misgivings behind her enthusiastic gaze.

Billy had managed to understand that last comment in Spanish. And he had heard the same reassurances many times before. Nothing in the land of dodgy business deals was guaranteed.

Then the persuading started. Natasha, who was vaguely related to Andres on her mother's side, seemed naïve to Billy. Maybe it was because they were family that Natasha had turned dead-set keen. Or maybe Andres had said something to her that she didn't translate. Something to free her of any hesitancy. It was as though she had fallen under Andres' spell. Billy took in the persuasiveness in his manner, his eagerness, his enthusiasm, but it was Natasha who carried all of that determination through to Billy without a filter of caution.

Billy felt himself getting sucked in. The way she presented it, the deal sounded bombproof. Besides, where was the harm? All he needed to do was part with five grand, wait a few weeks and double his money. It wasn't as if he was hard up. In the end, he let his heart do his thinking. Or maybe it was his gonads. More likely his desire not to disappoint his sweetheart was borne out of fear that if he did, she would shift her sights to Andres, never mind he was a blood relative already fucking a ravishing woman in pink. By the time the tapas were gone and the beer bottles empty, it was handshakes and kisses and an arrangement made to hand over the money next week.

'What exactly am I investing in?' Billy said on their way home.

'Andres said it was some cargo coming from Morocco.'

'Cargo?'

'Yeah, I know it isn't how you say kosher, but I wanted to help him out. He's my cousin.'

'Distant cousin.'

'In your world perhaps. But here in my culture, no cousin is distant.'

She made it sound as though everyone on the whole island was related to everyone else. If you went back far enough, they probably were.

Long before they reached his low house on the cliff, he felt certain he had agreed to kiss goodbye to five thousand pounds for the sake of keeping Natasha.

14

GOLF COURSE, COSTA TEGUISE, WEDNESDAY 20 MARCH 2019

THE MORNING WAS SUNNY AND WARM. With a cup of tea in hand, I sat out on the patio, gazing at the volcano, thinking I could get used to this lifestyle. Something about sitting outside in the shelter and privacy of a walled patio, protected from the wind, all the while looking out at an enchanting view.

But there was work to be done, a purpose to fulfil, risks to take. With no other lead, I had no choice but to return to the golf course. This time in different attire. I went inside to get ready.

I donned a maroon polo top tucked into khaki shorts, something I was able to do at my age thanks to a naturally trim figure not altered by childbearing. I dug out a new pair of white low-cut socks to go with my black runners. Observing myself in the bathroom mirror, I definitely looked the part. But now, I had no disguise. Even the large sunglasses would look out of place on the golf course and attract unwanted attention. I needed to blend in, disappear, fade into the background. Come on, Marjorie. The chances were high no one from forty years ago would recognise you. Ageing was its own mask. And there had never been anything distinctive in my visage. Besides, there was no choice. I had to risk it.

Still, I felt uneasy, exposed, almost naked as I forced myself out the door knowing the Maloney boys were most likely on the island. I would need to keep my wits about me. Avoid letting anyone stare into my face. Keep my eyes peeled. Be ready to duck or turn and disappear from view.

I left Guatiza a bit later this time, gauging my arrival at around morning tea, which would be when anyone arriving at opening time might be leaving.

The car park was almost full. I parked at the end of a row of cars and took a deep breath. Here goes.

There was no one about as I entered the clubhouse. I passed the reception desk and went on through to browse the apparel in the shop, keeping an eye out for anyone wandering by. All remained quiet. I thought I could stay put for quite a while as I pretended to browse the hat display. That thought was dashed when I glanced into the shop and inadvertently caught the eye of the assistant at the counter who then seemed poised to ask if I needed help. Not wanting her attention, I left the shop and went over to a photo display on the wall by the entrance to the restaurant. Odd I hadn't noticed it the day before.

I spent a long time gazing at every single head and shoulders in all of the group photos. In one, I spotted Billy seated at a table at a function. He wasn't easy to spot as most of him was obscured by the rotund man seated beside him. Yet what there was of Billy was unmistakable. His fiery hair, going white around the edges, was tied at the nape of his neck in that telltale ponytail and then there was that beard. Hair aside, he didn't look a day older than when I last saw him, which sent a shiver through me. If he was that easy to recognise, what about me?

Stop it, Marjorie. Get a grip.

The photo was dated about ten years before. Maybe since then he'd aged. Gone white. Did redheads go white early? Or was that just in dogs?

Feeling brave, I went out onto the terrace. An elderly couple strolled past me. Otherwise, the terrace was empty. All the golfers were out with their caddies potting balls. I ventured onto the course, wandering around beside the various fairways and greens, choosing the cover of rows of palm trees. None of the people on the course looked anything like Billy or the Maloney brothers.

Harbouring a mix of disappointment and relief, I went back out to the car park and sat for about an hour and a half, keeping an eye on any cars entering and whiling away the time thinking of all the things I might be doing if I hadn't been tied to my obs.

Hunger caused me to drive down to Costa Teguise for lunch. Then I spent another two hours in the car park that afternoon but there was no sign of Billy. It felt like a lost cause. And I was sick of the sight of golfers and their caddies.

On the way home, I considered asking Clarissa if she would help but thought better of it. She had enough on dealing with Trevor. Besides, I hardly knew her and she was staying on a different island. It was quite a trek getting up here. Pity. With her cool, no fuss manner she would have made a useful accomplice.

GOLF COURSE, COSTA TEGUISE, THURSDAY 21 MARCH 2019

Another day was another opportunity. I figured Billy was obviously an avid golfer and at least one day in any seven-day period, he would play golf. I just had to stick at the obs.

I donned the clothes I had on the day before and drove to the golf course. When I got there and observed the near empty car park, I grew confident that nothing would happen. It was a cloudy day, a little on the cool side, and golfers must love the sunshine.

I parked near the entrance, away from the other three cars – a white hatchback, a red coupe, and a black sedan. As I sat there behind the wheel with my seat belt still on, figuring a game plan, pessimism soon took hold. I feared I was losing confidence in my own abilities. How hard could it be to track someone down on this tiny rock of an island? Then again, when I thought back to my policing days, I knew that surveillance took months, not a few days, of constant watching. I must not be defeated, my more stoic self argued. This was my only lead. With this inner tussle going on, I all but marched into the clubhouse.

Not wanting to appear suspicious to those behind the reception desk who might be wondering what a non-member was doing entering the premises three days in a row without so much as buying a pair of socks, I made a beeline for the shop. There had to be something affordable to buy, something not totally meant for golf.

I decided on a hat. The shop assistant was no doubt by now wondering why I was so given to standing at the wire rack displaying the headgear. This time, I would please her with a sale. I took my time sifting through the hats, the various colours and styles, all the while keeping an eye on anyone passing by. I settled on a navy-blue hat, repressing a gasp when I saw the price. I got my wallet to the ready and went and paid.

With a paper bag advertising the golf club shop tucked under my arm, I felt brave enough to go on through to the terrace.

I didn't get far. I'd scarcely taken a step outside the door when I came to a sudden halt.

Seated at the far end of the terrace watching members head off to the first hole or stroll back after completing their round, with most of his face hidden behind a newspaper, was Mick Maloney. If it wasn't Mick Maloney, it was the spitting image of him – tall, heavyset, square shoulders, long nose, and that telltale protruding chin. He sat there looking like the gangster that he was in black sunglasses and a trilby hat. The glasses and the hat might as well have been identical to those he wore forty years ago.

Even though I had half-anticipated one of the brothers turning up – it was an obvious location on an island of this size if you were trying to track down an ageing Brit – seeing him there was a shock. It was also too much of a coincidence. I suddenly felt set-up, but by who?

My mind raced. Could Jim Ackland have tipped Mick Maloney off about seeing Billy at the golf course? What about me? Had Ackland told them I was on the island as well? The Maloney boys knew I had been in the squad, but did they know I was Billy's handler? I didn't think they did. Clive would never have betrayed a colleague to the Maloney boys. It wasn't in his nature. But Ackland? Clive Plant had always told me to be wary of Ackland. I pictured him laughing his head off on the flight home. It was something he would do. I was sure of it. At least he didn't know I'd come to Lanzarote to track down Billy. I was wise to be cagey with him. Not give myself away.

I turned my attention to the terrace. The man who looked

like Mick Maloney now had his back to me. I went inside and observed him through the glass. It had to be Mick.

Unlike me, he didn't care if he was recognised. And his presence meant I couldn't risk entering the clubhouse again. I would have to remain tucked away somewhere in the car park. Even that was risky. My surveillance had shifted from clocking Billy to clocking Billy before Mick did. Which put a different perspective on the situation. I now also had an additional task. Surveilling Mick.

I had planned to drive into Costa Teguise for lunch but that was now out. I sat, sweating in my car for four hours before I spotted Mick Maloney leaving the clubhouse. He was driving the black sedan. It was the only black car in the car park. And with tinted windows. Typical. Still, he was his own advert. Which would be handy.

My decision was instant. I was confident Mick hadn't spotted me sitting there, boiling hot in my golf gear, sunglasses, and navy-blue hat. My rental car was nondescript. The risk was worth it.

I waited for him to reverse and kept my eye on which way he turned as he exited the car park. A swift manoeuvre and I was a safe distance behind him, on the road to Costa Teguise.

From there he headed south to Arrecife. Damn. I kept my distance, kept my eye on the black sedan, kept hoping he wasn't planning on taking me down the riddle of one-way streets. But he took the ring road and the next exit to Tahiche. It was a strange route, as he had almost gone full circle. Force of habit? Was he paranoid someone, anyone could be following him? Or had he in fact spotted me?

I hung three cars back. It was a risk. I could easily lose him. Although with no bushes or hedges or trees or rows of buildings to obscure the view, I pretty much had him pegged.

He headed north towards Teguise before making a left for Mozaga. From Mozaga he made a right and followed the road to Tiagua. Seemed he was planning on zigzagging his way to wherever he was heading. Was he lost? He sure was taking the most roundabout route possible short of circumnavigating the whole island.

I couldn't risk following him much further. Not with him going every which way. He was sure to spot me. In the end.

The village of Tiagua was small and sprawling. He turned off the main road and I hung well back, turning off at the same intersection just in time to see him pulling into the driveway of a farmhouse up ahead, a farmhouse on the outskirts of the other side of the little village. I couldn't do a U-turn on that narrow street, not without drawing attention to myself, and there were no side streets. Which left me no choice. I drove on by, checking out the farmhouse and making a note of the street name before heading back to Guatiza.

In case I had inadvertently set up a game of cat and mouse, I took an even more convoluted route home.

15

GREENWICH, 1979

Tension was building in the squad. The pressure was on. It was mid-December and we needed to nab one of the Maloney boys soon. Funding was drying up and those seconded from the regions would soon be heading back to their regular postings. Tempers were frayed as a result, as everyone wanted to be a part of the action and accrue some of the glory that went with it. And the sergeant and constable seconded from Birmingham were behaving like animals. Worse than animals. DS Trower and DC Brice were uncouth and vile. Rumour had it they had trashed all the places they stayed in. Gave just cause to civilians calling us pigs.

It all came to a head one Friday night in the public bar of the Ship and Anchor. It was Clive Plant's birthday and the whole squad was there celebrating. Liz had had a whip round and organised a cake which was due to come out from behind the bar any moment. Everyone there was either sloshed or well on the way. Loud voices and raucous laughter. The usual jibes and gutter jokes. Liz and I stood clutching our drinks beside the bar. There was only one person in the pub that night who'd decided to let drink turn him sour.

For a reason known only to himself, Sergeant Trower was in a filthy mood. He was standing at the bar shooting his mouth off, oblivious to the reactions of all those in earshot, when a cat wandered through the pub and came up to him and rubbed against his leg. Poor choice of leg, I thought, sipping my drink. That cat needed to be more discriminating.

Trower shooed the cat away with his foot and carried on with his story. My gaze followed the feline as it wandered off for a short while. But the poor cat wouldn't take no for an answer and came up to Trower again, rubbing against his calf. Maybe it smelled food. Maybe whoever usually stood in that spot was a cat lover who petted the animal and fed it treats. Not Trower. He slammed his pint on the counter, reached down and picked up the cat. Then, to the horror of everyone who happened to be looking in his direction, he held the cat up and wrung its neck and tossed it aside as though it was an unwanted bag of rubbish.

Trower's sidekick DC Brice cheered. No one else did. One of others on the squad walked up to Trower and socked him in the jaw. Trower was quick to react and launched a retaliatory punch. The officer fell back into his friend. Deciding I was too close to the action, I grabbed my drink and headed over to the other side of the pub with Liz. A brawl threatened. DI Brace intervened and told Trower to go home.

As Trower and Brice left the pub, the others started downing their drinks. The cake had not appeared.

'It was Frank's cat,' Liz said.

'Shit.'

Frank owned the pub.

Clive, who didn't drink, not since he drove home drunk one night and hit a tree and smashed up his feet, came over and offered to drive me home.

'But it's your birthday,' Liz said. 'We got you a cake.'

'I can't face it.'

'I'll bring it into work tomorrow. We'll have it then.'

I left Liz to organise that with Frank and followed Clive outside.

'Those two should be sent back where they came from,' I said once we were on our way.

'What gets me is Trower will get away with it. You can bet your life nothing will happen. Never does.'

Clive sounded grim. He'd been cheated out of his own birthday celebrations, and it hardly seemed fair. Came as a shock, too, that folk like Trower existed in the force. Gone the halcyon days of my early career in policing when all I seemed to meet were benevolent souls. A veil had lifted. What I now saw I didn't like one bit.

THE FOLLOWING MONDAY, as I sat down at my desk, the phone rang. It was Billy. 'Meet me behind the toilet block in Greenwich Park at ten.'

I had enough time to drink the tea Liz had deposited in front of me – we took it in turns to make each other a cup in the mornings – and then, after clearing my absence with DI Brace, I was out the door.

The weather was foul. Rain threatened. I pulled up in the car park and pushed open the driver's door as an icy north wind pressed against it as though determined not to let me out of my car.

Billy was huddled against the back wall of the men's toilet, copping the full brunt of the wind. He didn't see me approach. When I said his name, he flinched.

'You alright?'

He looked at me through paranoid eyes. His face had a rigid set to it. I could see he was terrified. In fear of his life. He needed to lose the expression. It was a dead giveaway. He must know more than he's letting on, I thought. A lot, lot more.

For a long time, I'd sensed I was being drip fed. But what he did give me, with a couple of exceptions, had proved gold. I knew all informers took huge risks passing on information. There were coppers who thought informers were lowdown scum betraying their own kind. There was nothing noble about being a snitch. I saw things differently and I couldn't help feeling sorry for Billy. Although nothing about him provoked my sympathies. It was more that I wouldn't have wanted to be in his shoes.

'What's going on, Billy? Anything I should know about?'

He shook his head.

'I'm dealing with it.'

'Dealing with what?'

'Can't say.' He leaned in close. 'Will you do something for me, Marjorie?'

'If I can.'

He shuffled where he stood, hands in pockets, collar turned up, scanning the park.

'Talk to your boss. See if I can get witness protection. Things are getting hot, too bloody hot.'

'You'll have to give me more, Billy. Not just tip-offs. For witness protection, you need to give me evidence that will lead to a conviction and you'll need to testify. You prepared to do that?'

'Might be the only way I'm not gonna end up dead.'

I promised that if it came down to it, I would have a word with my superintendent. He seemed satisfied with that.

'I've got something for you. There's a prison officer getting drugs into Brixton prison.'

'Details, please.'

'I don't have any.'

'Oh, come on.'

'Go talk to Craig McIntyre. He's the prison officer in charge. He'll fill you in.'

Billy hurried off, leaving me standing behind the toilet block in Greenwich Park in the freezing cold as the skies opened up and the rain teemed down. I ran back to my car, twisting my ankle as I negotiated the kerb and cursing my stupid platform soles.

When I relayed Billy's information to DI Brace before lunch that day, he warned me to keep quiet, told me to pretend I had nothing to do with the tip-off.

'There's a lot of talk on the squad. Big egos. Especially now there's that reward. Everyone wants their snout to provide the tip-off in the hope of a kickback. Better you keep your head down.'

'But will you set up an obs?'

'You and Liz pay the prison a visit, see this McIntyre. If the tip-off proves accurate, we'll set something up.'

It was almost lunchtime. I went over to Liz's desk and suggested a pie and pint.

DC Brice seated at the next desk pricked up his ears.

'A girlie lunch, is it?'

Then DS Trower piped up.

'Not inviting us fellas, eh?'

'I told ya. Couple of dykes.'

'Sure you don't want some company? We'll just watch.'

Liz stuck her fingers up at the men as we headed out the door.

'Be glad when those dicks go back where they came from,' she said as we made our way downstairs.

'The dog pound?'

We both laughed.

Brixton was about half an hour's drive from Charlton. We stopped off at a pub on the way. Not for a pie, neither of us fancied one after that ribbing. We went for scampi and chips.

Safe and reliable.

At the prison, Craig McIntyre explained that the prison officer under suspicion was in charge of a workshop.

'He's getting the drugs in here somehow. I'm sure of it.'

'Do you have his photo?'

He opened a file and produced a headshot. Liz took it. He told us Barry Legg went for a couple of pints in the Royal Oak each lunchtime before he went on duty.

'When's his next shift?'

'Tomorrow.'

With that, we headed back to the station. The following day, Brace sent us down to the Royal Oak with Plant and Ackland. DC Jones would be parked outside the pub.

We entered the Royal Oak and settled in at the back, pretending to be two couples. Liz and Jones had their backs to the door, giving Plant and I a clear sightline of who entered and left the pub. After his first pint, Plant started taking his role a little bit too seriously. He sidled up close. Whispered in my ear. And then slipped his hand on my knee beneath the table. Ackland seemed not to notice but Liz gave me a knowing stare. I'd confided in her about Plant's pass at me in the car that day on the way back from Southampton and she'd rolled her eyes. My instinct now was to stand up or slap him round the face, but I was beaten to any action when the suspect entered and ordered a pint and sat at a table near the entrance. Soon after, another guy walked in and then our suspect stood and both men left the pub. Ackland radioed Jones. He radioed back to say he couldn't see what the guys were doing but he'd got the number plate. Plant then called the local uniformed police – no one on the squad wanted to be known by the local criminal fraternity – and told them to stop the vehicle as it was entering the prison. By the time we got back to the station, the arrests had been made. They'd found the drugs hidden in car parts.

Not much was said about the nabbing of the prison officer

on the squad. No one was interested. In his office, Brace acknowledged us all for a job well done and in a private moment when no one was in earshot, he thanked me. I couldn't help feeling peeved that I got no credit for the tip-off. It wasn't enough that Brace knew. I needed acknowledgement up the chain of command. I needed the whole squad to know how good I was. How good my informer was. But I kept quiet. I wouldn't disobey the inspector.

It proved to be an eventful week. The offer of a reward bore fruit. While we were hanging out in that Brixton pub, Mick Maloney's girlfriend had got in touch with DS Drinkwater.

I found out when I arrived at work fifteen minutes late – there'd been an accident at a set of traffic lights in Shooter's Hill and I'd had to make a detour – and a squad meeting was in full swing headed by the DS. The room was packed, and Liz had already done the honours of the round of teas. Brace looked over as I entered the room but no one else took any notice. I stood at the back beside DS Pierce, a giant of a man with flaming red hair which he wore like a helmet, and listened. DS Drinkwater said the girlfriend had arranged to meet Mick in a park in Plaistow the next day. Someone had drawn a map of the park. The super stood to the side and Brace explained how the capture would work. We'd form an inner and an outer circle. We would have eyes everywhere. Detectives would be placed as lookouts in a block of flats overlooking the park. Two officers would be in the church opposite. And we would be armed to the teeth. We would have people in cars, vans and three on motorbikes. Roles were assigned. Everyone knew what they had to do. Detectives filed out or returned to their desks. The mood in the office for the rest of the day was subdued in anticipation.

That night, I found it hard to get to sleep. All I could think about was the capture. We had to get Mick Maloney. It was the squad's major arrest. To fail would be a disaster. My role was small. I was put in the outer circle for my own safety. It felt like a do-nothing role, but Clive had pointed out I was to stand near where the girlfriend would be, not on the other side of the park like many of the others. 'Don't worry,' he'd said. 'You won't miss the action.'

Those words were what kept me awake half the night.

I GOT to work early the next day. Brace had told everyone to carpool. Turned out Liz and I were to travel in Plant's car. He was all ready and waiting. When Liz showed her face, he left his desk and summoned us both. We followed him out of the office.

Down in the station car park, we found Ackland already in the passenger seat and Jones in the back. Great.

'After you,' I said to Liz.

'No, no. After you.'

She stood back. Plant fired the engine.

'Get a move on, children.'

I relented.

And I was sandwiched between Jones and Liz for duration, which thankfully was only about fifteen-minutes.

Plant pulled up in a side street well away from the park. We'd been told to filter into our various positions drawing minimum attention to ourselves over the course of a couple of hours before the appointed time. Plant and Ackland headed off. Jones hung back, then took off in the opposite direction. He was part of the outer ring. Liz and I had been told to remain in the car until needed.

We had an anxious wait.

Would the girlfriend go through with it or bottle out? It was a question on everyone's mind. But the woman was hungry for the reward. The message came through on the police radio. She'd pulled up beside the park and sat waiting in her car.

Ten minutes went by and then we got word that a second car had pulled up a few cars back in the street, a blue hatchback. A guy had got out and gone to the newsagents on the corner and bought a paper.

Is that Maloney? someone asked.

Not sure. Different haircut.

He's gone back to his car.

Was it him? Or wasn't it?

No one knew. Nothing happened.

We waited.

By now, Liz had got fed up. 'I'm not sitting here while all the blokes enjoy the action,' she said and opened the car door. 'Come on.'

I hesitated. I felt uneasy. She was disobeying an order. Then again, we were so far away from the action no one would even know unless we were spotted.

Liz walked off. Not wanting to be left behind, I grabbed my radio handset, got out of the car, and hurried to join her as she marched on up the pavement. We found a spot on the corner of the street with a good view of the park. Liz pretended to retie a shoelace while I had a good gander. I located both of them.

The girlfriend got out of her car and approached the man's blue hatchback. It had to be Mick Maloney. His little visit to buy a paper had been a ploy. He suspected something.

The inner circle started to move in. I clocked Ackland, Plant, Jones, and Brace.

Maloney clocked all us cops in an instant and tried to drive off, slamming into the car in front and then the car behind, and, realising he wasn't able to get out into the road, he mounted the pavement.

There was a terrifying moment when I felt sure he was going to tear across the park and get away. Then, out of nowhere, Pierce, that giant of a man with the wild red hair, came screaming towards Maloney's car, a baseball bat raised up above his head. He leaped straight onto the car bonnet and pounded the bat into the windscreen. There was an explosion of glass.

Plant was next on the scene. I ran over, keen not to miss the action. Liz was right behind me.

Plant yanked open the driver's side door, grabbed Mick's arm, and tried to pull him out. I gave him a wide berth. That was when I saw he had no idea another officer was doing the same with the other arm through the shattered windscreen. Maloney was being yanked in two directions hollering for one of them to let him go. There was blood everywhere. And the girlfriend was standing nearby, hysterical.

Without needing to be prompted, I went over and scanned her injuries. The cuts on her forehead and cheeks and hands were superficial. Little more than scratches. No ambulance required. On Brace's instructions, Liz and I took her back to the station in Plant's car. The girlfriend screamed, cried, and blubbered the whole way.

'Calm down,' Liz said unsympathetically. 'We got him. Think of the reward.'

All I could think about was how she really didn't deserve to get it. That Billy was much more deserving and took far greater risks every day, helping to be my eyes and ears. Without the likes of Billy, detectives wouldn't detect much. It was all about receiving information and not so much about actual sleuthing. But whatever way you looked at it, that day we nabbed Mick Maloney, and there was one less gangster on the streets of London. All that remained was to find his brother.

16

TIAGUA, LANZAROTE, SATURDAY 23 MARCH 2019

TRACKING DOWN BILLY WAS GETTING TEDIOUS AND MUCH TOO risky. After two more days staking out the golf course, I decided on a change of tack. At dawn, while the rest of Lanzarote enjoyed a Saturday morning lie in, I donned my full disguise and drove to Tiagua and parked a few houses up the street from the farmhouse I'd seen Mick Maloney return to the other day. I was far enough away not to arouse suspicion and close enough to witness any movement.

All of the houses on the street were set back from the road, the gardens fronted by low whitewashed walls. Those inside might notice a strange car parked in the street, might wonder at the person seated inside, but on an island always packed with tourists, I figured the locals and expat residents wouldn't bat an eyelid.

I wound down the window to let in the cool morning air. Then I turned on the radio with the volume low, adjusted the focus of my binoculars, and set them down on the front seat beside my beach bag. I reached into the bag for my digital camera and a short book on the history of the Canary Islands and settled in for a long wait.

I'd slipped into the rhythm of surveillance with ease, but as I sat there gazing at the unchanging scene, I found it a lonely activity. I wasn't sure I was cut out to be a private detective, although I supposed if I was paid well enough, I could be persuaded to sit in a car for hours on end.

It might have been the glorious spring weather, it might have been the holiday mentality or perhaps just the need to eat breakfast out, but whatever the cause, I didn't have too long to wait before action up ahead meant I was on the move.

The same black sedan I'd seen the other day nosed out of the farmhouse drive. I grabbed the binoculars. Mick Maloney was behind the wheel. Eric sat in the passenger seat. There was no one in the back. They made a right turn. I waited and then pulled out, trailing them a good hundred metres behind.

This time, there was no turning off this way and that. The Maloney boys drove straight through San Bartolomé and on to Playa Honda. I thought they would be heading to Arrecife but instead they crossed the arterial road and cruised through the town to the coast, pulling up in a side street. I made a quick left and found a park, grabbed my bag, and scrambled out of the car.

I hurried back to the intersection just in time to see them corner the end of the street. Running was not my forte, but I had no choice. I sprinted, feeling the less than taut flesh of my sixty-something torso rebound with every footfall.

Before I reached the corner I stopped and caught my breath. Then I hurried on, stepping out onto the promenade, and catching sight of the brothers as they entered a restaurant up ahead. Perhaps I was not such a bad sleuth after all.

Keen for my heart rate to settle back to normal, I strolled on, planning my next move. Would I brazen it out and enter the eatery or choose a table outside? Or maybe I should hover down on the beach? It was at that moment I realised I didn't know what I hoped to discover from my surveillance. Keeping tabs on the brothers' movements wouldn't yield much unless they somehow led me to Billy. Yet I suspected they had about as much hope as me of locating him if he never showed up at the golf course. And there was no guarantee they were in fact looking for Billy. Although Mick's presence at the golf club did suggest that was the case.

For all I knew, the Maloney boys were after me as well. Although after forty years, picking off members of the crime squad seemed rather farfetched. And I hadn't done anything notable as regards their arrests, other than handle Billy. Despite what Clive Plant thought, as long as I didn't somehow announce myself to the Maloney boys, I would be safe.

There was nothing to be gained by standing on the beach. If anything, I would start to look suspicious, become an object of curiosity or puzzlement. Especially garbed as I was in an outfit that certainly drew the eye. I faced the same issue sitting al fresco. There was nothing for it but to walk into the restaurant and locate a table further back from wherever the Maloney boys were sitting. That way, I would be looking at the brothers who would no doubt be looking out at the ocean. Bolstering myself with fake confidence, I marched on in, narrowly missing colliding with a waiter loaded with a drinks tray thanks to my ludicrously dark sunglasses which had rendered me instantly blind in the dimly lit interior.

Only, I couldn't take them off for fear I'd be recognised.

I steered a course past the arrangement of tables fanning out along the length of open windows, all of them occupied. I clocked the brothers seated at a table for four over by the wall on my left. Neither man looked in my direction. As expected, many of the tables towards the back were empty. I went and sat at a table for two, two rows back and three along. I was too far away to hear any conversation but close enough to observe. I took up the chair positioned to enjoy the view as a waiter came and handed me a menu.

I felt terribly self-conscious and exposed. My only comfort was that the sun streaming in from the east meant many of the other diners were also wearing their sunglasses. I deposited my camera on the table. When the waiter returned, I ordered an orange juice and an almond croissant and sat with my face half-buried in my book.

Halfway through my juice I began to wonder if my latest plan to tail the brothers was either a lost cause or an insane risk or both, when a tall and enigmatic man in his late sixties breezed in. Accentuating his classic Hispanic good looks, he wore a loose and brilliant white shirt unbuttoned to the diaphragm revealing a deep tan and a well-formed chest. I imagined him on a yacht. And I was not the only one in the room to stare as he went by. He looked around and then to my astonishment he went straight over to the brothers.

What were the Maloney boys doing in cahoots with a man like him? Had to be drugs. Armed robbery had gone out of fashion decades ago. Going by the look of the stranger, I would hazard a guess it was cocaine.

I had another hypothesis. The dazzling stranger could well be aligned with the local criminal fraternity at the highest level which meant he might be a good contact if you were trying to track down someone with a dodgy past. Maybe they now knew he was living on the island. Like me, they'd clocked him in that photo display at the golf club. Doubtful, but unless Billy had lived the life of a saint since he got here, in all likelihood someone from the island's underworld would know something about him. It would be worth investigating, and it looked like the Maloney boys were doing just that. And going by what Ackland had told me in Arrecife the other day, Billy was not given to keeping that low a profile. Maybe, after all these years, he'd got overconfident. Mind you, he was no fool. By now, he would have to know about the murder of Oscar Cribbs. And he'd be lying low. Which explained why he hadn't shown his face at the golf course. Maybe he'd even slipped the island for a while. In which case I was on a hiding to nothing.

I wished I could get closer and hear what was going on. A waiter approached their table. The man shook his head, pointed at another table outside, and the waiter cleared away the plates. Eric said something to the waiter, and he nodded and walked away.

I quickly finished my croissant and juice and asked for the bill. Now, I had to leave. And I had to make up my mind who to follow. What would be the point of tailing the Maloney boys all day? Then again, there was little to be gained tracking the movements of the stranger. When Eric and Mick stood and made to leave, I fiddled around with the bag on my lap, keen for neither of them to get a good look at my face, sunglasses or not. When I looked up, they were gone.

I knew too much about tailing a hardened criminal to be in a rush to leave. It would be better to lose them for the day than have them see me following them. Instead, I went to the bathroom. When I came out, the stranger had left the other table. That gave me an idea. I approached the waiter at the bar and asked if he knew who that stranger was. It took several attempts as his English was not that good and my Spanish was non-existent, but in the end, he seemed to know who I was talking about. 'Andres,' he said. 'Andres Ortega. Why do you ask?'

'I thought he was that famous actor. Javier Bardem.'

The waiter laughed. 'Bardem is from Gran Canaria,' he said, as if that made a difference. To me it didn't. What mattered was I had managed to plausibly excuse my curiosity. It was another tick in the plus box of sleuthing attributes. You had to be quick off the mark.

I went for a stroll along the promenade, heading in the opposite direction to my car. I let about an hour slip by before I went back to that side street and headed home. The Maloney boys were long gone. Even so, caution made me take another circuitous route back to Guatiza. I breathed quite a sigh when I entered the farmhouse.

I was straight on my laptop, searching the name Andres Ortega in combination with the island and various words like drugs. Drogas, as it turned out, and I had far better luck finding out about Andres using Spanish. Crimen was another word I learned. And carcel. Back in the 1970s, Andres had spent two years in the same prison as Trevor. He should have served longer but was released early. At first, I couldn't understand why. But I surmised some sort of corruption at play. Andres and his family had friends in high places. I found that out by researching the Ortega family name. Someone had even done their family tree and made it public. Convenient. Among Andres' relatives were politicians, mayors, lawyers, a judge. I wondered what they all thought of their wayward relation. Who was, by the look of him earlier, doing very well for himself. Maybe his family of origin didn't find him all that wayward.

'What do you make of this?' I said to the air, realising with a lurch that Jess wasn't with me. That Jess would never be with me. I then felt guilty as I hadn't thought of her all morning. That lack of thought seemed wrong, like a betrayal. I felt I had to atone for the oversight. And grief filled my heart and radiated through me. Keeping the pain at bay, I wondered what Jess would have made of my sleuthing. I didn't think she would be all that impressed. But she would be pleased I was keeping busy, surely.

Dear Jess.

When we met, I was thirty. I had recently resigned from the force and was transitioning into probation. There was an induction course. Jess was one of the lecturers. Her pet topic was restorative justice. I didn't have an opinion about that either way, but the rest of the class did, and things got quite heated, and Jess became upset. I approached her afterwards and offered my sympathy. In her presence I felt unexpectedly drawn as though she was a magnet and I an iron filing. There was a spark behind that hurt expression, a definite fire in the eyes. Did she feel that magnetic pull, too?

I suggested on impulse that we went for a drink. She warmed to the idea. In a nearby pub, we sat together and chatted. She was still het up about the reaction of a particularly nasty man in the back row of the class who thought all criminals should be banged to rights, end of. Fail him, I said. And she laughed.

She did in fact fail him – not for his poor behaviour; he didn't complete a single assignment – and the probation service was saved from years of his attitude. A public service had been done. We laughed about it later, in a bed and breakfast in Leeds that weekend we went to see her parents for the first time. Not long after, Jess moved into my terraced house in Welling. Not long after that we bought a place together in Clapham and started a new life.

She'd never had any interest in the Canary Islands, and I suspected Billy was the reason. She wasn't into revenge. And she wasn't into delving into the past on the hunt for answers. Her policy was to let things go. She didn't want me dwelling on my past. She said it took me away from her. It was like theft. Jess could be possessive like that. In some ways she had been awfully insecure. I pictured her face, those kind, compelling eyes, and soft lips.

I was sinking into longing and regret and the raw pain of missing when my phone rang. It was Clarissa. She said Alvaro's killers had all been charged, fresh evidence had emerged, and she needed to be at the court at nine o'clock on Monday for Trevor's acquittal hearing. Luckily, the court had a vacant slot. Only, there was no way of getting to Arrecife in time.

'I'll have to book a hotel. I wondered if you would like to catch up tomorrow for an early dinner.'

'I can do one better. Stay here.'

There was a short pause.

'I couldn't impose.'

'I insist,' I said, thinking I could do with some company. 'This farmhouse is far too big for just me and I'm only ten minutes from the prison and fifteen from Arrecife. I'll take you in.'

'That is awfully kind.'

'Nonsense. You will be doing me a favour.'

'How so?'

'I'll tell you when you get here.'

'Is there a bus to Guatiza?'

'I'll pick you up from the ferry.'

'Make it Arrecife. No point driving all the way down there when the bus whips its way up the coast in half an hour.'

'Text me the time and I'll be there.'

Which meant I now had no choice but to figure out the best route to the bus station.

17

LOS COCOTEROS, SUNDAY 24 MARCH 2019

Billy eyed himself in the wardrobe mirror. He looked gaunt. He turned side-on and sucked in his belly. There was a definite concave below the diaphragm. And he could see his ribs. He went closer and examined his face. His cheeks were hollow. He could tell that even through his beard. He was wasting away.

And he was ravenous.

There was no point going to the kitchen. He was down to the knob of his last salami. He had an old packet of potato crisps in the pantry – the use-by date was last year – and half a jar of olives in the fridge. Tea bags. No coffee. The UHT milk was long gone, and the freezer contained a tray of ice cubes and a bag of frozen spinach he bought last month and never fancied. He should throw it out. Although he supposed he could fry up tiny cubes of the salami and toss in some of the spinach for bulk. It was stupid thinking. Never mind the spinach or the salami; it was Sunday, not his designated shopping day, but he had to go shopping.

Before fear trumped hunger, he fed Patch, gave her a good pat then grabbed a hat, sunglasses, and his keys. She looked up at him, mournful, her tail wagging. 'Sorry, Patch.' It was cruel to have to keep her in, but the risk was still too high. Out there somewhere were the Maloney boys. No matter how much he tried to pretend that they'd already left the island, instinct told him they hadn't. Besides, he knew exactly when they were leaving. It would be the last day they'd booked the Tiagua farmhouse. As he went outside, he looked ahead to golf on Wednesday with grim resignation. In the end, he might well have to suffer his fate. In the meantime, he had to eat.

As the rising sun reflected on the white of the patio, he stood outside in the shade cast by the house, trying to make up his mind which supermarket to visit. The Maloney boys were renting a farmhouse which implied that they were self-catering. That meant visits to supermarkets in their area. He could duck into the little supermarket in Guatiza, the safest option, but it didn't stock much. Neither did the supermarket in Tahiche. He wouldn't risk driving into Costa Teguise in case that was where the Maloney boys were searching for him. It was a prime resort town, after all, filled with Brits. He could head all the way into Arrecife and bank on the anonymity. There was a Eurospar just off the ring road. But that would be the most likely supermarket you would use coming in from Tiagua. He could head south, all the way to Puerto del Carmen or Playa Blanca. Or he could head north to Arrieta.

He settled on Arrieta. The petrol station on the corner on the way into the village was well-stocked and would have everything he needed. He figured he would be less likely to bump into the Maloney boys in there. A petrol station was not an obvious choice to shop for groceries. Unless you knew it was there, you would pass right by.

He went and unlocked the gates and reversed out his car before he changed his mind. He felt safer, too, on his way there, taking the backroad through Mala before joining the main road north.

He arrived at Arrieta a few minutes later. The petrol station forecourt was empty. He parked in front of the adjoining shopfront beside a red hatchback. He didn't look behind him at the road on the way in. Scanning the location would only attract attention.

He grabbed a trolley and pushed it down each aisle, piling in everything he could think of in bulk. Jars, cartons, boxes, tins, frozen packs of meat and fish, his trolley was piled high by the time he got to the bottled water. He had to use a second trolley to carry it all. When he got to the checkout, he remembered he'd forgotten cheese and, leaving his trolleys parked to one side to let other customers get served, he went through to the back of the supermarket to the refrigerated goods.

He was trying to decide whether to buy two packs or three when a voice right behind him said, 'Hello, stranger.'

Billy swung round and came face-to-face with Andres. The bottom fell out of his world. He beheld a dazzlingly handsome man dressed in white, a suitable mask for someone black on the inside. He'd done well for himself, by the look of things.

'I haven't seen you in years,' he said, all cheesy smiles.

He hadn't. Andres had been a notable absence at Natasha's funeral.

'How're you doing, Andres.'

'Couldn't be better. And you?' He took in all the cheese Billy was holding. 'Looks like you're buying for an army. Got visitors coming?'

'Yeah, a house full,' Billy said, realising Andres must have seen him at the checkout.

'Good for you.' He paused, his face filling with fake sympathy. 'I heard about Natasha.'

Billy nodded and grabbed a fourth pack of cheese and said, 'Best be getting on.'

'We must catch up sometime. Where are you? Still in the old place?'

Billy couldn't think fast enough to lie. Then again, why lie? It occurred to him in a sudden rush that despite his loathing of the man, Andres could be a godsend. If Billy played his cards right, this relative of Natasha could prove an ally, offer him protection, somewhere else to hide. Andres could even put a hit out on the Maloney boys. Yes, he was to be cultivated, not shunned. In the end, Billy avoided an answer by rebounding the question.

'And you? I thought you'd moved to Las Palmas.'

'I'm in the Tao house.'

Tao was the village before Tiagua. He recalled the one time he went there with Natasha and repressed a shudder.

'It's really good to see you again, Eddy.' Andres slapped him on the back. 'You must come over. Any day. Here, take my number. Be great to catch up.'

He pressed his business card into Billy's hand and then took off. Billy hovered by the fridges, grabbing a few packs of ham and chorizo while he waited for Andres to leave. Five minutes passed. Then he braved a walk to the front of the shop.

The packing and paying was fine. But loading the car proved an ordeal. Any one of those cars driving by behind him could contain a Maloney. He couldn't bundle the groceries into the boot fast enough and he was hampered by the wind threatening to blow his hat off. He felt pent up with eyes everywhere all the way home. He only started to relax when his gates were closed, and he could take his time filling his fridge and pantry.

Still, his choice of supermarket had turned out to be opportune. Meeting Andres had given Billy some unexpected hope. Andres was family of a sort, after all, and his loyalty to Natasha would surely extend to her life partner. Besides, even after all these years, Andres owed him. Never too late to call in a debt. With a touch of hope in his bones, he pulled a beer from the now well-stocked fridge and opened the sliding door to the back patio.

'Come on, Patch.'

The ocean heaved on a heavy swell. The wind out on this exposed outcrop could be fierce. There was little shelter but his need for some air around him outweighed the discomfort. He watched Patch trot down to the end of the terraces, blithe, content to sniff around and water a few spots. Dear Patch. His best friend.

'Hello, there, Eddy.'

The voice was so loud and so close, he nearly choked on his beer. He looked in the direction of the sound. The crown of a head appeared over the top of the side wall to the south. Then a face. 'Only me.' It was his neighbour, Tom. 'Sorry to disturb you. I rang the bell, rattled the gate, but I couldn't rouse you. Knew you were home. Saw the car drive up.'

Billy gave him a sullen look and said, 'Right.'

Tom emitted an awkward laugh.

'I have a favour to ask.'

'Shoot.'

'I need to take Penny to the vets. She has a thorn in her paw. Only, I have no one to look after young Patty.'

'The pup.'

He'd brought a pup home on Saturday. It was yet another intrusion on Billy's peace. Even from this distance, even in the wind, Billy could hear its yap when he was outside. Tom gave Billy an imploring look.

'She's too young to take with me. I wonder, would you mind dog-sitting till I get back?'

'Sure. Bring her over.' And I'll wring her neck, he thought.

'I would prefer it if you would come to mine. She's a delicate little thing.'

'What about Patch?'

'She'll be alright without you for a couple of hours, surely?'

Billy was outraged over the injustice. But his indignation gave way to opportunism when he realised it would be something of a reprieve. No one would find him at Tom's.

'Sure, no problem.'

'Terrific.' And Tom's face disappeared.

Billy called to Patch and took her inside and gave her a brief pat. Then he told her to go to her bed and wait for him. She cocked an ear, turned her head a little to the side.

'Sorry, Patch. Duty calls.'

He went out the front and opened the gate. It was a short walk over to Tom's. He got about halfway and was almost looking forward to the interlude when he heard a car. He looked back up the road. Whorls of dust trailed a vehicle heading his way.

The usual thoughts skittered through his mind. Maybe one of the farmhouses had a visitor. No, the vehicle had passed by the farm entrances. So, the vehicle belonged to a tourist. He had to assume that. And he had no choice but to keep walking. If he ran, he would draw attention to himself.

His feet felt like lead. He got to Tom's front gate as the car passed by behind him. It was all he could do not to cower. He scrambled to open the gate. But Tom, in his wisdom, had shut it. There was no way to get in without hitting the buzzer.

He heard Penny's loud bark. Then Tom called out, 'I won't be a minute.' And Billy had to stand there, a thin old man with his wild reddish-white hair and salt and red-pepper beard, recognisable to anyone who knew what he looked like.

He waited and waited as whoever was in that car did a three-point turn and headed back the way they'd come. They were taking a long time about it, too. The view from here was not that impressive.

He dared not turn, dared not see who it was. When he heard the engine near and then pass by behind him, he risked a glance and saw a woman behind the wheel and a couple of kids in the back, and he breathed a sigh. This vigilance was getting to be too much.

Then the gate opened, and he crossed Tom's immaculate grounds and was soon standing with the bull terrier pup in Tom's living room.

He'd only been inside his neighbour's house twice before. The first time was when his car had had a flat battery and he needed a lift into Arrecife for a replacement. He recalled having to readjust his attitude to his neighbour, the one single neighbour intruding on his solitude with his house and his dog. Without his presence, Billy would have faced a long walk to Guatiza where he would have had to hitch a ride. The second time was when Tom needed help moving a wardrobe. On neither occasion had Billy taken much notice of Tom's home. This time, with a couple of hours to kill and nothing to do except keep an eye on Patty, he did.

The wall facing the ocean vista was dominated by a large painting of a volcano. Not a regular landscape painting. The proportions were wrong. Things were on the skew somehow. It was not to his taste. On inspection, it was the volcano behind their properties, viewed from a different angle. Modern art? He had no idea. He wondered if Tom did, or if he had what they called taste. Looking around at the leather sofas, the smoked glass and chrome coffee table, the bookshelves filled with books of all sizes, he thought he'd probably underestimated Tom. Then there was his vinyl record collection. Scanning the covers and finding Frank Zappa, Captain Beefheart, and Van Morrison, he began to wonder if the next surprise would be a neat silver pipe or a bong. Old hippies did not necessarily look like old hippies. Who'd have thought. Still, Tom would remain the Tom he'd come to know over the decades, a slightly pesky retiree who preferred dogs to women when it came to company and was a tad too curious when it came to Billy.

He went and opened the fridge and helped himself to a

slice of cheese and another of cured ham, then moved onto the grapes, grabbing a handful before taking a slug of orange juice straight from the carton. He closed the fridge and wiped his mouth, casting an eye over the black marble countertop and the stainless-steel appliances – Tom had a new kitchen installed last year, with all the disruption that had entailed – before wandering through the rest of the rooms, taking in the furnishings, the eclectic array of wall hangings and ornaments and table lamps. This lot wasn't from Ikea. Tom had led quite a life.

He was interrupted on his house tour by a high-pitched bark and Patty, who had been wrestling with an old sock up till now, came scampering towards him. She came to a halt a few paces away and started barking furiously as though Billy was an intruder and not the man Tom had introduced her to about ten minutes earlier. Billy looked down at the feisty little bull terrier called Patty and thought of giving her a good hard kick in the ribs. But he wasn't into animal cruelty. Using his sternest voice, he told her to go back to the living room and then marched right past her. She trotted behind him and started attacking a chair leg. Then she attempted to chew Billy's shoe. He fetched some dog toys from a box by the back door and let Patty grip and tug and growl to her heart's content.

While he sat waiting for his neighbour to come back from the vets, doing his best to attend to the demands of Patty, it occurred to him he hadn't thought about his situation in all of what? – half an hour? The relief that came with not having to do that was remarkable. The stress had almost entirely fallen away. But it was there in him, bubbling under the surface, poised to rise up again, and he craved an escape.

He toyed with the idea of skipping the island. It would do him good to get away. But he couldn't leave Patch. The only place he could think of to go was Fuerteventura. The idea of a week or two on Lanzarote's sister island began to grow in appeal. It was by far the safest option. Using Andres for protection was all very well, but he should really be a last resort. Yes, yes, better off not going down that path. There was no telling where it might lead.

The more he thought about a trip to Fuerteventura, the more he warmed to the idea. Tom's laptop was sitting on the coffee table. He opened the lid and the screen lit up. Fantastic. No need for a log-in password. He went straight to a holiday booking site and started exploring dog friendly accommodation. The further south, the better. He plumped for Morro Jable, then changed his mind and made a two-week reservation in Costa Calma starting from the next day. Nothing much there except a bunch of hotels and a beach. A really very good beach. Patch would be in doggie heaven.

He allowed himself to get excited. In his mind, he was already there. As soon as Tom got back, he would rush home and start packing. Never mind all the food in the fridge. Most of it would keep and he could take supplies with him. Patch would love the little road trip and the ferry crossing. He berated himself for not thinking of the idea before. Why had he spent a whole week in lockdown when he could just as well have fled to Fuerteventura. Then his phone rang, and he knew why it hadn't crossed his mind.

Ramona.

'I have Alvaro's ashes,' she said. 'I want to scatter them on the water out at El Cotillo. He loved El Cotillo.'

'Ashes? What do you mean? They never found his body.'

'I went to Villa Winter and collected the ash out of the incinerator.'

'You did what?'

'I just said.'

'You have no idea that's Alvaro.'

'I know it is Alvaro. I can feel his energy. I am his mother.'

She started to cry. Then she added, 'And I think you should be there when I do it.'

'There's no need.'

'There is every need. You were his father. You should say goodbye.'

'To cinders that may or may not belong to our son. Ramona, I think you need to get some counselling.'

'I don't need counselling. I need you there. You have to come. I'm telling you now.'

He hung up. Then he revisited the hotel website and cancelled the booking. Nothing but nothing would see him set foot on Fuerteventura. Instead, when Tom came back with a forlorn Penny in a dog cone, her front paw bandaged to the elbow joint, Billy made his excuses and headed back home.

Patch rushed over the moment he opened the front door, wagging her tail, all optimism and devotion, and then she started sniffing his trouser legs. He let her out to have a sniff around the front patio while he gave the plants a water. Then he sat at the table in the corner where he'd enjoyed many an al fresco summer breakfast with Natasha, and phoned Andres.

He arranged to meet up with him in the morning out at Tao. He had no clear idea what would come of the meeting, but it felt a whole lot better to be doing something about his predicament. Maybe get it resolved permanently. Then he went indoors and fried himself a large steak, threw together a salad, and opened another beer, breaking a rule and feeding Patch before he ate.

18

ARRECIFE, 1982

A MONTH WENT BY AFTER BILLY HAD PARTED WITH HIS FIVE-grand investment in Andres' supposed bombproof scam and Billy had not heard a word from him. With every passing day came fresh awareness that he knew almost nothing about the business deal other than that he was due to receive ten grand sometime soon, according to Natasha. Billy didn't want to have to nag her to find out more, but Andres had gone to ground, as far as he could tell, and the longer the situation dragged on, the more concerned Billy became.

One day, as Billy neared the end of his rope and feared he would explode in fury over the lack of news, Natasha came home from work with an invitation. Andres wanted to talk, she said. Tonight. In the same restaurant as before. She stood in front of Billy in a bright-red shift, lips parted, eyes flitting to the floor. Something was wrong. He didn't dare ask. Instead, he mooched about the house until twenty minutes before the appointed time of eight o'clock and then sat in the passenger seat of her car with his arms folded across his chest, his head turned to the passenger side window as though he was captivated by the scenery. In the dark. Natasha didn't comment. She parked outside the restaurant behind Andres' car and gave his thigh a quick squeeze. He didn't respond. All he could think about other than anticipating a tirade of excuses from Andres was the fact that Natasha had not changed out of her figure-hugging, bright-red shift.

This time, as he pushed open the restaurant door, he spotted a solitary paint tin sitting on the floor and the restaurant carried that smell of fresh paint. The floor had been redone and a new counter installed. There was a lot of banging and clattering out the back. And no other diners. Just Andres, who stood and greeted them both, giving his cousin an appreciative sweep of his gaze along with the customary hug and kisses, before offering Billy a firm handshake and a cheesy, 'Eddy, Eddy, Eddy.' They all sat down, and platters of food appeared immediately, along with a bottle of local white. Then, they were left alone. Billy had the sense the restaurant was open only for them. It was a ploy. Next would come the sweet talk, the charm, the excuses, and of course, no cash.

Billy's gaze bored into Andres. 'Tell him I want what I'm owed,' he said to Natasha without turning his head.

Andres seemed to guess what he'd said and spoke before she had a chance to convey the demand, all imploring gestures and ingratiating smiles. Natasha was caught in a sudden exchange of words, not knowing who to translate for first.

'Let's at least eat,' she said with a weak laugh.

Keen to reinforce her point, she reached for the serving spoon nearest her plate. Billy followed her lead. Andres did the same and then poured the wine, but he was not about to obey Natasha. With his hand gripped around the stem of his glass he proceeded to talk rapidly, pausing to shovel some fish or potatoes into his mouth. Billy tried to understand his Spanish, but Andres spoke too fast and with a heavy accent. He only caught a word or two here and there. He studied the man closely as he spoke and even closer when he stopped, and Natasha offered an explanation.

The deal had gone belly up. The cash, the gear, gone. Andres was sorry. There was nothing he could do. His contacts had either left the island or were lying low. Billy's face hardened in the listening. He growled and told Natasha to remind her cousin that he had guaranteed the investment would be returned twofold and anything less was not good enough. Only then did he start eating. When Natasha relayed the comment, Andres threw up his hands in a kind of theatrical despair before launching into another longwinded explanation. By the time he'd finished speaking, Billy, who found himself surprisingly ravenous, had devoured half of the food on his plate.

When Natasha spoke, he put down his fork and paid close attention. The food had calmed him. He began to feel for her caught in the middle. It was not her fault. And he could see she was getting upset. Despite the length of Andres' second and apparently highly persuasive speech, she said comparatively little as she relayed his words to Billy.

During a brief lull in the exchange, Billy heard laughter and a shrill giggle coming from the kitchen. At least someone was having a good time. He reached for his wine, took a large gulp, and felt the sharp tingle on his tongue.

Eventually Andres came up with the real reason for the dinner: a second scam. If Billy was prepared to wait a few more weeks, Andres would recoup his original investment. But only if Billy parted with another couple of grand for another deal. As Natasha relayed the message, Andres uttered a name. Billy could scarcely believe his ears.

'What did he just say?'

'That you would get all your money back plus the five thousand profit from before.'

'No, not that. The name. Who is he talking about?'

'The other deal. He says he won't be having anything to do with Oscar Cribbs. That this new deal he's working on has nothing to do with the Brits.'

Billy paused, stunned, his past colliding with him like a steam engine going full throttle. He could barely disguise his reaction.

Natasha went on, oblivious to the cause of his shock. 'Andres is not stupid. He was just unlucky. He didn't know who he was dealing with.'

He sure didn't, Billy thought.

Oscar Cribbs had a finger in a lot of pies. The Maloney boys used him as hired help, but he was loyal to no one, or to everyone, depending on your perspective. When it came to gangland London, Cribbs popped up all over. He knew fences, fraudsters, forgers, money launderers, dealers, getaway drivers, safe crackers, thieves, burglars, and pickpockets, all the way up the chain to the masterminds and their wives. If there was a decent deal going down in London, you could be sure Cribbs would know all about it. If Billy had known before of Cribbs' involvement in Andres' scam, he would never have parted with his cash. Not because he thought the man spelled trouble, but the risk of someone letting slip that a Londoner newly moved to Lanzarote had helped finance the deal would have drawn unwelcome attention. People would have wanted to know who he was. His alias Eddy Banks would not have satisfied. They would have been after a description, even a photo. As it was, Billy had no way of knowing and no way of finding out if Andres or any of his cronies had divulged that information. He would just have to stew and hope for the best. He did consider making a discreet call to Marjorie, but then remembered she'd already left the force. His old handler Graham Spence was long gone, too. There was no one he could turn to without risking blowing his cover. He just had to hope Andres had enough sense to keep schtum.

Billy drained his glass and Andres refilled it. A second bottle appeared. Natasha and Andres conversed in lowered voices. Billy waited.

'This latest deal is much better, Eddy,' Natasha said at last. She sounded enthusiastic. Andres watched her intently. She shot him a nervous glance then carried on, ignoring Andres' overly keen manner, and directing her words at Billy. 'Andres knows everyone involved and they are very reliable. You have to remember he has also lost a lot of money. He's seriously pissed off.'

Billy believed none of it. But that wasn't the point. He reached for more of the salty potatoes and the spicy dipping sauce. Andres started on the second bottle. There was an extended pause in the conversation while they all finished their food. Having had scarcely a chance to eat throughout the whole exchange, Natasha was the last to finish.

When she set down her fork on her near empty plate, Billy said, 'Then tell Andres I'll give him another two grand, but I want it back. And the rest.'

Natasha looked relieved. She relayed the message and Andres' face lit. He reached across the table and clasped Billy's hands, then called through to the back for brandy.

'Don't worry. You'll get it back,' he said in English. It wasn't the first time Billy wondered how much English the man actually knew.

Maybe it was the wine and the brandy doing his reasoning, but Billy wasn't overly bothered if he lost more cash. Sure, no one liked getting ripped off. But there was a philosophical element to the entire situation. He was prepared to lose the whole seven grand investment if it meant Natasha lost respect for Andres. A small price to pay. And besides, it was for him a fraction of what he'd managed to squirrel away here. Natasha didn't know that. Some things were better left unsaid. Let her think Andres had taken his last pesetas. It would reinforce her contempt for her cousin. The moral part of Billy, that ultra-thin slice of sparsely filled pie that was his makeup, felt ashamed of his deception. No relationship should weather secrets. Then again, when he thought of the jam he would find himself in if Ramona ever got wind of his wealth, he all but shuddered. That really didn't bear thinking about.

Still, there were other factors at play. Even though he felt okay with the potential financial loss, Billy had never been comfortable financing dodgy deals and scams, especially when he had no clear idea what Andres was up to other than that drugs were involved. Coke, most likely. What was he, Billy Mackenzie aka Eddy Banks doing financing a drug deal?

On the way home, he told Natasha he was only taking the risk because Andres was her cousin. That he was doing it because it was what she wanted. But this was not the path he wanted to go down. He needed her to understand that. She demonstrated her gratitude at home once they were in bed. And all of Billy's quibbles evaporated. The woman in red was his and no one else's. Final.

CORRALEJO, FUERTEVENTURA

The following day, they drove down to Playa Blanca and took the ferry to Corralejo as foot passengers. Ramona was living in a flat in Puerto del Rosario. She'd recently moved, but she'd said when they last spoke that she didn't mind taking the bus up the coast if it meant Alvaro seeing his father. Billy knew that meant she would be hitting him for more cash. Resentment curdled in his belly. He'd deposited in her account the usual two thousand pesetas already that month, two days ahead of schedule.

He had failed to tell her Natasha was coming as well. It was only after they disembarked and were walking along the short stretch of promenade beside the harbour heading towards the café on the corner that he realised he'd also failed to tell Ramona that Natasha even existed. Oops. That was one mother of an oversight. At least Natasha was dressed in a loose and unrevealing top tucked into baggy knee-length shorts. If she'd been wearing the red dress Ramona would have exploded.

The reality of his faux pas sank in the closer he got to the outdoor tables and read the expression on Ramona's face. She stood with Alvaro propped on her hip, gave Natasha a hostile glare and then turned to Billy. 'You wasted no time,' she hissed in his ear as they exchanged customary cheek kisses.

His face reddened beneath his beard. He didn't know where to look. He made to take Alvaro, but Ramona held onto him and took a step back. Natasha hovered and said nothing. The other patrons gave the group quick glances. Heads turned. Realising there was only one way out of the situation he said, 'Ramona, this is Natasha.' Even as the words spilled from his mouth, he thought he might have got the introduction the wrong way round but then again, the other way would have been worse.

The two women acknowledged each other warily. There was no proper greeting, no kiss, just a tilt of the head. An embarrassed smile. Ramona sat back down propping Alvaro on her lap and holding him tightly. Billy pulled up a chair for Natasha before taking up the one beside it. A waiter made an approach then got sidetracked by someone wanting to pay their bill. Ramona and Natasha stared at each other without speaking.

'We thought we would take Alvaro to the park,' he said for want of something to fill the air which had turned electric.

'Oh, we did, did we?' Ramona said. 'And who's this we?'

'Ramona, please...'

Natasha leaned forward.

'It's okay. I understand. Eddy should have told you about me. Men, eh! The social graces of a donkey. How about we have lunch right here. I'm looking forward to getting to know you and Alvaro. It's important. You will always be a big part of Eddy's life and I want to share in that, if it's okay with you. Come, let's order something to eat.'

It was as though she'd rehearsed it. Ramona looked gobsmacked but then something in her manner changed. She let Billy take Alvaro. The waiter came and they ordered sandwiches and coffees. Natasha asked Ramona how she found Fuerteventura and that sparked a cordial exchange between the two women. At one point, they both laughed. Billy zoned out, preoccupied with his own stupidity as much as with his son who began arching his back in an effort to get down and toddle about. Alvaro had started walking. Billy did what any parent would do: watched him, poised to scoop him up if he strayed too far or looked about to hurt himself. When Alvaro grabbed the leg of a nearby table, teeter-tottered and threatened to topple over and take the table with him, Billy rushed to the rescue and plonked Alvaro back on his lap amidst smiles and reassuring words from the other diners.

The food arrived, which proved a welcome distraction. Ramona leaned over and handed Alvaro a crust.

The breeze picked up. A few small boats bobbed and pulled on their moorings. Beyond, another ferry was pulling into the harbour. A smell of grilled fish filled the air. It was a typical day on the island. Tourists outnumbered locals but Corralejo still retained its quaint fishing-village charm. Just. Although for how long? Billy had no idea. Seemed a shame to ruin the island, but when there was money to be made, there would be no holding back. The Andres's of the world would make sure of it.

Natasha continued to make a huge effort to engage Ramona. Billy left her to it. He rode out the ordeal playing funny little games with Alvaro and after they finished eating, and Natasha paid, Ramona finally agreed to let the couple take her son for two hours.

'Where will you be?' Billy said. 'You won't be late?'

'Don't worry. I'll be on time. I have an appointment in town at five.'

Leaving the stroller parked up beside her chair, she marched off and disappeared.

'Let's take your son to the little beach.'

Natasha took Alvaro from Billy's arms and popped him in the stroller. Then, she grabbed the handles and pushed. She was a natural when it came to mothering and Billy wondered if he might persuade her to have children. But it was a passing fancy, and he was soon put off the idea when Alvaro started to arch his back and grizzle.

'Should we let him out?'

'Let's wait until we get to the beach.'

She quickened her pace.

Billy couldn't have been more grateful for the presence of Natasha who had much more experience with small children thanks to her extended family and seemed to know exactly what to do in every eventuality. Alvaro was a fractious and demanding little tot, but with Natasha he beamed, chortled, and laughed. Billy watched, superfluous. She removed Alvaro's shoes and socks and let him paddle in the ocean. She made sand mounds for him to knock over. She spun him around and threw him in the air and was there with open arms as he came towards her. Alvaro even took what Billy thought might have been his first running steps. That was something they both chose not to tell Ramona who was waiting at the appointed time near the ferry terminal.

Billy was grateful for Natasha's presence for another reason. In front of her, Ramona didn't ask Billy for a single peseta.

19

GUATIZA, SUNDAY 24 MARCH 2019

Sunday afternoon proved warm and sunny with a soft haze on the eastern horizon. I set off at four and found the afternoon traffic light. I had no problem navigating my way through the roundabout connected to the ring road that wraps around Arrecife. From there, I headed down Calle León y Castillo, keeping my eye out for a roundabout up ahead that would take me to Calle Rambla Medula. So far, so good. No awful warren of one-way streets to get lost in. My main concern was parking. As I neared the bus station, I saw I needn't have worried. Clarissa was standing at the curb outside with a travelling bag at her feet. I pulled up beside her and opened the passenger side window.

'Thanks for this, Edna,' she said, bending to peer in, and once again I had to remind myself of my fake name. I would need to confess at some point if we were truly to be friends.

And something told me that we would be friends. There was something about her, something I liked. Admired even. She was intensely practical and thoughtful. Considerate.

Those were assets to be coveted in a friend. And I knew I would be able to ignore any spiritual side to her, just as I ignored Jess's.

She wasted no time bundling into the car and we were away. I knew the route back across the ring road and on through Tahiche would be easy – the bus station was conveniently situated – but avoided striking up a meaningful conversation until we were safely on the road to Guatiza. There was something about circumnavigating roundabouts in the opposite direction to what you're used to and the constant need to make sure you're looking for oncoming traffic in the right direction. It needed concentration. Probably accounted for a lot of prangs on the island.

As we cruised through Tahiche, Clarissa craned to view the prison.

'How's it all going?' I said.

'Good. Really good. The police have found DNA evidence that puts Alvaro at the scene of the priest's murder. Trevor is a free man, bar the formalities.'

'Will they let him out tomorrow?'

'Might do.'

Clarissa seemed to relax the further north we headed. Like everyone else, she was taken by the scenery. As we neared a passage between two volcanoes, I took the turnoff to the old road north. That was when I felt myself relaxing as well. The road wrapped itself around the base of the volcano on the eastern side before straightening on the approach to Guatiza. Fields of black gravel planted up with maize or potatoes gave way to the ubiquitous prickly pear.

I made a right turn in the heart of the village and drove slowly past the plaza and the old church and on down to the next T-junction. The farmhouse was opposite. I pulled into the driveway.

'Here we are.'

Clarissa got out and stood, hands on hips, looking around. 'Very different from Fuerteventura.'

I gathered my things and joined her on the gravel. 'I suppose there must be drier, wilder.'

'Has an entirely different energy. You'll have to come down one day.'

I didn't answer. Clarissa heaved her bag onto her shoulder, and I led her across the gravel to the front door.

Inside, she took in the open layout, the arrangement of furniture, the style.

'Rather grand.'

'I wanted somewhere off the beaten track.'

'If I drove, I would have chosen the same.'

She put down her bag by one of the dining chairs. It seemed heavy, too heavy for an overnight bag.

'You said you were renting an apartment in Puerto del Rosario.'

'For now. You haven't been to Fuerteventura at all?'

'Not yet.'

'My niece renovated an old Canarian ruin in one of the island villages. Tiscamanita. The house is magnificent if a bit monastic.'

'Cloistered.'

'That's a better word.'

We both laughed.

'What does your niece do there?'

'Creative things. Her partner is a photographer. A local. They met when she was building. They've made a rich life for themselves.'

'Sounds marvellous.'

'It's what happens when you win the lottery.'

'Seriously?'

'The jackpot, in fact. Up until then, Claire was a humble bank teller. She's still humble, mind you.'

I led her through to the kitchen. 'Tea? Coffee?'

'I brought something better.' She went back to her bag and dug out a bottle. 'You do drink, I take it?'

In answer, I went and fetched two glasses.

We sat out onto the patio with her bottle of white wine. It was from one of the local bodegas. She poured. Someone else might have found her pushy, but I liked the way she took charge.

'And what about you?' I said. 'What's your story?'

'Me? Nothing glamorous. Never married. Reared Claire after her mother died.'

'I'm sorry.'

'It was a long time ago. Ingrid stepped out in front of a bus. Devastated the poor child. Claire witnessed the accident.'

It was a lot to take in. From the way she spoke I sensed she had lived with the impact of that moment all her life, her matter-of-fact tone evidence of something like being at peace with the tragedy. I envied that peace in her and hoped one day to achieve the same.

She took a sip of her wine, sat back, and gazed out over the patio wall at the volcano. 'Do you have children?'

'No.'

'Ever married?'

'No.'

There was a brief pause. I had the distinct sense that she was figuring me out. I wasn't sure how I felt about that. She shifted in her seat, turned her face, and pinned me with her gaze.

'Sorry to pry. Only, you've lost someone. I can tell.'

Was it that obvious? I realised there was no point holding back. If we were to be friends, she needed to know.

'Jess. My partner.'

'Oh, I see.' No subtle freeze, no dismissive look flashing into her face, no uncertainty, nothing. I went on. 'I was a police officer as you know, but for most of my life I was a probation officer.'

'And Jess?'

'A lecturer. Her passion was for restorative justice.'

'Good woman. You must miss her.'

'Terribly.'

'Recent then.'

'Very.'

She nodded and returned her gaze to the view. 'Into and through,' she said softly. 'There's really no other way.'

I knew exactly what she meant without knowing how or why. It was just that there seemed to be no choice but to move through my grief as there was no repressing it and no bypassing it either. I thought vaguely that I ought to have provided some nibbles to go with the wine, but I couldn't summon the will to stand. The sky was beginning to dim. The wind was dropping, and all went still in anticipation of the sunset. The temperature was dropping, too. Somewhere off in the distance a dog barked.

I wasn't sure where next to take the conversation. I was relieved when Clarissa filled the void, skirting my mention of Jess and sticking to the theme of careers.

'I did a stretch as a mortuary attendant, of all things.'

'I've attended a few autopsies. Funny where life takes us.'

Clarissa laughed.

'The mortuary slab would not be my top pick. I mainly earned my living as a psychologist. I'm also a psychic. I hope that doesn't bother you.'

'Not at all. I noticed the Capricorn pendant you had on the other day.'

'That was a gift from Claire. I come from a long line of occultists. It's an odd talent, I must say. Often puts people off.'

'Or they don't understand.'

'Do you?'

'Jess did. So, I guess I do. I must.'

'Did she have a specialism?'

'Tarot and Reiki.'

'Good combo.'

'She was an excellent masseuse.' I put my hands on my knees. 'Will you excuse me?'

'Can I help?'

'No need.'

I stood and left Clarissa out on the patio while I put together something for dinner. Salad, some cured meats, the local cheese, the little salty potatoes, some salsas, and tapas. There was no cooking, just unpackaging and arranging on platters. Clarissa wandered in with two empty glasses and the empty bottle.

'Did we get through all that already?'

'I thought we might. Never fear. I have another one in my bag.'

I wasn't a big drinker and anticipated a fuzzy head in the morning. Still, there were occasions that warranted getting a bit sloshed, and I saw already that this was one of them.

We took everything out to the patio. Sunset brought out the reddish hues of the volcano and the sky began to darken. There was nothing to disturb us, not even a fly. The dog was quiet.

'You haven't told me yet why you are here. Other than to recover from the loss of Jess. You took a strong interest in that letter. It's Edwin Banks, isn't it? That's the score you want to settle. With him.'

'My word, you've a good memory. And your suppositions are correct.'

I ate an olive. Clarissa speared a potato.

'Forgive me for prying. You don't have to tell me anything.'

I felt the wine lowering my defences but stayed quiet.

'I've also figured out that your real name is not Edna Banks.'

I turned in my seat. My knife clattered to the floor. I reached down to retrieve it.

'How?'

'It was just too obvious.'

She speared another potato. She had a stabby way of eating, I thought. Maybe that was just the wine, too.

'I'm Marjorie. Marjorie Pierce.'

'Hello, Marjorie. I really am Clarissa.'

We both burst out laughing. That definitely was the wine.

'Have you found him yet?'

'No. But I do have a lead.'

I filled her in on what I knew so far, including his real name. Her interest was avid. She even came up with suggestions. What harm could it do, having her input?

I shunted some salami around on my plate. 'The hardest part is doing this alone.'

'I can imagine. You really need another pair of hands.'

'Back up. Someone to talk to. There are all kinds of reasons sleuthing is easier with two.'

'Absolutely. As long as your partner is effectual. Honestly, I could have throttled that Richard Parry on numerous occasions in Villa Winter, god rest his soul.'

'He probably wasn't cut out for the role. You need some experience.'

'In policing.'

'Or psychology.'

It was the second time in my life I'd felt an irresistible pull, although on this occasion, the pull was not amorous. We locked gazes.

'I'd be more than happy to help. If you want me, that is. For a trial period, let's say.'

I found her last remark strange. A trial period? That implied much more than simply finding Billy.

She echoed my thoughts. 'Tracking down Edwin Banks is just the start.'

'Is that a prediction?'

She didn't answer. There was a brief moment of silence. Then she said, 'From what you've told me about Billy, the Maloney brothers, and the golf course connection, I do wonder about this Jim Ackland character. Do you think he tipped them off about you as well?'

'I did wonder that, but it makes no sense. If he was concerned enough for my welfare to warn me about Billy, he wouldn't then betray me to the brothers.'

'One thing we can rely on, then. If you are sure of Ackland, we can assume the brothers are not looking for you.'

It was a mildly comforting thought.

We ate, drank, and chatted long into the night. I told her more stories from my policing days, happy to find that Clarissa took a keen interest. She was the first woman I had spoken to in a long time who shared the same outlook on life. I found I not only tolerated her psychic tendencies but thought they might even be put to some use. You never know. When we said goodnight, she offered me a hug and thanked me for the bed. And I thanked her, for what, I didn't know, but she seemed to understand.

20

FARNBOROUGH AIRPORT, 1979

WHY WAS IT WHEN I HAD A GOOD TIP-OFF, I WAS FORCED TO KEEP quiet about it and when things went awry, I managed to land myself in it.

My confidence in Billy had grown after the tip-off about the Brixton prison officer. So far, his information had been mostly good, if only partial at times. The only time he'd got things completely wrong was that sighting of Mick Maloney on the Isle of Sheppey. But then, that wasn't his fault. He'd been given the wrong information. It was his tip-off that had led to the arrests of two members of the gang down in Littlehampton and another two in Southampton. And he had put me onto the armed robbery itself. Even though the location wasn't precise enough to mount an operation. As for the tea bags we found in that otherwise empty lorry, I preferred not to think about that.

I knew Billy was feeling the heat, and since he was close to the source, he was also privy to the lowdown. When we next met behind the toilet block in Greenwich Park, I had no reason to doubt his latest news. Especially when he sounded so convinced himself. He stood there all paranoid and hunched, his red hair hidden beneath the hood of his jacket, his eyes darting every which way.

'I can't keep doing this, Marjorie,' he said as I handed him a tenner.

'What have you got for me?'

'Eric Maloney's planning a getaway.' He directed his speech at the ground between us.

'How?'

'By plane.'

Billy went on to explain that Eric had scheduled a private plane at the airport near Farnborough. Nine o'clock at night next Wednesday. That was two days away.

'Will I get the reward?'

'If we make the arrest.'

'I'll be needing it to get away. Right away. And fast.' He lifted his gaze to my face. 'Did you talk to your boss?'

'It's all in the pipeline,' I lied.

We went our separate ways. On the drive back to the station, I vowed to summon the courage to talk to DS Drinkwater at the first opportunity. But first I needed to clear it with Brace. Wasn't that the protocol? Ask to speak to them both, state my case, Billy's case. Which would only be strengthened by this latest tip-off. If his info led to the arrest of Eric Maloney, he would be due for the reward, too. Maybe I should wait until after that arrest before broaching the topic of Billy's safety.

When I got back to the station I was bursting with this latest info. I went straight into Brace's office, left the door open, and said I had information on the whereabouts of Eric Maloney.

'Shut the door.'

'Why must I keep this quiet? Why can't the squad know these tip-offs come via me? I feel like you are holding me back, sir.'

He raised his eyebrows and stood. 'Have it your way,' he said and ushered me out of his office.

He raised a hand to attract the attention of the others and said, 'Marjorie's had a tip-off. Seems we are about to nab Eric Maloney.'

Instead of the cheers I anticipated, the squad went quiet. Liz looked over at me from beside the photocopier, her mouth open. Plant gave me a cautious smile. As did Ackland. But Jones looked venomous. I could hardly believe the pettiness. Brace reinforced my deflation when he ordered me to go and make tea for the lads while he briefed the squad.

I spent the rest of the day doing paperwork and chatting to Liz by the photocopier. The mood in the office was mixed. There were a few murmurs among the squad about the reliability of the source and a few dubious looks at me as if to say who the hell do you think you are? But with Drinkwater and Brace backing the operation, those dissenting voices were not that loud. Everyone assumed the DS and the DI knew how to spot good info. Somehow, the entire squad assumed the tip-off had been verified.

Most were excited, keen to make the arrest and wrap up the operation. Those seconded from regional areas were especially eager to get their lives back. Then there were those who resented the fact that the information had not come through them. Those after the glory. Those Clive Plant had warned me about. Liz was indifferent. Her mind was elsewhere. She'd met a guy in a pub the other week, and she thought they were falling for each other. Which meant her mind was not on the job. She was happy to collate, file, photocopy, make tea and take home her DC's pay each week, with or without any overtime. She had even started talking about having babies. I hated to admit to myself that my only real friend on the squad was driving me up the wall with her gooeyness.

Later, at home in my tiny, terraced house in Welling, I was

still buzzing with excitement, convinced that the operation would be a success thanks to my policing. I phoned my parents with the news.

'Don't count your chickens before they've hatched,' my mother said.

I wasn't sure she had the right saying, but I knew what she meant. And I took no notice. Ever the cautious schoolteacher, ready with sensible advice in the face of a teenager bobbing with excitement. Only, I wasn't a teenager. I was a grown woman in her mid-twenties filled with ambition and desperate to succeed, to receive accolades, acknowledgement, a commendation. She knew that. My father knew that. And they wished me all the best. I could have had no idea at the time the doubts they both harboured. The doubts that come with wisdom and age. I ignored their tone, and after I hung up, I indulged in a pre-success private celebration with a half-bottle of champagne I had tucked away for a special occasion, and a takeaway from the local Indian eatery, which wasn't half bad.

On Wednesday, DS Drinkwater came downstairs to oversee the capture. The local Kent constabulary were notified and on Wednesday evening, every member of the squad went down to Farnborough airport. There were police stationed all over the area, watching from every nook and cranny. The dog squad came down. Air traffic control were monitoring the taking off and landing of all private jets. There was a plane booked by a Mr Jeremy Carver scheduled for take-off at nine o'clock. That, we decided, had to be the one. Brace then told everyone if Maloney could be nabbed before he went to board the plane, so much the better. Everyone knew their roles. We were set.

It took under an hour to get to the Biggin Hill airport near Farnborough, but the super wanted us down there by seven that evening. That meant we needed to eat an early dinner first and I was put in charge of taking the takeaway orders, everyone agreeing on Chinese. It was all sweet and sour pork and fried rice, and Peking duck for those more adventuresome. The local Chinese eatery was delighted when I turned up a little before five with orders for thirty meals. I could have phoned ahead but preferred a long sit down in the small foyer where I could gather my thoughts and quell my excitement.

I wasn't that hungry, but I knew better than to pick at my food with a big operation ahead of us. The office smelled of prawn crackers and sweet and sour sauce and there was a fair bit of barely supressed belching amongst the men.

On the way down to the airport, I was sharing the backseat of Plant's sedan with Jones. Ackland sat in front. No one said much. Other than Liz, these were the colleagues I had spent the most time with on the squad and none of them approved of me having an informer. I put their silence down to that, and not to any looming indigestion.

We were among the first to arrive. Plant parked with a clear view of the hangar and the access road and unbuckled his seat belt. Ackland sat with a pair of binoculars pressed to his face. There was not much action on the shortwave radio. Brace had stressed we needed to keep chatter to a minimum.

At about half-past eight, Ackland, who still had his binoculars pressed to his face, must have been blinded when a vehicle approached with its headlights on full beam.

The car made a left and pulled up outside the hangar. A smartly suited man got out and marched over to where another man, the pilot, stood looking at his watch. They seemed to be expecting someone else. Then another car pulled up. This time a woman got out and rushed over to the men. The pilot went towards the plane and the man embraced and kissed the woman. Then the couple followed the pilot. No Maloney. Even from this distance and with no binoculars, I knew it wasn't him. Wrong height. Wrong gait. Soon we heard the thrum of the plane's engine and watched as it taxied to the runway and took off.

Plant turned round to me, incredulous.

'You and your big mouth,' he said.

I blushed. 'Could be a different plane.'

'Air traffic control said that was the last plane for the night.'

'They did?'

'What were you even thinking?'

'I didn't make this up.'

'Drinkwater will be livid.'

On the way back to the station, there was a lot of talk about wasted resources.

We heard the next day that Eric Maloney had in fact left the country by plane the night before. Only he had flown out of Farnborough airport, Hampshire, not the airport near Farnborough in Kent. The moment Brace heard the news he hauled me into his office. I knew I was in deep trouble. He wasn't sitting down behind his desk. He hadn't even taken off his leather jacket. He stood, feet apart, arms spread, hands gripping the desk, his chest heaving in his body shirt.

I stared down at the floor.

'It was an easy mistake to make, sir.'

'His mistake, or yours?'

That threw me. As if I would get the airport wrong. I thought back. I couldn't recall exactly how Billy had put it. Had he said Farnborough airport or an airport near Farnborough? Had he mentioned Kent? I should have questioned him, asked for clarification. But I had no idea about the other Farnborough airport. I had no idea about any airport other than Gatwick and Heathrow.

'I was just acting on information received,' I said weakly.

'Incomplete information, as it happens. Have you any idea what this cock-up has cost the force? Not to mention the fact that Eric Maloney has managed to get away.'

'Sorry, sir.'

'Sorry isn't good enough. This is going higher up the chain. Won't be the last you'll hear about it, believe me.'

Before anyone else dragged me over the coals, I contacted Billy and arranged to meet in the usual spot behind the toilet block in Greenwich Park.

He was already waiting for me when I arrived.

'How did it go?' he asked cautiously.

'You mean, you haven't heard?'

'Heard what?'

'Never mind. Answer me this: Which airport did you tell me Eric Maloney was flying out of?'

'Farnborough.'

'Farnborough where?'

'Hampshire.'

'Why in god's name didn't you tell me that before?'

'You didn't ask.'

No, *you* didn't say. You needed to make that clear. You would have known full well that Farnborough, Hampshire, and Farnborough, Kent, are two entirely different locations and simply telling me the airport was in Farnborough, or whatever it was you said, was misleading.

I didn't say any of it. What was the point? He'd failed to provide me with that one vital piece of information and made me look like a complete ignoramus.

Which was exactly how DS Drinkwater treated me when he called me into his office later that day. And we weren't alone. Brace stood in a corner behind the super's desk with his arms folded across his chest, head low, gaze pinned to the floor, and Plant was beside me.

After lecturing me on the skills and maturity needed to be a good detective and on how to be an effective handler when it came to informants, DS Drinkwater said, 'Who is this informer of yours, Marjorie?'

Derek raised his gaze and looked at me with interest.

'I'm sorry sir, but I cannot tell you.'

'I understand your wish to protect your source, but it might help your case if you told me.'

Plant stepped in. 'Sir, you know we cannot reveal our sources. It puts them, and us, at risk.'

'Constable Pierce?'

I offered no reply.

Drinkwater inhaled. I could scarcely look at the expression of utter disappointment on Brace's face. I suddenly saw that he had a lot to do with what was going on. He could have stood up for me, but he didn't. His silence boomed louder than the super's dressing down.

'This insufficient information has cost the squad a huge amount in resources. Not to mention a major setback in nailing the gang.'

'I realise that, sir.'

'I don't think you do, Constable Pierce. You must understand I cannot let this go. You're off the squad as of now.'

I could hardly believe what I just heard. Brace just stared at me, his face expressionless. Plant took a step back as though to leave the room. Both men looked ready to leave, but no one moved.

'Where do I go?' I said, fighting back the tears.

'There's only one place a trainee detective can go. Back into uniform.'

'I'm not going back into uniform.'

DS Drinkwater lost patience, 'You don't have any choice. You've been reprimanded. This is punishment. There are plenty after the position you had, Marjorie.'

It was then that I knew I'd disappointed him more than anyone on the squad. He was the officer who gave me the chance and appointed me. He was the officer who believed in my worth. I had never felt more humiliated and more crushed in my short life. All of my ambitions came crumbling down around me as though I'd been blasted by a bomb.

I called Billy. Asked to meet up. He asked again about witness protection.

'I'm scared for my life.'

'One of the Maloney boys is locked up and the other has left the country,' I said without sympathy.

'It's not that.'

'Then what is it.'

'Can't say.'

I shrugged.

Billy gripped my arm and looked at me imploringly. 'You have to help me,' he said. 'I'm begging you.'

I didn't have to help him. I didn't really want to help him. But he looked so desperate, and I still had a bit of loyalty left in my heart so I told him I would talk to my immediate superior.

'Who?'

'DS Plant. Clive Plant.'

'Okay, never heard of him.'

LATER THAT DAY, I had a quiet word with Plant without revealing Billy's identity. Plant proved surprisingly helpful. 'If you think you can trust me,' he said, 'then I will handle it.'

Then I arranged a second meeting with Billy and relayed the message.

'He says for witness protection, you will need to turn supergrass.'

Billy didn't speak.

'Plant said he'll help.'

'Who is this guy?'

'He's a colleague. You can trust him. You have to trust someone.'

'Why can't you do it?'

'I'm leaving the squad.'

In the week that followed, I managed to get permission to organise Billy's witness protection and arranged for Billy to meet Plant in a safe house. I was back in uniform by then.

Plant came over and conducted a series of lengthy interviews. Billy's information then led to Eric Maloney's arrest in Spain. And he was given the reward. Operation Rancho never did recover all of the stolen money.

The last time I saw Billy was just before he left for the airport to fly to Lanzarote. He was sitting in an armchair in front of the television with a bulging holdall at his feet and I'd made him a cup of tea. The news was on.

'Here,' I said, handing him the mug.

He reached out to take it between two trembling hands. Then I saw that his face had turned white, and he was shaking as though cold. He started panting. I kept hold of the mug.

'What's the matter?'

He wouldn't say.

I glanced at the screen. And there was DI Brace and DS Ackland and DC Jones all standing in a crime scene. A murder, the reporter said. The footage came to an end and the screen returned to the newsreader. I had no idea out of those three coppers, who had triggered that reaction. But something had spooked Billy, big time. Maybe it was the victim and not one of the coppers. I guessed I would never know.

I went and switched the television off and offered Billy all the soothing words I knew. Eventually he sipped his tea and then the taxi came, and he was gone.

Helping Billy move to Lanzarote was the last thing I did before I handed in my warrant card and resigned from the force. There was just no way I was going to go through the whole process of getting into CID a second time.

21

THE OLD SALT WORKS, LOS COCOTEROS, TUESDAY 26 MARCH 2019

BILLY WOKE UP LATE IN A TANGLE OF DUVET, SWEATING. He'd forgotten to draw the curtains and the morning sun was slowly turning his bedroom into an oven. He untangled himself and rolled over onto his back. His head felt thick. Too much beer the night before. When he had nothing to celebrate other than a full fridge after his shopping expedition.

The stress of his forced lockdown was getting to him. He'd begun to think it was good Natasha had died. Because if she hadn't, if she was still there beside him, he'd have been frantic. But then, he would have left the island. Definitely. He would not have ridden it out like a sitting duck. He should care more about his own safety. Take action. Leave. Not be a rabbit in a burrow, too scared to come out. Oscar dead, him next, that was all he could think about. That, and who the hell told Eric and Mick where he'd relocated to. Only Marjorie and Graham knew, as far as he was aware, and neither of them would have let something like that slip. Not back then and not ever.

He got out of bed and took himself to the kitchen. Patch followed and went and sat by her bowl. Billy refreshed her water bowl and put a handful of dog biscuits down for her. He usually made her wait until after he'd eaten, but he wasn't in the mood for a proper breakfast. Coffee and a few mouthfuls of last night's dinner straight from the fridge and he belched on his way down the hall.

After that meagre breakfast, he spent an hour in his home-gym, working up a sweat, making his muscles ache. Then he took a punishingly cold shower. Downed a bottle of water. Made more coffee. Ate fruit. This was the day he would have had lunch in Arrecife. Not happening. He went to the puzzle room.

The puzzles didn't hold his attention for long. He'd finished the German castle and thought about starting another. After breaking up the puzzle and returning the pieces to the box, he went over to the shelves and selected an old puzzle at the bottom of a pile on the lowest shelf. He vaguely recalled doing the puzzle many years before. It was a street scene of Lisbon. The mosaic wall tiles were the challenge. Only had 1,500 pieces but it was beautiful and would look good when finished. He might even frame it. He should do that, he thought, get another one framed.

He took the box to the table. When he opened the lid, he found a photo of Natasha inside. She was smiling straight into the camera lens with come hither eyes. His heart lurched. When was it taken? Looked like Corralejo in the background. Must have been on one of the access visits. No sign of Alvaro in the shot. With her hair draped about her shoulders she was stunning. Oh, Natasha. His heart ached too much in the looking. How did the photo get in there? He sighed and went to the living room to put the photo in with all the others he had of her, tucked away in a box.

An hour later, after sorting out the outside pieces of the

Lisbon street scene and putting together the frame, he lost interest. He was listless. He'd spent too long cooped up. That trip to the supermarket wasn't enough. He needed a change of air, a drive. Patch needed a walk. And he had an appointment with is lawyer in Arrecife. He knew he wouldn't be able to live with himself if he didn't follow through with that.

After seeing her photo, Natasha's memory wouldn't leave him alone. She was pressed up against him on the inside. Yet he couldn't get close to her. It was as though she was looking the other way, in disgust. Or was that just his own shame? There was only one way to get physically close to what was left of her. And he hadn't been to the cemetery since the Saturday before last. It felt like an age. It felt like he'd deserted her, Natasha, his one true love. He missed her more intensely than ever. Maybe the existential threat he faced had turned him sentimental. The isolation, the having to hide reinforcing the loneliness of his life without her. He had to think of the living again. Had to consider what he still had. Patch. He went and stroked his dog, got the leash, and went out with her to the car.

First, he drove into Arrecife. It was a risk, a huge risk, but the appointment was too important to miss. On his mind was his own mortality. And he needed to put things right. Isn't that what dying people do? Put their house in order. Go to the grave with a clear conscience. And it wouldn't take long. All he had to do was sign a document.

He came away from the lawyer's office ten minutes after arriving and headed back to Tahiche and then on towards Teguise, turning off at Nazaret and then taking the backroad to the cemetery. The road cut across a sweeping plain. It was one of the many aspects of the island he enjoyed, the sense of openness, the volcanoes dotted about breaking up the horizon in all directions. But not on this day. He took no interest in the cultivated fields he passed. It was not possible to derive pleasure from the drive when he knew that somewhere out there, Mick and Eric were looking for him. His attention was fixed squarely on who approached, who drove behind, who, if anyone, was around.

There was no one.

As he pulled up in the empty parking area outside the cemetery, he realised he had come without flowers. He slammed a hand on the steering wheel. Sorry, Natasha. Forgive me.

He left the window open for Patch. 'I won't be long,' he said, unbuckling his seat belt and swinging open his door. Then he changed his mind. No dogs allowed? Who would know?

With his dog close beside him, he slipped through the entrance beside the high iron gates. He scanned the grounds, just to be sure, then he let Patch have a good sniff and a bit of a water, before he followed the straight path to Natasha's niche. 'Sit.' Patch sat. Billy bowed his head. He couldn't bring himself to read the inscription. But he felt her there in the niche, her ashes.

A cool breeze brushed by him, pushing away the warmth radiating from concrete and stone. When the breeze eased, a fly tried to land on him. He shooed it away.

Natasha. His beloved. Gone. But he couldn't have saved her. It was her time. You can't alter fate. Time and again he told himself these things. It didn't ease the pain of missing. Nothing running through his mind helped him. Tears welled. For a short while, he sobbed.

The breeze gusted, kicking up dust. Patch cocked an ear as a car drove by, heading south. He listened to the engine until it faded and was gone. At last, he lifted his gaze and ran a hand down the marble of the plaque, tracing his fingers over her name. It was then he saw the date of her death and realised with a sickening start that he had lost her a year ago to the day. How could he have failed to remember the first anniversary of her passing? What kind of man was he? Then again, some part of him had known, the part that had motivated him to visit her. Not an especially dominant part of his personality. A timely reminder before he'd arrived, and he would have bought flowers.

Pointless waste of space. That was what he was. Useless.

What do I have to live for?

Think of Patch.

He was always thinking of Patch.

He walked back to the car. Loaded Patch into the back seat. Sighed.

Was he depressed? Was that the diagnosis? His life felt hollow, meaningless. What had he ever achieved? Little. He'd got a few criminals banged to rights and now they were free. And he wasn't any different from them. Cut from the same cloth. Really, he deserved whatever he had coming.

Still, he wasn't bereft of self-preservation. He surveyed the area. There was no other car parked outside the cemetery. No one parked up or down the road. Taking the usual care that he wasn't followed, he drove home.

With a glass of water in hand, he stood outside and watched Patch wander around the patio, bored. Poor mutt. She needed a good long walk. But not yet. It was still too risky. He'd already taken a big enough risk driving to Arrecife and then the cemetery.

There was only one thing he could do to release the tension that wouldn't stop building up inside. He needed to find a way to put an end to the situation. He called Andres.

'Sure thing. Come on over. You know where to find me. I'm at the Tao house.'

22

TAO, LANZAROTE, 1982

BILLY WAS RELAXING ON A SUN LOUNGER OUT ON THE BACK PATIO, enjoying a beer and the afternoon sun. He'd finished renovating the Arrieta house and was having a well-earned rest. He enjoyed watching Natasha sitting on the edge of the pool slurping on an orange, her feet dangling in the water. The winds were light, the ocean calm, the sky the clearest blue. And it wasn't only the beautiful setting and the quiet achievement that were lifting his spirits. The island felt a lot freer without Andres.

Natasha said her cousin would be gone for a week or two and Billy aimed to make the most of his absence. They'd been spending a lot of time together, too much time, Andres popping over at all hours, inviting them out or over to his. He wanted to keep Billy close, keep him sweet. That was Natasha's perspective. But Billy didn't care for the way Andres eyed his girlfriend.

He also didn't like the way his lack of Spanish prevented him from knowing what was really going on. He only had Natasha's word for everything. He'd been making a big effort, studying the language every day, practising, practising, but he didn't find it easy. All the different verb endings were confusing. And they put words in a back-to-front order. By the time he'd wrapped his head around one sentence, the speaker had moved on to at least two more. That was the other thing he found hard, the speed at which Spaniards spoke. As for the local accent, that was plain impenetrable. He couldn't make out a single word any local said unless they slowed right down and enunciated their words. He would have given up, relied on Natasha for a translation, but that hurt his male ego and besides, he wanted to know what she was saying when she muttered under her breath, when she was cross with him or upset about something, or when she was talking on the phone, and he felt an urgent need to earwig.

Billy's reprieve from Andres didn't last long. The day he landed back in Lanzarote, Billy and Natasha were invited to his house. Or was it summoned?

'Shouldn't we be heading down towards Arrecife?' Billy said as Natasha headed north at the first roundabout in Tahiche.

'He's living in Tao, now.'

'What happened with the old place?'

'His sister has it. They did a swap.'

'Odd.'

'Why odd? The houses belonged to various grandparents. And it makes sense for Andres to live in Tao. More private. You'll see.'

The farmhouse was not in the village itself. Natasha turned left off the main road as they neared the village outskirts and made for the volcanoes to the south. The gravel road tracked between two of the volcanoes, a much larger one tucked behind the volcano closest to the village. At the end of the track, sandwiched between those two volcanoes, was a large house. And before they got anywhere near it, Natasha parked at the end of a long line of cars. They had to make the rest of the way on foot.

Up ahead, celebrations were in full swing. She never said they were going to a party. Billy hated parties. You never knew who might be there. Strangers, he could count on that, but what if one of those strangers was another Brit, someone from London, from his old patch. Andres collected friends like rotting flesh attracted flies. And one of those flies could likely as not be Oscar Cribbs.

Billy caught up with Natasha who had marched on ahead. He grabbed her arm and said, 'I think maybe we should go home.'

'You've got to be joking,' she said, snatching back her arm. 'I'm not going anywhere. Come on. It'll be fun.'

Will it?

Filled with misgivings, he walked beside her, facing into the blaring music that enveloped them when they arrived at the house. There was a strong smell of roasting meat. Concrete paths snaked through garden beds mulched with black gravel and filled with cacti and succulents, leading to a large, paved area on the southern side, a grape arbour, and figs protected by arcs of stone. The grounds were peppered with partygoers. He followed Natasha inside.

The place was huge and sparsely furnished with traditional furniture. Men congregated in some of the rooms and women in others. The internal patio was crowded. Who were all these people? What drew them all here? And no children. That itself spoke loudly. A party for adults only meant one of two things, or both: drugs and sex. Which begged the question why Natasha had insisted on dragging him here, other than that Andres had insisted on their presence. And maybe that was why she had chosen to wear that skimpy black dress and high heels.

Andres exited one of the doors, greeted Natasha with lingering kisses and a warm embrace, and then, after waving her off in the direction of two women chatting near a stand of pot plants, he wrapped his arm around Billy's shoulder and steered him into a room accessed through a doorway partly hidden by a stone staircase leading up to the roof. The room was small, dark, windowless, and contained two tables and a few chairs. On the table, lined up in a row, were five piles of cash. Andres grabbed the one at the end, stuffed it in an envelope and handed it to Billy.

'It is all there,' he said.

Billy stuffed the cash in his jacket's breast pocket. He was uneasy. With the house flooded with revellers, it wasn't good to have so much cash lying about. Then Billy looked at the other table and saw the mirror, the white powder, the credit card, the rolled-up note. Andres was insane to have both the drugs and the cash in the one room. More over-confident than too trusting. Untouchable. Is that what he thought he was?

With his jacket pocket now bulging with cash, Billy wanted to leave then and there. But he couldn't find Natasha. He toured the house and the grounds, and he couldn't see her. Then he heard a voice call his name. He looked up. She was on the roof with a couple of girlfriends. They each held a bottle of beer.

Natasha gave him a wave and said, 'Come on up.'

'Natasha.' He said no more. He couldn't tell her to leave, not in front of the others.

Maybe he would feel safer if he put the cash in the car. Then again, maybe not. He was standing around, dithering, not knowing where to put himself, when a car sped down the road and came to a screeching stop just before the front garden, kicking up clouds of dust. Heads turned. Then the party carried on as though nothing had happened.

Billy sensed trouble. He backed away from those around him. His steps left the concrete path and landed in the gravel mulch of the cactus garden. He glanced behind him and stepped further back, keeping an eye on the four men exiting the white Audi. Four grim-looking men in muscle shirts tucked into tight jeans striding down the garden path with set jaws and hooded eyes. Whoever they were, they had not come to the party to have fun.

Billy glanced up at the roof. Natasha and her friends had formed a huddle and were chatting and laughing, oblivious to the unfolding situation down below. Once the men had disappeared into the house, Billy reached down in the gravel for some larger stones and hurdled one then another up at Natasha. His aim was not brilliant, and he didn't want to hit her. Just attract her attention. But his last throw missed the mark, or rather hit the mark he was trying to avoid, and Natasha yelled out and looked his way, rubbing her arm. She was furious.

He waved at her and mouthed his apology and gestured for her to come down. She put her fingers up at him and turned her back. A natural coward, Billy braced himself. He was no hero rescuing his damsel, but he had no choice. He ran into the house.

The stairs to the roof were on the other side of the internal patio, running up the south wall. The party was still pumping and there was no sign of the men. But something bad was brewing. He was sure of it.

Beneath the stairs, the door to the drug and money room was shut. No doubt those men were in there with Andres.

Billy budged past a couple canoodling by the lava-stone water filter recessed in the east wall and bolted up the stairs. He went straight over to Natasha who saw him and turned back to her friends. There was a titter of girlish laughter, no doubt at his expense. He was still catching his breath when he said, 'Come on. Let's go home.'

'Are you serious?'

'Natasha, please.'

'You might not be in the mood to party but I am.'

She said something to her friends in Spanish and they all laughed.

'For god's sake, Natasha. It isn't safe.'
'What the hell are you talking about?'
'Four guys turned up just now. Really mean guys.'
'They're probably friends of Andres.'
'Friends?' He stared at her in disbelief. How hard could it be to persuade her that she was in danger. 'Jeez, Natasha, you gotta believe me. These guys had hate in their eyes. I'm not kidding.'

'Alright, alright. I'll go and find Andres. See what's going on.'

She shrugged an apology at her friends and made towards the stairs. Billy followed.

'Finding Andres is not a good idea,' he said to her back. 'We need to leave, now.'

But it was too late.

The first crack of gunshot came just as they were about to head down the stairs. He had no idea where it had come from, but it sounded like inside the house. Women screamed. Down in the patio, people started running off in all directions. Billy grabbed Natasha's arm and pulled her back away from the stairs. He closed the door to the roof. Looked for a bolt or a lock. Nothing. Something to form a barricade. But Andres kept his roof clear.

'You three sit down here and wait,' he said, pointing at a narrow stretch of wall well away from the door.

Natasha went and sat with her friends in a tight huddle. They were terrified.

It was down to him to display bravery. He inched his way over to the edge of the roof, dropped to his knees and peered down, anxious not to be seen.

Some of the revellers had made it to their cars. They were driving away. Others were running down the track. The music kept blaring, but he could hear intermittent screams beneath it.

He pulled back, glanced over at Natasha and her friends, and wondered what to do. They just had to wait it out up on the roof until those hoods drove off. There was no other option.

The smell of roasting meat was strong. Suddenly seemed a pity to waste all that good food. Maybe the situation would blow over. And they could eat.

Instead, the music grew louder.

Then the shooting began again, guns firing like fireworks, barely audible above the music. Must be a blood bath down there. What the hell was Andres mixed up in?

Billy went and herded the women further away from the door. They all hid behind a water tank, hoping no one would bring all that gunfire upstairs. In every movie he'd ever seen involving a shootout in a house, someone headed for the stairs, someone ended up on the roof. But that was the movies. What happened in real life?

They waited. His pulse was racing. Natasha was trembling, her friends hyperventilating. He tried to get them to slow their breathing. 'It'll be okay,' he said. No one was convinced. Least of all him.

They waited. The shooting had stopped. Then someone killed the music, and all went quiet.

Billy heard voices, footsteps, car doors slamming. He told the women to stay put. Then he crawled on his hands and knees over to the edge of the roof and peered down. The white Audi was driving off. Just the driver and a passenger in the front seat. No one in the back. They'd arrived as a foursome. Now there were only two. That left two downstairs, somewhere.

Dead?

He went back to the others.

'They've gone.'

'Are you sure?'

'The car just drove off. It's over.'

No one moved.

'We can't stay up here. Come on.' He waited. 'Vamos.'

'Estoy esperando a que venga la policía,' one of Natasha's friends said.

Waiting for the cops to come? She could suit herself. Probably have a long wait. Her friend showed no sign of moving either.

'Natasha, we need to leave, right now.'

She obeyed, at last, gave her friends a weak look and followed him downstairs. He wasn't sure how she would handle seeing dead bodies, but he knew he would soon find out.

The patio itself was empty. He turned to Natasha.

'Are you ready for this?'

'I've seen dead bodies before.'

'Not like this, you haven't.'

He began looking in all the rooms. He recognised one of Andres' associates splayed out on the floor of the kitchen, blood pooling behind his head. His eyes, staring up at the ceiling, blank. One of the men in the Audi was slumped by the back door. A bullet had exited his chest. Billy's first concern was Natasha. A hand covered her mouth. Eyes wide. Horrified. He tried to steer her away, but she wouldn't move.

'Carlos,' she said.

'You knew him?'

'He was Andres' best friend. Rosa's boyfriend.' She pointed upwards. Looked about to move.

'Leave her. She doesn't need to see this.'

Andres came staggering out of one of the bedrooms. He wasn't hurt, not that Billy could see. No blood.

'Eddy,' he said. Then he saw Natasha and spoke in his native tongue.

She turned to Billy and said, 'We need to get rid of the bodies. Clean up before the cops get here.'

'We?'

'Who else will do it?'

'Stretching a friendship, I would say.'

'We have to help.'

'You think?'

Natasha closed the kitchen door and followed Billy and Andres into the small dark room. All the cash had gone. Hopefully into the pockets of those whose money it was and not those thugs.

'Atrapa,' Andres said, throwing a bag of coke at Natasha.

'What do you expect me to do with this?' she said in Spanish. For once, Billy understood, mostly due to the expression on her face.

'Keep it. Hide it. He'll come and get it later.'

Andres started clearing away the rest of the evidence. Billy and Natasha left him to it.

Out in the patio, partygoers started reappearing. In the rooms, they emerged from behind furniture or inside cupboards. Some were walking back in from the surrounding fields. It was a strange sight to watch such a large group recongregate, dazed, drawn by the music that had started playing again, the alcohol, the drugs, the roasting meat, and a profound lack of common sense. Billy steered Natasha back into the kitchen.

'We need to keep that lot out of here,' he said, looking around for something to barricade the door. He resorted to dragging the heavy wooden table across the floor.

Natasha went over to the sink and started opening cupboards. She extracted cleaning products, a bucket. A sponge.

The back door opened a fraction and a voice called out. Natasha answered in quick terse Spanish. Then she tried to drag the body out of the way of the door.

'Let me.' Billy heaved the corpse and two men walked in, surveying the situation. There was a short exchange, a few nods. Billy caught sight of a third body slumped near a red sedan.

Then the men picked up the first body between them and carried it outside.

'What's going on?'

'They're removing the bodies.'

'I can see that. But where are they taking them?'

'Didn't say. Make them disappear, that's all I know.'

What was the point? The police would come. They'd interview the witnesses. And there were scores and scores of witnesses. No way you could hide the killing.

The men came back for the second body and then Natasha said, 'Here,' and threw him a sponge and Billy found himself on his knees mopping up blood.

The moment the mop up was done, Billy said, 'You got everything?'

'What do you mean?'

'We need to leave before the police arrive. I cannot be seen here.'

She tipped the bucket down the sink, had a quick wipe around and left the kitchen.

In the patio, Andres was back to his grandiose self, laughing and joking and making everyone feel as though nothing had happened.

'We have to go,' she said to him as they headed out the front door, and he planted a kiss on both her cheeks and called her cariña which meant sweetheart.

'What is Andres telling those people?'

'That some men were wounded but they'll be alright.'

'And people are believing that?'

'Sure. They all ran away or hid, remember. No one saw a thing, not properly.'

Billy had never felt more relieved to be driving away from anywhere in his life. He was glad Natasha was behind the wheel. The effects of the afternoon hit him with force, and he began to feel weak and nauseous.

'I can't believe there are no cops here yet,' he said.

'There will be.'

As they were turning off at the Tahiche roundabout, three cop cars sped up the road to Tao.

'That is the last time we have anything to do with your cousin. You promise?'

'I promise.'

'Good. Because if you do, I can't be with you. That is not a threat, Natasha. It just isn't safe.'

Billy had no need to worry. The bodies were never found, which came as no surprise with all that ocean to dump them in. Even so, those two men were still missing. Yet the police didn't care or were hamstrung. No one would talk, no one was charged and Andres got away with his shenanigans scot-free.

Billy was relieved when, not long after the night of the party, Natasha came home from work one day and told him Andres had moved to Gran Canaria.

'Things weren't working out for him here.'

That, Billy thought, was an understatement.

Billy hadn't anticipated the relief he would feel at the man's absence. He felt liberated, no longer burdened with jealousy and apprehension that he would lose the love of his life. With Andres out of the way, he could move forward with his life. A new optimism infused him. He enjoyed a spurt of fresh energy and set about renovating his latest purchase, a rundown farmhouse in Tiagua. No longer anxious, he spent less time drifting back to those months before he went into witness protection. Less time dwelling on the terror he had felt back then. Less time mulling over that time when Marjorie had told him about the reward for information leading to the arrest of Eric and Mick Maloney and how hungry he'd been to get it, hungry for a way out of the mess he found himself in. And how that hunger had unforeseen consequences, for her.

Dear foolish Marjorie. She'd had no idea how hot things

had been getting for him. Gang members knew they had a grass in their midst, someone close. Someone who knew or had some means to hear about their every move. His name was mentioned. A friend of a friend had warned him. And if that hadn't been bad enough, there was the not so small matter of a certain murder he should never have witnessed.

Yep. If it hadn't been for Marjorie, he'd be dead.

23

HARÍA, TUESDAY 26 MARCH 2019

The kettle was on the boil, the toast browning, and the egg mixture was ready to slosh into the frying pan. All the crockery and cutlery ready to take outside. I had full mastery of the Guatiza farmhouse kitchen. And that felt good.

Clarissa was sitting out on the patio enjoying the early morning sunshine. She was staying an extra couple of nights, and I rather enjoyed her presence. Besides, it seemed the right thing to do. After joining her at the Arrecife courthouse after the hearing the day before, it felt natural to invite her back to stay. I couldn't very well let her travel all the way to Fuerteventura on the bus on tenterhooks when she so dearly wanted to be there to greet Trevor when he walked out of the prison. There was a process to go through, paperwork to deal with. Her lawyer had told her to expect him to be freed in two days. Which meant we had the entire of this day to ourselves.

And I couldn't help sharing in her excitement at the prospect of Trevor's release after the success of his acquittal hearing. I hadn't met Trevor, although I had heard a lot about him, and I was pleased for him and for her. She was a trouper. Not only did she survive that terrible ordeal at Villa Winter – locked in an attic, twice, and narrowly escaping with her life – without her relentless campaign, Trevor would still be rotting in a cell with no prospect of freedom on the horizon.

With Clarissa under my roof, my quest, the entire reason for my presence on the island, had changed a little. I was still keen to continue tracking down Billy, but as Clarissa had pointed out over dinner last night, if he'd gone to ground there was little point hanging around the golf course day in day out, especially with the Maloney boys doing the same. It could get dangerous. And then there was the matter of that man Andres. We needed to find out more about him. We'd toyed with the idea of getting up early and heading out to Tiagua for a spot of spying, but we'd both quaffed a little too much wine again and neither of us fancied a day of obs boredom. Besides, Clarissa's hip was playing up and a day spent sitting in my car would have done it no good. 'Even sleuths need a day off,' she'd said before we went to bed last night, and I agreed.

And now there she sat out on the patio, plainly dressed in practical and well-tailored clothes, and I knew that whatever we did with our day, I was not going to be seen by her side garbed in that ludicrous hippy outfit. I'd put on cotton pants and a smart blouse and that, I decided, was how I would stay.

Another five minutes and I had our breakfast all prepared.

'I have a suggestion,' Clarissa said as I stepped out onto the patio with a loaded tray. I handed her a mug of coffee and set down her omelette with slices of tomato and buttered toast and jam.

'That looks nice.'

'I thought we needed something substantial.'

'You thought correctly.'

'Your suggestion? Do tell.'

Clarissa took a slurp of her coffee before she spoke. 'Let's drive up to Haría. There's an artist I would like to meet. Some old friends of Richard's.'

Although I couldn't quite marry her idea to my desire to find Billy, it sounded like she had a plan. She said she knew nothing much about Paula and Celestino, but they had been important to Richard, in a fashion. 'Would have been a lonely existence for him here, home alone all day trying to write books.'

'Trying?'

'Writer's block. I never really understood it existed as a condition, if you see what I mean. But meeting Richard made me realise it can be quite serious. He was in a terrible state about it. I thought his wife was the root of his problem. In the end, he agreed. He even announced, just before he fell to his death, that he would leave her. Such a terrible shame and possibly a waste. He might have ended up writing something worthwhile about the islands.'

'I can see they're inspiring.'

'And awfully fragile.'

I didn't know what she meant but then, I hadn't been here long enough to know anything much.

The wind picked up a little, lifting a corner of her napkin. She reached for the salt cellar to weigh it down. I went and fetched my breakfast, and we ate in silence for a while. Clarissa soon finished her omelette and moved on to her toast.

'Delicious jam,' she said, taking another bite.

'The local supermarket stocks it. Cactus jam. I never knew there was such a thing.'

'Stick around and you'll soon find there's a lot to discover here.'

I didn't doubt it. I only had a postcard impression of the place. Even an island this small would have its secrets and special places few knew about. Jess was forever on about the hidden and the little known when it came to England, especially along the coast. I had lost count of the number of beach walks she took me on, the number of times we got blasted by the wind, sprayed with salty water from crashing waves. And I would never forget the time we had to wait it out in a sea cave until the tide went back out. In Kent that was. The Thanet coast. And all because she wanted to hunt for fossils.

'You'll be returning to your home in England soon, I take it,' I said, thinking it might be nice to keep in touch, catch up with her there.

She put down her cup.

'I'm not sure. I've been toying with buying a small flat in Puerto del Rosario. It's a jolly nice little city. You should visit sometime.'

It was the second time she'd invited me there.

'I'd like that,' I said, succumbing to the possibility that she had warmed to me as much as I had warmed to her and that I had in fact found a friend. In the next instant, I felt I'd betrayed Jess. She'd have wanted me to be happy, though. She did say that, towards the end. Don't give up on life, Marjorie. You go and grab it by the horns. Do it for me. Maybe, eventually, when my heart stopped aching, I would.

It was a lovely drive up to Haría. I had only driven north of Guatiza once, on my mission to acquire hippy clothes, and I hadn't paid much attention to the scenery as I was forced to tail a clutch of cyclists the whole way and the day had been cloudy. Since my time on the island, I'd focussed on heading south. This time I was treated to a nice surprise as we entered an elevated valley cradled by the mountains, and I beheld an oasis of palm trees and pretty white houses huddled right up against the narrow streets, all splendid in the sunshine. Clarissa directed me to the village centre, to a car park behind the main plaza.

'Everywhere is walking distance from here,' Clarissa said, opening her door.

'You've been here before?'

'I studied the map.'

We headed down to the plaza, slipping beneath the dense canopy of large trees, the plaza more a closed off street, paved and turned into a functional and pretty municipal space. The café at the end looked to be doing a steady trade. We plumped for a table outside.

A waiter approached us almost immediately. We ordered coffees. I watched the locals going about their business, the easy way of life here. Tranquil, compared to the hustle and bustle of Arrecife and the tourist areas. It was like another world. Although there was plenty of evidence that the village catered for passing trade, with gift shops and cafés and an abundance of civic pride.

When the waiter returned, Clarissa wasted no time with her query. With a pleasant smile and an innocent if determined gleam in her eyes, she said, 'Do you know where we can find Celestino?'

'Who's asking?'

'I'm Clarissa. A friend of Richard Parry.'

A look of sadness appeared in his face.

'Ah, Richard.' He paused. 'Are you the woman he was with when...?'

She nodded. 'I have a message from him for Celestino.'

He directed us through the village to a house on Calle César Manrique. 'You can't miss it. There's a sign outside.'

Clarissa paid the bill before the waiter left, providing him with a generous tip, and then she downed her coffee in a few gulps, and I was forced to do the same. Not that I minded. Her forthright manner was refreshing. I found I could relax because of it.

We followed the waiter's directions through the village,

heading down narrow one-way streets, passing the town hall and numerous old and impressive buildings. We hadn't gone far when I saw that Clarissa was wise to have us park in the centre. It was much easier and far more pleasurable to walk than drive. So many pretty old houses to enjoy. And the higgledy-piggledy nature of the lay out.

The house the waiter had directed us to was obvious, standing out from the rest due to the decorative front garden and a large plaque by the front door. The home exuded pride.

I hung back while Clarissa went and knocked. A woman answered. She was slender, blonde, pretty, looked about forty, with few signs of ageing beyond some wrinkles beneath her eyes. Obviously English.

'I'm looking for Celestino,' Clarissa said. 'You must be Paula.'

The woman looked doubtful, cautious.

'Excuse me? And you are?'

'Clarissa Wilkinson. And this is Marjorie. Sorry for the intrusion. I thought I owed you both a visit. I've come about Richard. I was with him when he died. Is Celestino home?'

Paula relaxed a little. Her gazed darted behind us as two women walked down the street. Tourists. The bum bags were a dead giveaway.

'You better come on through.'

She led us down a short passage to an enclosed patio out the back and invited us to sit down. There was an array of seating options scattered amongst numerous potted plants. Clarissa chose a straight-backed chair, as did I.

'He won't be long. He went to the shop. Tea?'

There was no possibility of saying no. I began to wonder if my bladder would go the distance. She didn't have time to put the kettle on before we heard a door open and a male voice echoing down the passage.

He stopped short at the sight of us, a grocery bag hanging

227

from each arm. He was swarthy and olive-skinned and medium in height, with strong features, notably his liquid brown eyes. I put him in his late thirties.

Clarissa stood and went and held out her hand. He set down the bags at his feet as Paula came out from the kitchen and explained who we were. Only then did Celestino accept Clarissa's handshake.

The couple stood together and waited as Clarissa sat back down.

'Richard mentioned you both when we were held up at Villa Winter. Fondly, I should add. He held you in high esteem.'

She failed to tell them what she'd told me in the car earlier, that Richard blamed them for his presence at Villa Winter. They were the ones who'd encouraged him to visit, to unlock his writer's block. It was a matter uppermost in Celestino's mind. 'Instead of inspiration, he met his death,' he said bitterly.

'The perpetrators, they're all locked up now. I doubt any of them will be free for a long time. My lawyer says they are certain of a conviction.'

'In this country? Bah! Simon Slava and that Salvador character, they know too many people in high places.' He launched into a tirade about the island's corruption and Paula drifted back into the kitchen.

'Talking of corruption,' I said, cutting in. 'What can you tell us about Andres Ortega?'

He hesitated, a deep loathing appearing in his face. He shook his head and exhaled. 'Where do I start?'

He explained how Andres was the son of a businessman, property developer and owner of a number of hotels. His family had been implicated in numerous corruption scandals, but no one had ever been convicted. Andres was the wild child, involved in serious drug trafficking. His associates ran a brothel. He moved to Gran Canaria to escape the heat sometime in the 1980s.

'Why the interest?'

'He's back,' I said.

'And we think he's connected to someone Marjorie used to know.'

Her candidness took me aback. Then again, this was the reason we were here, the real reason, I suddenly realised.

'I'm trying to find the whereabouts of Edwin Banks. Eddy.'

He thought for a moment. 'Never heard of him.'

I felt deflated. My hopes had been raised and dashed so fast. I scarcely had time to take it all in.

Celestino seemed to lose interest. He fidgeted where he stood. The shopping bags were still at his feet. It was a weekday and no doubt he was itching to get on. Paula reappeared, tealess, and stood by the kitchen door. I was both grateful and surprised. Didn't take that long to boil a kettle. Perhaps she was waiting for the whistle or hiss. That was when I suddenly recalled a vital clue that might help the situation. I dived into my bag and extracted the only photo of Billy I had, taken before he left England. I handed it to Celestino, and Paula went over to have a look.

'Wait a minute,' she said taking the photo. 'That's Tom's neighbour.' Celestino shrugged and Paula handed me back the photo. She went on, addressing her husband. 'You know Tom, the guy who lives on the coast near Los Cocoteros. He bought one of your paintings and got us to deliver it to his house on the pretext of inviting us to dinner.'

Celestino still looked puzzled.

'You do remember. The dinner was disgusting. And the painting was the one you did of Montaña Tinamala.' She turned to us. 'That's the volcano near Tom's house. Hence his interest.'

The penny dropped and recognition lit his face.

'That recluse with the dog.'

'That's the one. He went on about his weird neighbour with

the crazy red hair.' She looked over at me. 'The guy you're talking about, I reckon that's him.'

I put the photo back in my bag. A shrill whistle interrupted us, and Paula asked how we took our tea. We told her. She disappeared into the kitchen. Celestino followed behind with the shopping and then came out and bid us both goodbye.

There was no choice but to be polite and drink our tea and make small talk with Paula. In any case, they were very nice people.

On the way back to Guatiza, I said, 'We didn't go up there to talk about Richard at all. That was just a ruse.'

Clarissa chuckled. 'A good one, as it turns out. Richard mentioned Celestino came close to being murdered once for his work in anti-corruption.'

'Blimey.'

As I drove down the main road, dodging cyclists and ignoring tailgaters, I had to fight off feelings of inadequacy. I'd spent all my time on the island trying to figure out a way to locate Billy, and Clarissa had managed to pinpoint his whereabouts in one morning. Perhaps I wasn't cut out for this caper after all. Then again, it was my sleuthing that had revealed a beguiling connection between the Maloney boys and Andres Ortega. We were equals, I decided, which was a pleasant thought. Although I cautioned against getting too attached to the woman. Despite what Clarissa had hinted at the other day, I suspected once Trevor was free, they would both skip off to Fuerteventura and then back to England. Neither of them had any good reason to stay in the Canaries. And neither did I for that matter, not once I'd had it out with Billy. We would all go our separate ways, and I would never have to negotiate any sort of power share in some bizarre amateur sleuth duo. Suited me. Although the thought of going back to London, to the house I had shared with Jess for all those years, made my blood leaden in my veins. What sort of life did I face going back there?

Drudgery and depression were all I had to look forward to. Just one endless grey existence until I joined Jess on the other side of life.

I turned off the main road before we reached Mala. Guatiza was the next village on. After that, I followed Clarissa's directions and we ended up on a dirt track heading for the east coast a little to the south of the village.

He was so close, all along. Walking distance. My original assessment of where he would have most likely chosen to live had been spot on. In the time I had spent on the island, I would have had better luck going door to door than staking out the golf course.

Tom's house was easy to spot. The track came to an end shortly after. I turned the car around and pulled up outside the neighbour's gates. Looking around I could see this was exactly the sort of place where Billy would hide. Isolated, wild, with a magnificent ocean view.

'I can hardly believe he was less than a mile down the road all along.'

Clarissa gave me a knowing smile.

I got out and approached the gates. They were locked. There was no bell. I peered in through the metal grille at the stark white patio with its seating and plants, and at the house itself, the few windows, the front door. I called out, but there was no reply. I walked around the side of the property, found a large rock to stand on and peered over the high wall. Some terraces. A swimming pool. The ocean view. The place was neat and tidy. No evidence of a woman's touch. On this side the house the windows were large. But I couldn't see inside.

A dog barked. As I headed back to the car, the neighbour Tom appeared and strode over. A nosy neighbour, then. Clarissa was still in the car.

'Looking for Eddy?' he said when in earshot.

'Do you know where he is?'

'Out.'

'Any idea where?'

'Can't help you there.'

Pity, but understandable. Still, he had confirmed Eddy lived here. Only, we couldn't very well keep watch on the place, not with Tom right next door and with nowhere to hide. I thanked Tom for his trouble.

'Can I take a message?'

'No need.'

Tom wandered back to his place, and I got back behind the wheel. I suggested we park up a bit further on out of Tom's line of sight and wait.

'After lunch. I'm starved.'

Now she'd mentioned it, I was too. And I needed to pee.

We headed back to Guatiza.

'What should we do?' I said as much to myself as Clarissa. 'Keep an eye on the Maloney boys or wait for Billy?'

'They are our only options. The thing is, what's the hurry. We know where he lives. He's not going anywhere. And the Maloney boys can wait as well. We know where everyone is, which is a powerful position to be in, don't you think?'

She was right again. And tomorrow was another day.

24

TAO, TUESDAY 26 MARCH 2019

Billy stood, phone in hand, gazing out at the blue expanse, his heart a great weight in his chest. That it was the first anniversary of Natasha's passing lingered at the forefront of his mind along with an army of self-recriminations. Uppermost, that he should have realised what day it was before he went to the cemetery, not after.

He made an effort to clear his mind. He had to resolve the situation he was in. Take action. Do what he thought was best. As he readied to visit Andres in the Tao house, he was catapulted back to that day of the party, with Natasha on the roof, the dead bodies. Then the clean-up. It was as though the party had occurred only the night before, and he was still youngish, foolish, although also quick to learn, quick to decide he'd had enough of that sort of life. Now he was about to hurtle back into it.

He was pulling out of his property for the second time that day when Tom came rushing over. He was holding a tea towel and his hair caught on the wind, two wispy locks rising above his ears like wings. He was so out of shape he was panting. He tapped the window and only then did Billy open it. He looked up at his neighbour standing beside the car catching his breath.

At last, Tom spoke. 'A couple of women were looking for you just now.'

Women? He didn't know any women. Weird.

'What did they look like?'

'About your age. Nothing much to distinguish them. One didn't get out of the car.'

'And they asked for me, specifically.'

'They did.'

'What did they want?'

'Didn't say.'

And you didn't think to ask. What a useless neighbour.

Billy took his foot off the brake and made to reverse. Tom didn't step away from the car. What did he want now? A reaction? Some explanation?

'No idea what that's about,' Billy said, and wound the window back up.

But whatever it was, it couldn't be good.

At least they didn't ask for Billy Mackenzie. That really would have been alarming. Some of Natasha's friends? Relatives? Or Ramona's? Could be something to do with his holiday lets, too, he supposed. Whoever they were, he would just have to wait and see if they came knocking again. Maybe the women were coming round to see if he was okay. Nice, charitable women. He wasn't sure he wanted that sort of company, but any sort of company might be better than none at all, as long as it was decent.

He felt more relaxed driving to Tao. As he drove through Tahiche, taking the back road across the flat dry plains of the island's interior before reaching the more fertile land around Mozaga, he thought about what he would say to Andres. How much he should divulge. What help he should seek. Maybe he could hide out on his boat. Maybe Andres had other ideas. His place on Gran Canaria? Maybe he could stay there. If Andres still had it. Plenty of options. He hoped.

He was able to drive right up to the property and park outside. No line of cars belonging to partygoers obstructing his way. In fact, there was not another car in sight. But he noted the garage. Was that new? He didn't recall there being a garage before.

He took the path through the cactus garden which appeared much the same, and when he reached the house, he had no need to knock. Andres swept the door open in a grand welcoming gesture as though Billy was a long-lost friend. His manner was fake. The charm layered on too thick. As was the cheesy grin and sparkling eyes.

Andres was immaculately dressed in crisp white that accentuated his tan. And his hair was more white than grey. He had aged magnificently. It hardly seemed fair. The man even wore perfume. Billy followed him through to the back of the house, expecting others despite the absence of cars, a harem, hoods and heavies, but there was no one. The place was too quiet. He began to wish he'd stayed away.

Too quiet and too opulent with it. Billy was half-anticipating a tray of fruits and cheeses to appear at any moment, presented by a demure yet supercilious servant. No one appeared. But his anticipation was rewarded out on the rear patio with a confirming arrangement of tapas piled on a long wooden board and a bottle of white chilling in a bucket all set out on a table positioned beneath an arbour supporting grape vines in full fruit. The Last Supper without the other guests. And so obviously a trap. What did Andres want now?

They sat down and Andres chatted about nothing much as he poured. His English had improved. Billy's Spanish had too. They were able to hold a half-decent conversation. Andres led the way.

'What keeps you here?'

'What brings you back?'

'Ah, Lanzarote.' Andres raised an appreciative hand. Billy had to admit the view out the back of the farmhouse was pleasing and typical of the island – neat black fields meeting barren volcanoes. Andres returned his gaze to Billy's face. 'Life treating you well?'

'Can't complain.'

When were they going to get to the point? Was there any point? He reached for some Iberian ham. A couple of figs. Andres sat back, waiting. Billy went next for the olives. He felt observed. After a while Andres said, 'Can I interest you in a little business?'

Here it comes.

'If its drugs...'

'Not drugs. That is the past. An investment. Property. A winery, in fact. All above board.'

'Why me?'

'Just chance, my friend. Providence. We met and someone pulled out.'

Andres waited, toying with his wine. Billy took a large mouthful of his.

'I need details. Time to think.'

'Sure, sure.'

Andres stood and crossed the patio, entering a room on the right – a room in a new extension running off the back of the house – and returned with a folder.

'Here.'

Billy took the paperwork and flicked through. It was a real estate brochure.

'If you're in, I'll get a contract drawn up. It's just shared ownership. You won't be involved in running the business. Neither will I.'

'How do we profit?'

'From the business. And when it's time to sell, from the property itself. You know how it works, surely?'

Billy wasn't about to admit that he didn't, at least, not clearly.

'How much are you needing?'

'A hundred thousand.'

Billy exhaled. 'You think I have that kind of money?'

'Can't you sell something?'

'Not that fast.'

'Borrow it.' He looked at his watch. 'The bank is still open.'

'I'll think about it.'

'Don't think too long. There are plenty I can ask. Am asking.'

'What's the rush?'

'Competition. Another buyer. The agent is on my back. It's why I returned to the island. The chance to own one of Lanzarote's wineries does not come along that often.'

'I never took you for a wine man.'

Andres laughed. It was not a convincing laugh. It occurred to Billy that he was being set up. Maybe the whole proposal was fake. He would need a lawyer to look it over. And then a second lawyer to make sure. Did he even want to go into business with Andres? Probably not.

'Think you'll stay?' he said.

'After the deal is done and a manager found for the winery, I will sail away.'

'And how long will all that take?'

'Days, weeks, who knows? You should come.'

'On the yacht?'

'I'll be heading down to Cape Verde.'

'What's down there?'

'Unimaginable beauty.'

And escape.

'Sounds great. But I have Patch to think of.'

'Patch?'

'My dog.'

'Bring it.'

'Her.' He paused. 'It's tempting.'

'Think of it as a thank you for going into business with a friend.'

A friend?

Billy drained his glass. He thanked Andres for the hospitality, told him he would think it over, and left, heading round the side of the house and back to his car.

The meeting hadn't gone as he had wanted. He'd gone there hoping for protection, a solution, and he'd come away with neither.

He drove slowly down the track back to Tao. At the turnoff to Mozaga, he had to wait for a stream of traffic to pass. He felt impatient, keen to get away.

Another car indicated to turn into the road he was trying to exit. The windows were tinted. As the car passed and he was close enough to see inside, he could have sworn he clocked the Maloney brothers' getaway driver Fred Timms.

Couldn't be. Surely?

Was Timms another investor? Or the Maloneys themselves? Is that why they were hanging around on the island?

He was taken back to that day Natasha mentioned Oscar Cribbs' involvement in that first scam he invested in, the one that went belly-up. Did that mean Andres had known the Maloney brothers all along?

His palms sweated. In the rear vision mirror he saw the car slow and stop. Fear held him like a vice. He pulled out in front of a lorry and had to accelerate his way out of a rear-end crash.

He didn't go straight home. He cut a path through the back streets of Mozaga and then made for Masdache, turning off for Montaña Blanca and heading back through San Bartolomé, all the time keeping an eye on the traffic behind him.

Convinced he wasn't being followed, he risked going home. Before he took Patch for a walk, he made the call.

Andres said, 'That was quick.'

'I passed another of your visitors on my way out of Tao. Looked like someone I know.'

There was a brief pause. Billy thought he heard music playing in the background. Then Andres emitted one of his fake laughs. 'You mean Mateo García.'

'If he was driving a black sedan with tinted windows, then yes.'

'Mateo likes to pretend he is cool, like a James Bond spy.'

Billy didn't speak. How could this Mateo character be a Fred Timms lookalike? They weren't even the same nationality.

'Why do you ask?'

'I thought he might be the competition. I wanted to know what or who I was up against.'

'Mateo is not competition. He's an old friend. That's all.'

There was a short pause.

'I'll leave you to it,' Billy said.

'Speak soon.'

Billy threw his phone down on the couch. He'd had enough of his own paranoia. He couldn't live like this. It was worse than when he was in fear of his life back in London. When he'd begged Marjorie to get him into witness protection after Oscar Cribbs had told a mutual mate that Eric Maloney had put out a hit on him. He never told Marjorie that was one of the reasons he was so scared. That, and the actions of a certain bent copper.

He snatched the leash, called Patch, and went out for a good long walk along the cliff path to Los Cocoteros.

25

GUATIZA SUPERMARKET, TUESDAY 26 MARCH 2019

ON THE WAY BACK FROM BILLY'S PLACE, I REALISED I WAS GETTING tired of all the investigating. I wasn't getting any younger and needed to pace myself. Above all, I needed to figure out what I wanted to say to Billy before we met. I also needed the bathroom after that tea at Paula and Celestino's.

As I was turning back onto the main road, I remembered we were out of milk and eggs.

'Let's swing by the Guatiza supermarket,' I said, thinking my bladder could hold out that long.

Clarissa remained silent. It was not a remark that required an answer.

I pulled up outside the little supermarket located in a building that was no more than the size of a large family home. 'Coming in?'

'Why not.'

We both grabbed a wire basket on our way inside and browsed the narrow aisles. Clarissa gravitated to the fridges in the back corner. I searched for eggs, bread, and milk.

As I turned down the last aisle, I narrowly collided with a man dressed head-to-toe in black. It was when I looked up into his face that my insides flipped over. Eric Maloney held my gaze.

'Excuse me,' he said. He paused and I knew he'd recognised me. Why, oh, why hadn't I worn my disguise? I'd taken a monumental risk in trying to mirror Clarissa in apparel and now I had paid the price.

He hadn't taken his eyes off me. 'Marjorie, isn't it?'

'I think you must be mistaken.'

He emitted a cynical laugh. 'If you say so,' he said and paused. 'Constable.' He emphasised the first syllable. Clarissa approached, and he took one look at her and walked away.

'Who was that?' she said, touching my arm. She could see I was shaken. I could barely hold my shopping basket.

'Eric Maloney,' I whispered.

'My word. What rotten luck.'

'We need to get out of here.'

'Let him get a head start.'

She was right. We wandered around the little supermarket, loading ourselves up with much more than we'd intended, and when we thought the coast was clear we made our way to the checkout and watched as all of our purchases ended up in bags.

Clarissa insisted on paying. I didn't have the strength to argue with her. My gaze was fixed on the exit, on what I could see of outside. Before we left, I stood by the doorway and poked out my head and scanned up and down the road.

Out by the car I said, 'We need to make sure we're not followed.'

'Should be easy enough.'

Both of us had eyes everywhere as we loaded the boot and got in the car. Despite my need to pee, I was taking no chances and following Clarissa's directions, I took a circuitous route back up to Haría, then on up the mountain, along to Teguise and back down to the coast road. After all that, I was as certain as I could be that no one had tailed us back to the farmhouse.

Inside the house, I bolted to the bathroom.

AFTER A LIGHT LUNCH, neither of us felt like filling the afternoon with entertaining activities. The excitement of Trevor's release had been dampened. We were both preoccupied with the same issues. What to do about the Maloney brothers now I'd been seen by Eric. And what to do about Billy now we knew where he lived.

'How long has it been since Oscar Cribb's murder?' Clarissa said.

I thought back. 'Ten days.'

'Then it's my guess the brothers know Billy is living here.'

'What makes you say that?'

'They'd have given up by now, otherwise.'

'I guess you're right.'

It was a disturbing thought. There was only one copper I knew that was aware Billy lived on the island: Graham Spence. Surely, he wouldn't have betrayed his old informer. Whether he had or not, one way or another, Billy's cover was in tatters.

'One thing seems clear,' Clarissa said. 'We can't chance returning to his house. The risk of being followed or surveilled is much too high.'

'We can be sure they don't know where we are, though. They are in Tiagua.'

'And we are here in Guatiza a stone's throw from Billy's place. What's to stop them climbing that volcano, binoculars in hand. They'll know your car. Or at least they'll have a pretty good idea. And they'll have taken down the number plates of all the cars parked outside the supermarket when we were there.'

And that would have amounted to about three vehicles.

'I guess I just want to confront Billy.'

'With what, exactly? Whatever it is happened over forty years ago. Not pressing, is it.'

Her remark took me aback. She was right. Besides, all I wanted was an explanation and an apology, or at least some sort of acknowledgement that he had ruined my career. That he'd set me up good and proper. He must have known. All these years the one thing that had played on my mind was why I lacked the courage or the nous to confront him at the time. Demand he tell me what had been going on. Yes, that was it. All I really wanted was the truth.

I was shaken out of that line of thinking by the sickening thought that Clarissa was right about the car. And it was parked on the gravel in the front yard in full view of anyone passing by. We'd been home two hours already. Anyone could have driven by and clocked the number plate.

'I'll be right back,' I said and grabbed the car keys.

As inconvenient as it was to have to park the car behind the back patio, I moved it there, cursing myself for not thinking of it before.

Clarissa gave me an inquiring look when I reappeared. 'I heard the engine,' she said. 'Smart move.'

'Probably too late.'

'Let's not be pessimistic.' She paused. 'What time is it?'

'Three o'clock.'

'The sun's over the yard arm somewhere on the planet. Come on. I have something in my bag.'

She produced a bottle of tequila.

'I don't want to give you the impression I'm an old soak,' she said with a laugh. 'But for me, this day is momentous. Trevor is out tomorrow. And for you, too. You now know where Billy is. Let's forget about the Maloney boys. I very much doubt they are about to murder us in our beds. It's Billy they're after. I'm sure of it.'

We spent the rest of the afternoon sipping tequila and sharing stories from our past. Clarissa had led an interesting life. And we'd both encountered an array of damaged people and had a storehouse of funny stories to share.

We had dinner late and went to bed early. And as my head hit the pillow I was filled with gratitude. I was not alone in the house. I had a companion, someone to share the load. Despite the nagging thought that Eric Maloney knew I was on the island, I went to sleep comforted and more contented than I'd felt in a long time. Anxiety seemed far away.

But it returned with force in the middle of the night when I awoke to the sound of stones skittering on the roof.

I lay on my back, hearing acute.

There it was again. No doubt about it.

I got out of bed, donned a dressing gown, and crept down the hall. I waited outside Clarissa's room, but she didn't stir. I decided not to wake her. Instead, I went to the rear of the house and stood by the door. I waited, listened. Sure there was no one out on the patio, I went outside and looked up at the roof. I couldn't see anything.

I went back inside and tiptoed through to the front door. This time, in a fit of bravery, I flung open the door and stepped outside.

There was no one in sight.

26

GOLF COURSE, COSTA TEGUISE, WEDNESDAY 27 MARCH 2019

Andres' business proposal had given Billy something else to think about. Could he trust the man? Did he want to go into business with him? What were the risks? How much did he stand to lose? Then again, should he even be contemplating investing in a winery considering the potential for exposure. His name might appear on some register. As for the proposal, that was written in real-estate sales speak and meant nothing to him. Nothing he could trust.

He was finishing his breakfast, his mood buoyed by the sun streaming in the living room window. Patch was outside having a sniff around down on the lower terraces. He'd left the sliding door open for her. And to let in the cool air coming in off the ocean. Offset the warmth radiating in. It was light and warmth reflected in the way he felt. As though a corner had been turned. And he could get back to how things were before he'd stumbled on the body of Oscar Cribbs.

After a successful run to the supermarket on Monday and a

safe passage to Arrecife and the cemetery, Billy felt confident a round of golf with his old mate Ben would do him no harm. It had been twelve days since he'd stumbled on the body and no one had come knocking on his door save for a pair of elderly women and so far, they hadn't come back. He'd already convinced himself they were friends or family of Natasha. And he'd become absolutely certain that if Eric and Mick were in fact out there looking for him, they would have given up by now. The booking agent Marisol had texted the night before to say the holidaymakers at the Tiagua house were leaving a week early and were checking out in the morning. By now, they'd be on their way to the airport. What he had originally found terrifying – that the brothers had managed to let his own property out of all the many thousands of holiday rentals on the island – had now proved providential.

Billy had arranged to meet Ben in the foyer at nine thirty. After attending to Patch and watering the plants, he arrived at the golf course a bit before the appointed time and parked at the end of a row of cars.

Without thinking to look for Ben's car, he heaved his caddy out of his boot, breezed into the clubhouse, and went and stood over by the photo display with his caddy beside him, eyeing that one photo of him seated beside Ben at the annual Christmas dinner a few years back. It would be a relief to spend a leisurely round of golf followed by lunch. Back to his old habits. There was even a bit of a spring in his step as, leaving the caddy parked where it was, he wandered over to browse the golfing apparel in the club's shop while he waited.

Time ticked by. He kept looking over at the entrance doors, but no Ben.

He waited a full fifteen minutes, eyeing this and that in the shop but still no Ben.

He sent him a text.

No reply.

He tried calling but his mobile went straight to voicemail. Strange. Ben was never late.

An accident? His health? Anything could have happened. How much longer should he give him?

He waited until five to ten and then toyed with heading home. Before he left, he went over to the restaurant and peered through the glass-panel doors. He was surprised to see Ben chatting to Aaron Tyler from the Location! Location! estate agents in Costa Teguise. Aaron was pointing at a brochure lying open on the table between them. Ben shook his head. Aaron persisted. Billy thought of Andres, the winery. Couldn't be the same brochure, surely? He couldn't know. He did know he wasn't going to interrupt.

He was about to pull away when Ben stepped to one side, and he noticed a third figure seated at the table. Disbelief rocketed through him. What in heaven's name was that crooked low-down cop Derek Brace doing in Lanzarote, never mind talking to Ben? How did he even know Ben? Or was it Aaron he knew? Was Brace buying real estate? Heaven forbid! It was bad enough having Oscar Cribbs and then the Maloney boys on the island. Not to mention that cop Ackland. And now Brace. It was all too much of a coincidence. How long had Brace been here on the island? Was he looking for him as well?

His past was catching up with him, that much was certain. He was catapulted back to the night he had stood in the lane behind the Cock and Bull having a quiet smoke when a sallow and gaunt drug addict had lumbered by. There was a commotion, shouts, a brief chase, and then gunfire, a single shot. The addict fell not five metres from where Billy stood. He tried to step back, but he was hard up against the side wall of the pub. Every bone in his body hoped he wouldn't be seen. He glanced to his left. Not three feet that way was pitch black. Craving that blackness, he started to inch towards it. He'd only managed a few sidesteps when his left foot hit a dustbin lid. There was a clatter. Billy froze. The killer looked his way and Billy knew he'd been seen. He thought he was a goner. The guy came over, gun in hand, grabbed him by the collar and hissed into his face, 'You breathe a word of this, and you'll end up like him.' Then the guy hurried off.

Billy found out later on the grapevine that the killer of that down and out junkie was a high-ranking copper by the name of Derek Brace.

And it wasn't any old junkie. It was Eric and Mick's cousin, Dan Maloney.

There was a cover up. Billy got wind that the death had been deemed a misadventure. Billy, the only witness, knew the truth. And then, in an effort to ensure he got away with murder, Brace started making Billy's life hell. He threatened his ex-wife, turned up at his kids' school, slashed the tyres on his milk float and left a menacing message under his windscreen wiper. Sing, and he'd wind up pushing up the daisies along with his wife and kids.

Billy was as sure as it was possible to be that Brace had no idea that he was an informer and Marjorie his handler. But if he found out, Billy would be dead meat. He never met Marjorie near the Cock and Bull again.

BILLY MOVED AWAY from the restaurant door before any of those three men looked his way and wandered back over to the golf-club shop telling himself Brace would probably head off with that estate agent Aaron, and Ben wouldn't be long, and as long as he stood behind the clothing displays, he wouldn't be seen. He did consider going home as he was losing patience and misgivings were swirling in him like bats, but he was loyal to Ben. Besides, if he did leave, he risked being seen by Brace.

Two couples sauntered in and stood beside him, wanting access to the apparel he was in the way of, and he made his way to the display of hats on the other side of the shop entrance. His gaze drifted to the terrace outside. Perhaps he would be better off on the terrace out of sight. He could keep a discreet eye out for Ben from behind a screen of plants. It was a risk, but one worth taking.

He left the shelter of the shop, grabbed his caddy, and took a few paces in the direction of the terrace. He glanced backwards at the restaurant door willing it not to open, and then turned and stopped dead in his tracks.

Outside, not six metres from where he stood, were Eric and Mick Maloney.

They had their backs to him and appeared to be surveying what they could see of the golf course. What were they doing here? Why weren't they on a plane back to London? And how the hell did they know he played golf on Wednesdays? If they knew.

He reached for his caddy, started to inch his way backwards and was about to turn and scurry into the relative safety of the shop when he felt a presence right beside him.

'Bang on time, I see,' Ben said, and Billy thought he must have got the time wrong.

'Ben, I...'

'Ready?'

Just as he was about to speak, someone came inside from the terrace and held open the door, and Ben stood right behind Billy and half shunted him out onto the terrace before he had a chance to protest, let alone walk the other away. He felt as though he were being jostled along towards certain death. But as his feet met the paving, the Maloney brothers were walking off towards the eighteenth hole, and they didn't look back.

Ben eyed him strangely. 'Whatever's the matter? You look like you've seen a ghost.'

'Shall we get going?' Billy said quickly, wheeling his caddy over to the first hole which was thankfully free of other golfers.

He insisted that Ben took his turn first. As his friend lined up his shot, Billy looked around, eyes probing every figure, every gap in the foliage. The brothers were nowhere to be seen.

Maybe they'd given up and left. Maybe their flight was due to leave, and they needed to head for the airport. Fat hope. All attempts at self-reassurance fell short. He felt naked and exposed. He might not be seeing them, but they might well be seeing him. And there was nothing in his apparel or his features that lent him a disguise. He was who he was, readily identifiable at many, many paces.

Ben's ball landed squarely on the first fairway. He stood back and Billy took his turn. He wasn't able to take much care but managed a decent shot. The two men wheeled their caddies on up the fairway, Billy coveting the row of trees and shrubs that screened them from onlookers on the second half of the course, doing his best not to glance over his shoulder in case he locked gazes with a Maloney.

Ben's next stroke sent his ball rolling on the green and straight into the hole. Billy's concentration broke as he took his next stroke, and it took him four attempts to pot the ball.

'Are you sure you're alright?' Ben said as Billy fished out his ball and they strolled off.

'Still recovering.'

'Bad stomach?'

Billy didn't answer.

'It's the water,' Ben said, answering himself. 'I always filter mine.'

'Must be the water.' It was much easier to simply agree.

Billy's anxiety rose as they neared the next tee; the second hole was awfully exposed. He wanted to crouch down and curl into a ball like a hedgehog but all he could do was stand, watch, and wait.

Ben went first again and got a hole in one. He was triumphant. He was all chirrupy banter as Billy lined up his stroke. He ended up hitting his ball well past the green and had to spend the next three strokes getting it out of the rough.

'We all have our off days,' Ben said with sympathy. Although also with a measure of doubt, Billy thought.

The third hole was little better. The only saving factor was that the fairway flanked the course's perimeter, giving him a decent view of who was around. Still no sign of the Maloneys. Maybe his hopes had been realised and they'd left. He did his best to concentrate on his stroke, but he put too much spin on the ball, and it veered off to the edge of the fairway.

Ben's ball sat neatly at the top end of the fairway with a clear sight of the hole. He was plainly satisfied with his stroke.

'Find any good puzzles since we last met?' he asked as they strolled over towards Billy's ball.

'I was looking online the other day,' Billy said. 'Didn't see anything that grabbed me.'

'I found a fabulous scene of a duck pond; would you believe it. Vintage too.'

'Two thousand?'

'And the rest. A monster and just how I like a puzzle to be. A complex and interesting scene.'

Billy took another three strokes to Ben's one. Ben made no comment.

The fourth hole was situated on the course perimeter as well, this time on the eastern side. The wire fence kept the golfers in and those on the small housing estate beside it out. Billy felt more secure standing with his back to the perimeter surveying the course knowing all he had to do was make it over that fence and he stood a chance of getting away.

He felt more secure with every passing minute that the brothers did not appear.

They'd been on the course for about forty minutes. Surely in that time Mick and Eric would have had ample time to scour the entire area.

They must have left.

They must have.

At the fifth hole, Billy and Ben encountered a bottle neck, those ahead of them not as competent, not as fast.

'Let's skip to the eighth,' Ben said. The tee was right in front of them, holes five to seven forming an inner circle.

'If you're sure.'

'Better for your health. We don't want you having a relapse.'

By the time it was his turn at the eighth hole and there was still no sign of the Maloney boys, Billy relaxed and his game improved. No one would stand around looking for him for all this time. They'd have found him, or somehow failed to see him and left. With those thoughts in mind, he managed to pot his ball on the ninth in two shots.

Before they headed off to the tenth, he broached the subject lingering at the fringes of his mind.

'That guy you were talking to in the restaurant just now...'

'Derek?'

'You know him?'

'Aaron met him in Costa Teguise. He'd wandered into his office for some reason and Aaron had offered to show him around.'

'And that included here?'

'Aaron wanted to show me a brochure. There's a winery for sale.'

Something in Billy froze. Had to be the same place that Andres had his eye on.

'And Derek tagged along,' he said, more to himself than to Ben.

'Why the interest? You know him?'

'He just reminded me of someone I once knew.' He paused, needing to deflect. 'But it's not Sam.'

Sam? He didn't know any Sam. But Ben didn't know that.

It was nearing noon. A rich smell of frying fish and meat

wafted on the breeze. As they stood beside the green, Billy stared through the palm trees and shrubbery over at the terrace, scanning the patrons. Despite the confidence he'd felt moments earlier, he felt a sudden impulse to avoid the terrace and veer off somehow either by going around the practice ground in the middle of the course or cutting through to the front of the club house and entering the second half of the course on the other side. He wasn't even sure that was possible or if access was blocked by a fence. As though making up his mind for him, Ben strolled off towards the terrace. Left with no choice, Billy followed, his stride leaden, his belly tight.

To his astonishment, he made it unscathed to the tenth hole.

Then, as Ben pulled out his club and went over to take his shot, Billy sensed someone coming up behind.

27

TAHICHE PRISON, WEDNESDAY 27 MARCH 2019

I AWOKE ON SUNRISE, EXCITED FOR WHAT THE DAY HAD IN STORE. Trevor was due to be released from prison at nine o'clock. We planned on inviting him back to the farmhouse since there was plenty of room, and with the Maloney brothers lurking around the island, the extra protection of having a man about seemed wise.

One single thought of those brothers and I rolled onto my side and stared at the wall as fear came rushing back. I had not completely recovered from the day before. That chance encounter in the Guatiza supermarket was unnerving enough, but the stones on the roof underscored the reality that those scoundrels knew where I was and wanted me to know it. Billy was their real target, and they'd be sniffing around me hoping I would lead them straight to him. Which meant I was relatively safe, for now, but I was being watched. And there was every chance they would come after me as well once they'd finished with Billy. I was, after all, a key witness.

I decided to keep my misgivings to myself. This was an

important day for Clarissa and Trevor. I was eager to share in the happy occasion. I didn't want the shadow of Billy and the Maloneys marring the day. I divested myself of my anxieties as I threw off the covers and headed straight for the shower. Then I dressed for the day in one of my hippy tops over plain pants. I'd grown fond of the bright colours and swirls.

Clarissa emerged from her room in her dressing gown as I was making my way through to the kitchen. One of the things I liked about our new friendship was the way we accommodated each other's routines. In the mornings, I used the bathroom first. No fuss. Those were the sorts of habits that made for a firm relationship of any kind. The minimum amount of domestic irritation. I had no idea what she wanted for breakfast or even if she was hungry, but I made coffee and settled on cheese, ham, and tomato on toasted sour dough.

It all went down a treat.

Clarissa had followed my lead and put on a vibrant orange and pink blouse over sage-green trousers. We made a colourful pair, two ageing birds out on the town. All we needed to finish off the look were a pair of floppy wide-brim hats.

I went and reversed the car out of its hiding place at the back of the house and pulled up for Clarissa who was waiting for me in the front garden.

The drive was a short one and we were at the prison on the dot of five to nine.

I reverse parked beside a few shipping containers dotted in a patch of land directly opposite the prison entrance. Before us we faced a high black gate set between two plain buildings. The one on our right stretched northwards towards Tahiche and sported two long rows of small square windows. I presumed it was the office block. On our left was a short row of houses. Could only be staff accommodation, I thought. No one would want to live butted up against a prison, especially when there was nothing else in the vicinity other than the shipping containers.

We waited and waited, watching the door, hoping to see Trevor appear at any moment. Even with the windows wound down to let a breeze blow through, the situation in the car was becoming unpleasant in the full morning sun. It was nearing ten o'clock when Clarissa said, 'I've had enough of this,' and went to find out what was going on.

I watched her cross the street. She hit the buzzer on the gate and stood around. The gate opened a few minutes later and there was a brief exchange before she disappeared, and the gate closed.

When she reappeared, she looked annoyed. She marched back to the car, got in and yanked the door shut.

'Unbelievable,' she said.

'What is it?'

'The release is delayed as the prison officer in charge of the paperwork has been called away. We are to come back after one.'

'At least it's still happening today.'

She didn't reply. There was a brief moment of silence.

Then she said, 'Sorry to chew up your time like this, Marjorie.'

'I had nothing else planned.'

'We have almost three hours. What would you like to do?'

'Go back to Guatiza?'

'Could do. But it seems pointless when the golf course is right there.' She pointed out the window at all the palm trees.

'Have another look for Billy?'

'Might as well. But first, let's stretch our legs.'

'Coffee and a stroll?'

'Sounds divine.'

We headed off to Costa Teguise. With so much time to kill, I forwent the cafés on the main drag in favour of a café overlooking the ocean. I found one after a few wrong turns and dead ends.

We sat outside beneath an umbrella on a large wooden deck, ordered our coffees and watched the holidaymakers down on the beach. Squeals and shouts, chatter, and laughter were caught on the wind. Sweet doughnut smells filled the air, and I saw those at the table nearest us were enjoying churros. Following my gaze, Clarissa said she felt a little peckish and when a waiter came, we ordered a small dish of churros to nibble on.

For a tourist resort, there wasn't much to fault Costa Teguise. I sat back and for the first time since I had arrived on the island, enjoyed the holiday vibe. Although a small part of me remained vigilant and both of us were disinclined to chat. The delay in Trevor's release seemed to be weighing on Clarissa. What else could go wrong? I tried not to what if.

As though she had been reading my mind, Clarissa said, as much to herself as to me, 'I might have known this would be a challenging day.'

'How so?'

She hesitated, shooting me an uncertain look before continuing. 'Saturn and Neptune are playing up. Or, I should say, linking arms. With Pluto pointing the stick. Always makes for a challenging time.'

I had no idea what any of that meant and I didn't want to inquire further.

Clarissa went on. 'I better not say more. The prediction is too grim. Besides, it might not impact you and me and Trevor. Someone will be impacted, though. I can feel it.'

I didn't dismiss her prediction. Rather, I tucked it away in a tray in my mind marked pending validation. Somehow, though, I sensed she was right.

We finished our coffees and churros, paid the waiter, and headed back to the car.

By the time we pulled up in the golf course car park it was just gone eleven.

'Do we have a strategy?' Clarissa said.

It was a touch unsettling the way she grew ever closer to being my sleuthing partner through these simple questions. And yet also comforting.

'Given the time, if he's here, he's somewhere between halfway through the holes and finishing up.'

'How do you know that?'

'Opening times and how long it takes the average golfer to play a round of eighteen holes. Jess had a membership.'

'Always amazes me the things we pick up along the way.'

'I figure we should go out to the terrace and then head straight over to the last holes.' I pointed to indicate their general direction.

'Shouldn't we try to fan out a bit?'

'Perhaps. Maybe once we get there.'

'Make up your mind.'

'Let's go together. See what happens.'

'Play it by ear. Good-oh.' And she unbuckled her seatbelt and was out of the car before me.

What had started out as a diversion and even a bit of an adventure took a dark turn as I joined her on the footpath and spotted the Maloney boys' car parked in the shade a few cars away. I stopped and stared, trying to figure out whether to change my action plan.

Clarissa turned. 'What is it?'

'Right now, I wish I had a gun.'

She followed my gaze and twigged. Making a quick appraisal of the situation, she said, 'Don't be dramatic. We'll be fine.'

'You think?'

'There's only one way to find out.'

We headed into the clubhouse. I went and snatched a

pamphlet with a map of the course from a display stand near the reception desk and followed Clarissa out onto the terrace. I already had a decent idea of the layout of the course imprinted in my mind, so I handed her the pamphlet. She briefly studied the map with the eighteen holes laid out with their fairways and greens. Then both of us started looking in every direction for Billy and the Maloney brothers. Once we were at the edge of the terrace, I steered Clarissa on to the eighteenth hole and suggested we work backwards.

'That way we are sure to bump into him if he's here.'

'You're sharp as a tack, Marjorie,' she said and off she strode all breezy and confident with her map clutched in her hand. I followed on, attempting to catch her up. She really had no idea how much danger she was in. These men were ruthless psychopaths. They wouldn't care if they shot us all in broad daylight in front of everyone. They'd probably enjoy the thrill of the kill.

28

GOLF COURSE, COSTA TEGUISE

Ben was poised to tee off on the tenth hole. Whoever was coming up behind them was getting closer. Billy glanced around.

It took a fraction of a second for the alarm switch to go off in his brain and a tremor shot through him. Eric Maloney was striding his way. There were about ten metres between them.

A quick assessment. No sign of Mick. Billy didn't think twice.

He left Ben standing with an incredulous look on his face and bolted up the fairway to the green, getting some distance between himself and his foe, all that working out in his home gym paying off despite his ageing joints.

As he approached the end of the tenth hole, he thought fast. Ahead was the perimeter fence. To his right were the remaining holes of the course. Having failed to spot Eric and Mick on the first half, he figured Mick would be hovering somewhere towards the last holes. Which meant his safest bet was to head left.

Someone shouted. A woman's voice. She shouted again. Could be anyone. He didn't look back.

He veered left and bolted down the fairway of the first hole, narrowly missing getting hit by a golf ball and wishing to god that that fate would fall to the brothers. Then he made a beeline for the terrace and the clubhouse, hoping for some kind of intervention, security, anyone who could, who would stop the Maloney boys.

Instead, people stood and stared.

He kept running.

Had he gained any distance?

He glanced back.

No.

He kept running, as hard as he was able.

He got to the terrace. Hope glimmered. He thought maybe, just maybe he could get into the clubhouse where someone surely would help.

Five more paces.

Four.

Three.

The door was almost in reach.

A sudden blow to the back of the knees and he buckled, stumbled forward.

As he was collapsing to the ground, he felt his arm being pulled up behind his back and he was forced to stand.

'Just walk,' Eric said in his ear. He was panting hard.

Billy was panting even harder. He could scarcely take in enough air. He bent his head, his mouth filling with saliva. He thought he might vomit. He spat. And spat again.

He looked up to find an elderly couple staring at him with disgust. Him? He was the victim here. Then he glanced to his left. And there was Mick, striding across the terrace wheeling Billy's caddy, an open-mouthed grin spread across his face. He waved. Called out a cheery greeting to put the onlookers at their ease.

Billy felt all the pairs of eyes of everyone on the course looking their way. No one came to his aid.

Where the hell was Ben? He of all people could see Billy was in trouble. Had he called the cops? Gone into the clubhouse to inform security? Or was he that much of a coward he planned on doing nothing?

They were at the club house doors.

'Keep moving.'

Mick held open the door and gestured for Billy and Eric to pass through with a mocking sweep of his hand and that big grin plastered across his face for the benefit of the gawkers.

Billy looked around. Ben was nowhere to be seen. Instead, that awful estate agent Aaron Tyler from Location! Location! stood with an even broader grin on his face than Mick had.

'You in a spot of bother there, Eddy?' he said and laughed.

Billy thought if he ever got out of his present situation alive, he would murder the bastard.

They were nearly through the clubhouse. Mick held open the next set of doors and Eric pushed Billy out onto the footpath.

'Stop!'

It was a woman's voice again. Coming from behind. The same woman? He couldn't tell.

'Leave him alone!'

Did sound familiar, though.

But they were out of the clubhouse, and he was being frogmarched to the car park and he couldn't look back. What could that woman do to save him? It was too late.

29

GOLF COURSE, COSTA TEGUISE

WE WERE HEADING ACROSS A LONG STRETCH OF ROUGH ON THE fifteenth hole when a commotion broke out ahead of us. It was hard to see through the rows of stout palm trees that edged all the fairways and greens, but others had downed their clubs and were staring in the direction of what I imagined to be the tenth hole. Then I caught a glimpse of someone running up the fairway. Couldn't be sure but I thought it was Billy.

I left Clarissa trudging up to the green ahead of us and ran as fast as my old bones would let me. I cut a course between two palm trees and crossed the fairway of the thirteenth hole as the man, who I now saw was indeed Billy Mackenzie, paused, taking a split second to decide which direction to head.

I called out. He might have heard me, but it made no difference and he headed off in the opposite direction. That was when I clocked Eric giving chase. He was unmistakable with his lean and gangly physique, unchanged in forty years. And he appeared to be gaining on Billy.

He whipped past and rounded the corner. There was no

way I was able to follow on behind. Whichever way Billy went he would be hoping to get off the course and away somehow. Probably back to his car. I backtracked across the fairway as Clarissa appeared between the palm trees, breathless.

'This way,' I pointed. 'Back to the terrace.'

She nodded and I left her to follow as best she was able while I rushed on down the fairway of the thirteenth hole, cutting across a swathe of gravel, dodging golfers standing around. I'd made it to the last stretch of fairway when I saw Eric frogmarch Billy into the clubhouse.

Everyone else just stood and stared. I ran across the terrace, entered the clubhouse and called out again. But it was no use. The brothers were forcing Billy out to the car park. And they were gone.

Clarissa caught up with me. We both stood with our hands on our hips, catching our breath.

'What do we do now?' she said between gasps.

'Back to the car,' I said, already on my way. 'It's possible we might be able to tail them.'

We had to push past a gaggle of onlookers crowding the entrance doors. Cowards, the lot of them. Had nobody in the golf club the presence of mind to stop those men from making off with one of their own members? I was furious and desperate to get outside. I barrelled my way through, elbowing people out of the way, and I soon made it out to the path with Clarissa behind me. We got as far as the edge of the pavement when I saw Eric Maloney bundle poor Billy into the black sedan.

'Will you leave off!' I cried.

There was no response. I wasn't even sure I was heard.

Behind me, Clarissa yelled at the crowd, 'Will no one assist? Has anyone called the police?' They all just stood there, open-mouthed. It was as though she was speaking Esperanto, and no one could make out a single word.

I raced to the car, fumbling in my pocket for the fob,

grateful we'd found a park close to the entrance. Clarissa was already waiting to open the passenger side door. We moved like lightning. We weren't fast enough to stop the Maloney boys, but at least we could tail them. Deploying what little of the advance driving skills I had acquired in the force, I swiftly reversed and manoeuvred the car.

We approached the exit. The sedan was ahead of us. Mick gave us a cheery wave through the passenger side window as they drove out of the car park and sped off.

I made to follow, scarcely looking for approaching vehicles before making a left.

'Hold onto your hat, Clarissa,' I said as I floored the accelerator. 'We're in for a bit of ride.'

'What about Trevor?'

'We'll be back before he gets out.'

30

LEAVING COSTA TEGUISE

'How did you find me? How did you know I was here? It was Andres, wasn't it?'

No answer.

He got the sense that they were heading out of the car park in the direction of Tahiche, but he couldn't be sure. It was hard to manoeuvre himself out of lying flat on his face on the back seat. Mick had tied his hands behind his back. But that wasn't why he struggled to sit up. When he finally did manage to twist his torso around and get himself into a sitting position, he winced with pain and the world spun. He'd cracked the side of his head on the door frame as Eric shoved him into the backseat.

But all that paled in the light of what lay ahead. This was beyond a nightmare. There was only one outcome, and it didn't involve waking up.

Billy's only hope was that woman in the car park, a woman he now realised was Marjorie. Had to be. What was she doing on the island? Looking for him? And she'd found him, almost, as it must have been her rocking up at his place that time. Would she manage to stay on Eric's tail and somehow prevent the inevitable? Could she save him?

Or maybe someone back at the golf course had called the cops.

Maybe.

But Eric had given the crowd of onlookers a cheery wave in the car park as though the whole situation was a prank or a joke.

Some joke.

After what happened to Oscar Cribbs, he wasn't holding out much hope that anyone would get to the Maloney boys before they got to him.

But this was broad daylight in the busiest part of the island. Surely someone would intervene.

His head throbbed but the dizziness had faded. He gazed without hope at the skyline, the volcano nearby, the barren landscape devoid of life. He thought of speaking, asking questions, but what was the point?

There was a screech of tyres as the car cornered a bend and Billy was flung hard to the right, his shoulder slamming into the door. They then screamed along the road to Tahiche.

There should have been cyclists. Cyclists blocking the road. Cyclists were everywhere on the island. But clearly not when you wanted them, needed them, three abreast, impossible to overtake, giving Marjorie a chance to catch up.

Was she behind him? He didn't dare look. It would only alert the brothers. Make Eric drive even faster.

As it was, Eric hurled the car into the next bend and Billy was flung sideways once more.

Mick gripped his seat. 'Take it easy,' he said.

Eric slowed a little, but not much.

At the roundabout, Billy was convinced Eric would veer right and head for the mountains. The easiest way to murder someone on the island was to hurl them off the sea cliff. The strong currents would sweep the body away and for all he knew it would turn up in Cape Verde.

But Eric turned left and headed straight for Arrecife.

They were through the roundabouts and on the ring road in no time, barrelling along well over the speed limit.

Where was a cop car when you needed one?

And where the hell were they taking him?

31

PUERTO DEL CARMEN

'WHERE THE HELL ARE THEY TAKING HIM?'

The black sedan was five cars in front, and I only just caught sight of it turning off the ring road at the next exit.

'Puerto del Carmen,' Clarissa said, reading the sign.

I had to slow to avoid rear ending the car in front.

I took the exit down the slip road. There was a roundabout up ahead.

'Which way?'

Clarissa sat forward, craning her neck.

'Straight ahead.'

I caught sight of the black sedan as I exited the roundabout.

I concentrated on the road as it snaked its way down to the coast. Another kilometre and we arrived at another roundabout just in time to see the black sedan taking the third exit which was really straight on. They were still heading into Puerto del Carmen.

Another couple of kilometres and another roundabout and we entered the main drag. Traffic slowed to a crawl. There were cars angle parked and holidaymakers everywhere. I'd lost sight of the black sedan.

'There it is,' Clarissa said, pointing. 'Quite a way up ahead.'

'Keep your eye on it.'

'Can't. Bend in the road. We'll just have to stay on this road and hope for the best.'

The traffic was getting heavier and there were people everywhere as we crawled by a chaotic array of shops, cafes, and resorts. I had no idea what was up ahead. Clarissa was reading the map.

'If they're heading this way, what are their options?' I said, braking as a woman with a pram threatened to step out in front of the car. She didn't even look.

'I was puzzling that. I thought they would take him back to their holiday let. They could have done away with him there and then dumped the body.'

'But that's Tiagua.'

'Indeed.'

'Unless they've rented two places.'

'Unlikely.'

There was a brief pause. Clarissa looked around.

'This isn't where you spotted them before,' she said. 'That day you tailed them?'

I didn't answer. Then I slapped my hand on the steering wheel.

'They'll be taking him to that man Andres Ortega. He'll be waiting for them somewhere.'

'Which leads me to think they're heading for the harbour.'

'What makes you think that?'

Clarissa folded the map and sat back.

'You said he looked like a sailor.'

32

PUERTO DEL CARMEN

Billy stared out the window watching normal life pass him by. Normal for Puerto del Carmen, all tanned tourists in shorts and sunglasses sauntering in and out of gift shops and eateries determined to have a good time. It felt surreal, a universe away from where he sat having a very, very bad time.

He wanted to open the window and plead for someone to help, but he knew that if he did, all that would happen would be stares of incomprehension and people hurrying off as Mick grinned and waved and Eric wound the window back up.

The road narrowed and became one-way as they approached the heart of the town centre, and if his hands hadn't been tied behind his back, he could have thrust an arm out the window and touched a wall, the pavement scarcely two feet wide. A left and then another left, and they approached the marina. Eric slowed to a crawl.

It was to be a watery grave after all, not thrown off a cliff but tossed overboard, typical of the Maloney boys. He might have known. Not that it would have made any difference.

'Just tell me one thing,' he said as they cruised along past the main car park.

'What d'ya wanna know, Billy boy?'

Did Mick really need to sound so upbeat? Was there any point in asking the question if all he was going to get in response was sarcasm? Then again, he might as well satisfy his curiosity while he had the chance.

'How do you know Andres Ortega?'

No answer.

'It was Oscar Cribbs, wasn't it?'

Again, no answer. But the brothers exchanged glances and Eric shrugged. Mick filled Billy in.

'We've known since we got banged up that Oscar had dealings in the Canaries. Then when Eric got out, he went straight home to Sally obviously.'

'And from Sally to Lanzarote,' Eric said. 'That's where she said Oscar had headed.'

'And Freddy had made it his business to log all of Oscar's connections.'

'Good 'ole Freddy. That was money well spent, Eric, as it happened.'

'Too right. And Andres was not hard to find.'

'Sticks out like the proverbial.'

They both laughed.

The world of gangland crime had always been far too tight knit for comfort. Billy should have known that. He should have got off the island the moment he eyeballed that copper Ackland in that restaurant in Costa Teguise. He should definitely not have wasted time in lockdown after finding Oscar's body. It had only ever been a question of time. And when he bumped into Andres in the supermarket, he should have seen that as an omen. He should have put Patch in the car and driven off. He'd had every intention of doing just that when he was puppy sitting at Tom's. Then Ramona had phoned with that crap about Alvaro's ashes. And what had he done? He'd reacted. And he forfeited the one sensible choice he'd made all week in booking that place in Costa Calma. He'd made a decision that was about to prove fatal. He knew it. He knew there was no way out of this. It was two against one and they held all the cards. Blame was useless. Self-recriminations were useless. He was done for.

He realised with a sick feeling in his guts that checking out of the Tiagua farmhouse might have been a ruse to draw him out. After all, if Andres had had cause to visit the brothers at their holiday let, he could easily have joined the dots and told them that they were renting Eddy Banks' aka Billy McKenzie's place. But then, surely Andres would have just told them where he was living. Then again, maybe not. Couldn't have done.

Billy paused in his thinking. Maybe Andres did have scruples after all. Probably did it for Natasha. Wouldn't have been self-interest. He'd have found some other mug to invest in that winery.

His thoughts stopped short as Eric pulled up at the far end of the car park. Ahead, the road continued, tracking along below the high harbour wall. Sheltering in the still waters, small fishing boats bobbed on their moorings in the breeze. White cuboid buildings cradled the harbour beneath the brilliant blue of the sky. An idyllic setting on any other day.

'Get out.'

Billy didn't have much of a chance to look around as the brothers led him across to the nearest boat ramp. There was a brief pause while Mick opened the iron security gate. A couple of women were standing at the water's edge some way off over by the main car park. They were looking everywhere. One seemed to be frantic. In a split second he realised it was Marjorie. She looked his way. She spotted him. They were coming over. Would they get to the boat in time?

He tried to struggle free of Eric's grip, hoping to buy some time.

'Pack it in.'

Eric pushed him on down the ramp as Mick locked the gate behind them.

Billy kept walking. What were the chances of making it to safety if he jumped in the water? Not high, considering his hands were tied.

'Whose boat is this?' he said as Eric pulled on his wrists to make him stop.

'Whose do you think?'

Andres wasn't much of a mate, after all.

The boat was one of the larger recreational fishing boats in the harbour. Looked like it had some grunt. Mick jumped aboard first and Eric pushed up against Billy. He used all the strength in his body to resist making that first step up onto the boat. Mick was already untying the moorings. Marjorie had made it to the security gate. She yelled. But there was nothing more she could do.

Billy tried again with all the strength he had. Then a hard blow between his shoulder blades sent him careening forwards. One big shove and he landed face first on the prow. Eric stepped over him and then dragged him by the shoulders towards the deck. Seconds later, the engine fired up and they were away. As Mick manoeuvred the boat out of the harbour, Billy managed to get up on his knees. He looked back. Marjorie was standing at the head of the boat ramp, waving and yelling. He couldn't hear a word above the boat's engine.

'I'm sorry,' he yelled, hoping she would. 'Marjorie, I'm really bloody sorry.'

A sharp pain gripped him in the chest. He turned and looked away from her, his gaze fixed on the other side of the harbour. And there, standing against the harbour wall with his hand raised in a casual wave, was his nemesis Derek Brace.

Had to be Brace. Even at this distance, that copper was unmistakable. He was standing with his feet apart, all cocksure and superior. He even had the same moustache.

Brace, the reason he got out of London and came to Lanzarote.

Brace, first at the golf course and now at the marina. Was he after him as well?

Was it Brace who'd told the Maloneys that he'd sung like a canary back in 1980? Someone had told them. But who? Not Marjorie, surely. She would never have betrayed him. Not then and not now. And neither would Spence. The only copper who had had it in for him back then was Brace.

That image of Brace waving him off stayed with Billy as the boat headed out to sea.

33

GUATIZA

'Well, that's that, then.'

Clarissa gave me a sympathetic look and headed back to the car. I stood watching until I could no longer see the boat. Even if I hightailed it to the local police station and explained what was happening, Billy would be dumped overboard no doubt with heavy weights tied to his ankles long before the cops mounted a response. And there was no way I was about to commandeer a boat and give chase. I had no experience with boats and no authority.

Defeated, I made to follow Clarissa when a man standing on the other side of the harbour caught my eye. He turned away before I had a chance to make out his features, but he seemed familiar. Like me, he'd been taking an interest in the goings on in the harbour. I told myself he could be anyone. Lots of people liked to watch the boats in a harbour.

It was a desolate walk back to the car.

'He did apologise,' Clarissa said once we were on our way.

'Billy? But for what?' I said.

'Could only be for one thing. He's sorry for costing you your job. I know it's not complete closure, but it'll have to do.'

It would. It was all I was going to get.

Clarissa directed me through a confusion of one-way streets until we were on one of the main roads out of town. After that, we found our way back to the ring road easily enough.

'What time is it?' I said.

'Nearly one.'

'A bit late. Better get our skates on.'

There really wasn't any need. The island was tiny. Fifteen minutes later, I turned right at the second roundabout in Tahiche, took the second right and taxied down beside the prison. Trevor was sitting on the narrow strip of pavement outside the prison gates.

As soon as I pulled on the handbrake, Clarissa flung open the passenger-side door and sprang out to give him a huge hug. In the rear-view mirror I observed the man who had just served several years for a murder he did not commit. He was thin, pale, drawn, and demoralised. He could scarcely raise a smile. But he was grateful, I could see that even from inside the car, and when they both got in and Clarissa introduced him, I absorbed his cultured voice, his humility.

The conversation petered out as I set off and we drove to Guatiza. Each of us had a lot to process: Trevor had his new freedom, Clarissa had the realisation of her success, and I had to come to terms with Billy's certain demise and fleeting apology.

The reason I was on the island had come to a sudden halt. For two weeks I had that major occupation of tracking down Billy. Now what? I didn't care to look ahead into my future. It presented me with a Jess-less void. Clarissa and Trevor's presence seemed to reinforce the vacuum. They had each other and everything to celebrate. Joy was ahead of them. Jess was behind me.

Once we were inside the house, Clarissa sprang to life, steering Trevor out onto the patio and cracking open the champagne. I hung around, feigned interest, laughed in the right places. But it was their celebration, not mine.

It was already gone three when Clarissa offered to prepare a late lunch. I made a few suggestions and followed her inside with Trevor trailing behind. He took up a stool as I prepared to muck in when my phone rang. I left them chatting around the kitchen bench and went back out to the patio to answer it.

It was Jim Ackland.

'Didn't you get my messages?' he said. He sounded frustrated.

I apologised. Said I'd had my phone on silent all day. When I checked I found I had ten missed calls and five unread messages, all from Jim.

'What is it?' I said cautiously. I wasn't sure I wanted to know what this man had to say. Clive Plant had warned me about him many times and he had never been nice to me in the squad.

'I found out this morning something you should know about Clive.'

'Clive?'

Mistrust swirled. But I had to hear him out.

'I was speaking to Jones,' he said. 'He's a detective superintendent now, did you know?'

I said I didn't.

'I always knew he was destined for great heights.'

'You were talking about Clive?' I said, impatience growing. Clarissa broke out in raucous laughter in the background.

'When you left the squad, we all knew something was going on, but everyone kept their head down. You know how it is. But word got out that Billy Mackenzie was a snout and we all put two and two together and guessed you were his handler. Clive should have kept quiet, but he let a few of us know that

Mackenzie had turned supergrass. He even provided us with a face.'

So, Ackland had known all along that I was Billy's handler. I was beginning to feel well and truly set up, by Ackland and by Plant, who had withheld all this for forty years. Worse, Ackland chooses this moment, this very day to come clean. He couldn't have known what had just happened to Billy, but even so, his timing was abominable. It was all I could do not to hang up.

'Why are you telling me all this now?'

'Don't you want to know who's been stabbing you in the back?'

Clive?

'But why?'

My mind flitted back to that day in Clive's car when he put his hand on my knee and I took it off. His cool, almost hostile reaction. But Ackland would have known nothing of that.

'We all had ambition back then,' he said. 'Clive more than most. He wanted promotion and didn't get it. And he loathed Derek Brace. He saw that you were in with Brace and with Drinkwater. And I guess that made you his target. An easy target. He didn't care a hoot about Billy Mackenzie.'

I'd heard enough. This was all just petty gossip.

'I better go.'

'Wait,' he said. 'It gets worse. Remember Fred Timms? He got caught on another job recently and to reduce his sentence he let a few things be known. He said that Clive had told the Maloney boys back when they were first arrested that Billy was a snout and you were his handler.'

Jim stopped talking. The betrayal was absolute. I could scarcely take in what I was hearing.

'Are you still there?'

'Yes, sorry, go on.'

'It's bad, Marj. Timms also said that when the boys were released and were on the hunt for Oscar Cribbs, Clive let it slip that Cribbs wasn't the only person of interest on the island. That Billy was there, too.'

So, Clarissa had been right. The Maloney brothers had remained on the island for as long as they had knowing that Billy would not be flying off home to somewhere else.

'How long had Clive known where Billy had set up his new life?' I said, thinking aloud.

'Can't help you with that one.'

I needn't have asked as it dawned on me that I already knew the answer. Clive had never pried into my plans for Billy. He hadn't needed to. Not when the *Let's Go* travel guide had lain open on the dining table in the safe house at a page titled Lanzarote. And Billy had stupidly dogeared that page. Drawers and blunt knives came to mind.

Jim went on. 'I wish I had known about Fred Timms before I told Clive that I had clocked Billy shooting his mouth off at the golf club.'

'You practically handed Billy to the Maloney boys on a plate.'

'I'm sorry.'

'You weren't to know.'

'I'm not sure, Marj, but there's every chance that scrote told the brothers that you were on the island as well.'

No doubt he had.

'What would they want with me?'

'You want me to spell it out? You always were wet behind the ears. You were instrumental in getting them banged up. Revenge. Settling a score. You know what they're like.'

Add 'getting rid of a witness' to the list. My mind flitted back to the harbour, to the little boat pulling away, and to a certain Eric Maloney clocking me and giving me a sly wave.

I thanked Jim and hung up. I didn't have much time to process the call. Clarissa was calling me inside to help with the food.

It was to be an afternoon of celebration whether I was in the mood or not. Clarissa was beside herself with enthusiasm. Over the platter of tapas she'd prepared, she entertained us with hilarious stories of her various ghost tour escapades, digressing into titbits of fascinating history. The second bottle of champagne disappeared as fast as the first and Clarissa uncorked a local white. Lunch morphed into dinner. While we waited for a spicy stew to cook on the stove, we watched the sunset quaffing the wine and listening to music on my laptop.

We were halfway through a second bottle of white and feeling thoroughly sated by the stew when stones skittered on the roof. I froze.

'What was that?' Trevor said, sculling his wine. He leaned forward and deposited his glass on the cluttered table between us.

A worried look appeared on Clarissa's face.

'Not sure,' I said.

'Do you want me to go and have a look?'

'I'll go. I'm sure it's nothing.'

Call it Dutch courage but in that moment, the wine was doing my thinking. That, and I had an urgent need to visit the bathroom.

I should have gone to the bathroom first. I didn't even get as far as the front door handle when I felt a presence behind me, and a hand wrapped itself over my mouth.

I was shunted outside. Eric was standing by the black sedan. He dropped his handful of gravel at the sight of me.

34

TAO

'Let's go.'

They tied my hands together and manhandled me into the back seat. I looked back at the house, but no one appeared. Clarissa and Trevor were too intoxicated to notice my absence. They would have had a reduced concept of time after all the wine. As the car pulled away, I kept looking, hoping, but there was no sign of anyone.

A couple of left turns and we were on the main road heading south. The mountain range loomed to my right, a dark mass beneath the darkening sky. Where were they taking me? Was I about to be ferried to that boat to face the same fate as Billy?

The brothers remained silent. Seeing no point in striking up any sort of conversation, I did the same. Keeping my wits about me, I paid close attention to the route. It seemed as though they were taking me to the Tiagua farmhouse, but we turned off on the outskirts of a village and pulled up outside an isolated house in a narrow valley sandwiched between two volcanoes.

I managed to open the door and step out before either brother had a chance to manhandle me again. Something I couldn't abide, being manhandled. Mick gave me a shove to let me know who was boss and then Andres Ortega appeared in the farmhouse doorway. What a surprise.

He stepped aside as we crossed the threshold. A vestibule led through to an internal patio where a wooden chair sat, vacant and expectant, the rope and tape ready on the ground beside the chair legs.

'Sit.'

I sat. Mick did the honours. He untied my wrists and retied them behind the back of the chair. Then came the tape over the mouth. I didn't resist. What was the point in resisting? Me, at sixty-seven against those three, all fit and able. And ruthless.

Eric looked over at Andres. 'Keep an eye on her till we get back.'

'One more rodent to go,' Mick said as they headed off.

Who else were they after?

How long before I would find out?

No need to ask what was about to happen to us. I needed to think my way out of this. Develop a plan. One thing was immediately clear. I couldn't escape. Not bound and gagged and tied to a chair. I needed another strategy. Andres. The traitor and my only hope.

I gave him a pleading look and made some distressed noises. He observed me for a while. I thought he was about to leave. But he walked towards me, stood over me, and reached out his hand and ripped off the tape.

I thanked him through smarting skin, but he didn't stick around to hear me. Instead, he walked off and left me.

The silence was enveloping. I took in the staircase that led up to the roof, the doors opening into various rooms, a passage at the foot of the stairs leading off somewhere. The sky above me represented freedom of a sort. The sort that can't be accessed.

I should have called the police back in Puerto del Carmen. Reported the crime. But we were so focused on Trevor after watching Billy disappear in the boat that it never occurred to me. Even if it had, saving Billy would have been hopeless. What amazed me was that the brothers had returned to the island to finish what they'd started as though they just assumed no one would be after them. The arrogance of that. Or the recklessness. Did that pair really think they could go on a murderous rampage on the island and get away with it? They might have got away with killing Oscar Cribbs and they might even have managed to leave the island before being arrested for the disappearance and assumed murder of Billy. But me as well? Or was I placing too much importance on myself? Surely the brothers knew that I had friends, allies, people who would be looking for me, people who would be notifying the police. Or was this latest crime spree their swan song? Go out in a blaze of glory.

Maybe they had a fast getaway planned.

That last thought grew legs when Andres reappeared, his phone pressed to his ear. He mentioned something about a yacht before wandering off to another room.

I'd already figured they weren't so stupid as to murder me on the island. They would wait until we were out in the ocean and then tip me overboard like they had Billy. Me, and whoever else they were after. Then they would no doubt head somewhere lawless, somewhere without extradition laws, somewhere they could hide.

I lost all sense of time. Fear gave way to a crushing need to pee. The booze back at Guatiza, the decision not to make that urgent detour to the bathroom before I opened the front door and was whisked away, and my bladder was fit to burst. The pain, the urgency, the need to hold on, it was all I could do not to let a single drop escape. The last thing I wanted was the return of Eric and Mick to my soggy bottom and a puddle beneath my chair.

Andres ended his call and pocketed the phone. He seemed as keen as me for all this to be over with. And he didn't seem like a bad man, a completely through and through bad man.

'Andres,' I said catching his eye.

'Quiet.'

He walked away.

'Andres, I...'

'I'm not interested.'

Before he left me alone again, I yelled to him, 'Please, for the love of god, I need to visit the bathroom.'

'The bathroom?' He turned and emitted a mocking laugh.

'I can't hold out much longer.'

'Those men are going to return any minute and then they will kill you and all you can think about is needing the bathroom?'

He obviously had no idea. My bladder was burning.

'Please untie me,' I said imploringly. 'I'm an old woman. I'm hardly going to make a run for it.'

He looked me up and down and smiled. Then he went around the back of my chair and untied the rope. I rubbed my freed wrists as I stood.

'Come this way.'

He led me by the elbow to a bathroom. Any thought I might have harboured of a miraculous escape out the window was dashed the moment I saw that the room only had a vent in the ceiling. But at least I no longer had to endure the strain of holding onto my bladder.

The release was liberating. I was now in full charge of my faculties. And I could die with a measure of dignity.

I flushed the toilet and the door flung open. I hadn't thought to lock it.

Despite his moment of goodwill, I knew by the expression on his face that Andres was not going to set me free. He seemed preoccupied. He returned me to the chair, tied up my hands, checked his watch and then replaced the tape over my mouth and headed off. My brief reprieve was an anticlimax to beat all anticlimaxes. A few moments later, I heard the sound of a car engine. Was he leaving me here alone?

The waiting grew intolerable. There were times when it was unhealthy to be alone with your thoughts. This was one of those times. I had to maintain hope and stave off the feeling of impending doom. As much as I wanted to be with Jess again, an undignified death at the hands of two gangland criminals was not what I had in mind. I wanted to live. Jess wanted me to live. She'd told me exactly that and she'd been emphatic about it. And while I still breathed, there was a chance I would get out of this mess, slim as that might be. Never in my life had I wanted a rescuer, but I wanted one now. I tugged at the rope around my wrist. Andres had tied it looser but there was no give in it, no way of sliding out a hand. All that happened when I tried was pain.

A car engine interrupted my thoughts. My insides nose-dived. They were back. Andres had abandoned me and now the Maloney boys were gearing up for the next part of their heinous plan. Hearing footsteps on the gravel, I braced myself. I wasn't about to slide into victimhood. If there was an iota of a chance of escape, I would seize it.

There were muffled voices outside the front door. A creak of the hinges as the door opened. Footsteps hurrying my way. Then I heard a female voice and Clarissa appeared in the patio and rushed over with Trevor beside her.

'One, two, three,' she said, and she ripped off the tape covering my mouth. I ignored the sting.

Trevor knelt down behind my chair and untied the rope.

'How did you know I was here?' I said, standing and rubbing my wrists.

Clarissa held up my phone.

'Fell out of your pocket, according to Andres.'

Fell out of my pocket? Really? Must have been when I went to the bathroom.

I caught the sound of an engine in the distance. As though on cue, Andres appeared.

'Hurry! They're back.'

'What'll we do?' Trevor said with alarm.

'Leave it to me.'

Andres was about to make for the stairs up to the roof when we heard footsteps on the gravel. His plan had failed. We were trapped. There looked to be no way out. I thought we could perhaps tough it out, but Andres and Trevor were no match for Eric and Mick.

Andres seemed to have a fresh plan. He darted behind us. Wasting no time, we followed him into the room under the stairs. Andres locked the door. Clarissa flicked on her phone torch and shone the light around. The room was small and just about empty, the walls bare. No window.

'Help me with this,' Andres said to Trevor.

They tipped a heavy-looking table on its side and used it to barricade the door. At the back of the room was a tall cupboard built into the wall. It was a store cupboard and gratifyingly empty and large enough for us all to squash into. Andres ushered us in and closed the door.

Clarissa killed her phone torch, and all went black.

I was sandwiched between Andres and Clarissa. Trevor stood on the other side of her. It was then that I realised if the brothers managed to breach the barricade, they would know we were in this cupboard. Where else could we be? The floor hadn't opened up and swallowed us whole and there was no other way out of the room. Not the smartest move on Andres' part but he had been left with no other option.

'Is there some other way out of here?' I hissed as I braced myself for an inevitable spray of bullets.

Beyond the cupboard and the room, Eric yelled, 'Andres! Where is she?'

Another voice, Mick's, a little distant replied with, 'Where's Andres?'

'They can't have gone far.'

Bonks, crashes, slams, shouting, the sounds fading and getting closer and fading again.

Should we make a run for it?

'I thought you were in cahoots with the brothers,' I said to Andres, hoping to clarify a niggle while I stilled breathed air. 'Why help me?'

His reply was immediate. 'I've always liked Oscar Cribbs.'

I was left puzzling their association when there was a loud pounding on the door to the room. Doom descended. It was the dead of night in the middle of nowhere. No one was going to come to our rescue. Would the barricade hold?

My heart felt like a jackhammer. I turned to Clarissa, felt her warm breath on my cheek. She grabbed my hand and gave it a squeeze. 'It's going to be alright,' she whispered.

Maybe her hearing was a lot sharper than mine, and she heard the sirens before I did. Although her hearing would have needed to be as sharp as a canine's to have caught the sound of the sirens above the pounding on the door. It was another minute before I heard that tell-tale high-pitched sound. Even then, I couldn't be sure they were heading our way.

They were.

The sirens grew louder and louder. The hammering on the door more frantic. There was a sharp crack, the sound of splitting wood.

Andres pushed open the cupboard door.

'Wait,' I said.

But there was no need. Loud voices spoke in Spanish and the hammering on the door stopped.

We filed out of the cupboard and stood together in the black of the room.

An English voice spoke and one of the brothers answered. I couldn't make out what they were saying.

Andres went and pulled the table away from the door. The next moment, light filtered in from the patio, and there, not metres from where I stood sandwiched between Clarissa and Trevor, stood Derek Brace. A much older version of the suave lady killer, but it was undoubtedly him. He'd lost the sideburns, but the moustache was still a fixture.

He turned and caught my eye and smiled.

Eric and Mick had been handcuffed and were being pushed forward across the patio to the front door. Before they disappeared, Derek said to their backs, 'Never play cat and mouse with a seasoned copper.' I realised then that he was the 'rodent' they were referring to earlier.

After the local police had taken away the Maloney boys, Andres offered to make us all some supper. Soon he was handing us each a glass of brandy along with slices of cake on small plates. We sat down in his spacious living room.

'How are you holding up?' Clarissa said, eyeing me with concern.

'Pretty well, considering,' I said, swallowing a hunk of cake. 'I still can't believe I'm here eating cake with my old boss.'

'You two know each other, then.'

'We sure do.' I gave Derek a grateful smile. 'I'm curious to know what brought you to the island.'

'I came to investigate Oscar Cribbs's murder,' Derek said setting down his plate.

'I thought you'd retired.'

'Not quite, as it happens.' He laughed. 'I had, but then this murder came to light and there's been quite a lot of interest amongst the old squad members once we all got wind that the Maloney boys were due for release. Everyone was watching.'

I found it ironic that after all the decades that had passed since I was in the force, it was Derek Brace who had saved my bacon and Clive Plant who had stabbed me in the back. For forty years I'd harboured the belief that it was the other way around. I'd always thought Brace was instrumental in me losing my position in the squad and Plant had tried to defend me. How wrong can you be?

'What about Billy?' I said.

Clarissa, Trevor, and Andres occupied themselves with their plates and glasses, listening.

'That scum. Always cropping up where he's not wanted.' Derek glowered. 'What about him?' Brace said.

'It was you, wasn't it, at the marina, the guy waving at the boat.'

'It was.'

'And you did nothing to help him?'

He shrugged. 'What was I supposed to do?'

'You've got the local police in tow. Surely you could have stopped the brothers?'

He shifted in his seat. I sensed unease in his manner as he gathered his thoughts. Then he launched into his defence.

'Have you any idea how long it takes to organise the maritime police? Not to mention the language barrier and the need for a lengthy explanation. Even if I had notified them, there was no way they could have got a boat out in time to save Billy. Besides, I knew the brothers wouldn't get far. The boat was too small, for one thing, and their business on the island wasn't finished.'

'You mean me?'

'And me.'

'Why you?'

He hesitated. I watched him closely. Everyone waited. Brace didn't seem to have an answer, not one he was prepared to divulge.

'Let's just say it was an old score.'

I wasn't satisfied but it would have to do. Derek set down his plate, sculled the last of his brandy and stood to leave. I had one last question. As he reached in his pocket for his keys, I said, 'How did you know to come here to this house?'

Clarissa coughed.

'I'll leave your friend to explain. Thanks for the cake.' And with that, he headed off.

I turned to Clarissa. She looked a touch wary as she spoke.

'Our paths crossed at Trevor's hearing. Derek gave me his card and asked me to keep him posted of any, um, eventualities.'

It was the day I had met her outside the courthouse and invited her to stay at mine until Trevor's release. She'd taken Derek's card and then accepted my invitation without so much as batting an eyelid. How much had she told him? Was it a betrayal? A deception? I decided to let it go. She was just being prudent. She had my back and, as it had turned out, she had saved my life.

On the way home, she surprised me. Without any preface she said, 'I think you should know I really don't care for that Derek Brace one bit.'

'Whyever not?'

'Too shifty. He's hiding something. Something dark.'

'The reason Eric and Mick were after him.'

'I'd go further than that. I'd surmise he's the main reason Billy came here in the first place.'

'We can't know that, though.'

'He despised Billy,' Trevor said. 'That was obvious.'

'Just because Derek saved your life doesn't mean he hasn't taken another. I can see it in his eyes.'

I shuddered. I respected Clarissa's insights but right then, it was all a little too much.

35

GUATIZA, THURSDAY 28 MARCH 2019

I thought that would be the end of my time on Lanzarote. I was preparing myself for the inevitable return to London, to the house I had shared with Jess, to memories and little else. And then, all the way from his watery grave, Billy hit me with a curveball.

It was Clarissa who first raised the matter of his will. We were out on the patio enjoying some fine Rioja the following afternoon when Trevor mentioned missing his kids. That remark caused Clarissa to sit up straight in her seat as though struck by a flash of insight. She turned to me.

'A man like Billy would have made a will,' she said slowly. Her eyes had widened. She was having one of her psychic turns.

'You think?' I said doubtfully.

Clarissa grew a touch impatient. This wasn't the first time I had cast doubt on her psychic abilities, and I could see she didn't like it.

'He had his two kids back in England who he hadn't seen in forty years,' she said.

'Sophie and Emily.'

'Girls. He would have made provisions for them, surely. No one leaves their situation intestate when living in a foreign country. Well, only an idiot.'

'She's right,' Trevor said.

I was dumbstruck. This was no time to be thinking about Billy's will. Or maybe it was, but I didn't want to think about it. Clarissa had other ideas. She stood.

'Let's go and find it.'

'Go where?'

'Billy's place, of course.'

'We don't have a key.'

'We do. I picked up his keys at the golf course. He'd dropped them, on purpose most likely.'

I was puzzling over what point in that chase and capture Billy had managed to drop his keys when both Clarissa and Trevor were calling for me to get a wriggle on.

THE NEIGHBOUR'S dog let out a string of barks. I glanced over but the man who had approached us the last time we were here did not appear.

Trevor pushed open the gates and we wandered in. The patio was spacious and neatly laid out. I wanted to take my time, absorb the atmosphere, but Clarissa was already at the front door. Trevor followed her. We went in to the sound of a few hapless barks. And then we encountered a dog.

It was a mongrel with a large white patch over its eye. One pointy ear. One floppy. Female. Neither old nor young. Friendly thing. And no doubt hungry and thirsty and lonely. Clarissa and Trevor walked straight past it. I bent down and gave it a pat. It sniffed my hand. My heart went out to the animal. It had, after all, just lost its owner. I wondered what its name was. There was no identity disk on its collar.

'Patch,' I said, and the dog pricked up its ears.

'Good guess.'

I looked up and Clarissa was wearing a broad smile.

With Patch beside me, I looked around. I was surprised at how tidy the place was. The layout was open and distinctly 1970s in feel. The large windows overlooking the back patio that reached down to the cliff and the ocean beyond were the making of the place. The property turned its back on the volcanoes in favour of all that blue.

We each went our own way poking our heads into the various rooms. There were five large bedrooms, one off the living room over by the front door, the others accessed via a corridor off the kitchen and dining area. There was a home gym in one and a room devoted to jigsaw puzzles. Four on the go, each on its own table. Billy must have spent most of his time here. The puzzles were large and complex and beautiful. A flutter of admiration passed through me. Someone should finish them off.

We regrouped in the kitchen.

'I'll search in here,' Clarissa said.

'I'll tackle the bedrooms down the hall.'

'Guess that's me holding the short straw then,' Trevor said and took himself off to the bedroom on the far side of the living room which Billy had used for storage.

It was Trevor who found the will, buried in the bottom of a holdall brimming with cash.

'You do have a knack for these things, I must say,' Clarissa said, and they burst out laughing as we all stood in front of the sofa, observing the holdall.

'Trust Billy to have a stash of cash,' I said.

'There's not that much here,' Trevor said, counting the bills. They were small denominations.

Clarissa read the will. 'He's got several houses here,' she said. 'The Tiagua farmhouse, an apartment in Costa Teguise and a property in Arrieta. Plus, this place.'

I hovered. 'And who has he willed them to?'

'Emily gets Costa Teguise, Sophie gets the farmhouse in Tiagua, Natasha gets this place and Alvaro was willed the Arrieta place.'

'That will now go to his mother, I daresay.'

'Who's Natasha?' Trevor said.

'Not sure.' She turned to the next page, read it through and gasped.

'What is it?'

'A codicil. Recent too. He only arranged this two days ago. He must have known his number was up.'

'And?'

'It says Natasha, his partner has died and he's left this house to you, Marjorie.'

I gasped. 'He's willed this house to me?'

I thought my legs would buckle. I sat down. Patch jumped up on the sofa and sat beside me with her head on my thigh.

'You've made a friend, there,' Trevor said.

I replied with a small smile.

Clarissa set the will down on the coffee table directly in front of me and pointed at the text.

'Written in black and white.'

'What will you do with it?' Trevor said after a long pause.

'I've no idea.'

'Sell it?'

'She should keep it,' Clarissa said.

'And then what?'

'Live in it.'

'But...'

'What have you got to go back to in London? Nothing. Take a risk. Start a new life.'

'But here?'

'Why not?'

I gazed out the huge window at the terraced garden and the ocean. Every day, whoever sat here would get to admire the sunrise. Who gets a view like that? Few. And Billy had gifted it to me. He knew he'd wronged me and this was his way of making amends. I was stunned. Did I want it? Did I want his old home? Could I be happy here knowing he had lived here for maybe decades in isolation from the world. And it was an isolated spot. How would I fare in such an environment? Without company. And just that one neighbour and his barking dog.

Trevor stuffed the cash into the holdall and handed me the will.

'You better pocket this.'

Clarissa went to the kitchen. She opened the fridge and pantry and let out a loud gasp. 'There's enough food here to feed an army. So much cheese.'

'We should go,' I said.

'He's even got organic coffee beans.'

'We have no right to be here.'

'From Colombia.'

'Nice,' Trevor said.

'We should take some of this food with us.' She set about finding bags and sorting out what she considered the most perishable. When she was done, she came back and stared down at me.

'What about the dog?' I said. 'We can't leave it here.'

'I've packed the dog biscuits.'

She exchanged a glance with Trevor and then they both pinned me with their gazes.

'Well?' she said with a sweeping gesture of her hand.

'It's far too big.'

'You think?'

'And lonely.' I looked from Clarissa to Trevor. 'I suppose I could sell it.'

They both protested at once.

'I'd kill for a place like this,' Trevor said. 'I mean that metaphorically.'

'You really need to think hard about this, Marjorie. Places like this are like hen's teeth.'

'It's the perfect retreat.'

'You could at least treat it as a holiday let and come and stay when you felt like it.'

Trevor turned to Clarissa.

'Does she even like it here, though? The island, I mean.'

'Of course she likes it here.'

Trevor turned back to me.

'Do you like it here?'

I laughed. 'I do. It's unusual. The island, I mean. It's nothing like anywhere I've ever been. And life does seem easy here.'

'She's warming to the idea.'

'You reckon?'

'I'll consider it on one condition,' I said.

'Well?'

I hesitated, not given to impulse.

'Spit it out.'

What was the point in holding back? You can't half-say something and then back-pedal. It was Jess, talking in my ear, egging me on, wanting me to have a happy post-Jess life.

'That you both stay here as well,' I said. 'Free of charge. Stay as long as you want. Regard it as your second home.'

'That's silly. You'll lose all that income.'

'I don't need it.'

'That's exceptionally generous,' Trevor said with a reflective glint in his eye. 'And you can always change your mind.'

'Meanwhile, we really ought to do something about all this food.'

'And the dog.'

'Patch. Her name is Patch.'

Trevor went over to the front door.

'Here's her leash.'

FACED with eating through all the groceries Billy had bought proved a welcome diversion. As did Patch. Back at the farmhouse over dinner that night, I began to warm to the idea of living in Billy's house. I could make it mine, replace the furniture. And Clarissa and Trevor were good company. I needed company. Time to heal.

Trevor grew enthusiastic at the prospect of somewhere to base himself on the island.

'I was dreading going back to England,' he said. 'To the old life. I hated it.'

He said he would give up ghost writing and apply for local jobs – gardening, house painting, whatever he could find – and make a go of it on the island.

'I'll rent out my place in Norfolk. See how things go.'

'And set to work on your next novel,' Clarissa said. She turned to me. 'I might as well hang around, too. Keep an eye on the boy.'

Thank you, Billy, I said to myself. All is forgiven.

WE RELOCATED from the farmhouse to Billy's place a few days later after squaring it with his daughters. No one minded. The first thing we all agreed on once we were settled was that since we were all serious about living in Lanzarote, we needed to organise a Spanish tutor.

The End

Dear reader,

We hope you enjoyed reading *Sing Like A Canary*. Please take a moment to leave a review, even if it's a short one. Your opinion is important to us.

Discover more books by Isobel Blackthorn at https://www.nextchapter.pub/authors/isobel-blackthorn-mystery-thriller-author

Want to know when one of our books is free or discounted? Join the newsletter at http://eepurl.com/bqqB3H

Best regards,
Isobel Blackthorn and the Next Chapter Team

ABOUT THE AUTHOR

Isobel Blackthorn was born in Farnborough, Kent, England, and has spent much of her life in Australia. Isobel holds a PhD in Social Ecology from the University of Western Sydney for her ground-breaking study of the texts of theosophist Alice A. Bailey. She is the author of *The Unlikely Occultist: A biographical novel of Alice A. Bailey* and numerous fictional works including the popular Canary Islands Mysteries series. A prolific and award-winning novelist, she is currently working on a trilogy of esoteric thrillers and a new mystery series set in Australia.

ALSO BY ISOBEL BLACKTHORN

Other novels set in the Canary Islands

The Drago Tree

A Matter of Latitude

Clarissa's Warning

A Prison in the Sun

The Ghost of Villa Winter

Dark Fiction

The Cabin Sessions

The Legacy of Old Gran Parks

Twerk

Other Fiction

Nine Months of Summer

A Perfect Square: An esoteric mystery

Emma's Tapestry

Esoteric Works

The Unlikely Occultist: A biographical novel of Alice A. Bailey

Alice A. Bailey: Life & Legacy

Other Works

All Because of You: Fifteen tales of sacrifice and hope

Voltaire's Garden: A memoir of Cobargo

Printed in Great Britain
by Amazon